ALSO BY EPHINY GALE

Stage plays

The Playbook: Six Plays and One Libretto

NEXT CURIOUS THING

EPHINY GALE

For Tara,
without whom these stories
would not have been written

CONTENTS

INTRODUCTION

I have a voracious appetite for the curious, for the strange and beautiful, and for intellectual input in general. Almost every day I view hundreds of new artworks and absorb an abundance of new ideas, and it feels like filling up a tank. Give me my next curious thing. Tell me something else that's interesting, show me something else unusual until my brain is all full up.

And at the end of the day, if I'm still not satisfied? I can come up with a multitude of curious things all on my own.

ON THE STORIES WITHIN

The following introductory notes include mild spoilers, and thus you may prefer to read them after the stories themselves.

In the Beginning, All Our Hands Are Cold

Sometimes I'll develop a clear idea of what another author's story "must" be about based on its title, and am then disappointed to learn it doesn't match my assumptions. In this manner, "In the Beginning, All Our Hands Are Cold" owes its existence to Carrie Ryan's popular novel *The Forest of Hands and Teeth*, which I have not read but understand to be about zombies rather than a literal forest of hands.

This story is about a *literal* forest of hands.

My deep thanks to *Syntax & Salt* for giving it such a good home and bestowing it with their coveted Editor's Award; it's been an honour.

Sickly Sweet

"Hansel and Gretel" is my favourite fairy tale. I remember having the idea for this story on the tram to work one morning, puzzling over what the witch's motivation might be beyond *delicious children* whilst also reviewing my top five fairy tales. Once I'd paired "Hansel and Gretel" with "The Girl without Hands" the rest of "Sickly Sweet" coalesced wonderfully quickly.

My hands have always been my favourite body part. I consider them to be the most beautiful part of me, but they're also my primary tool for work and communication and storytelling. I hope that I can keep them for a long, long time.

Emelia and the Undrowned

I really like cephalopods. That's the takeaway here. I wanted to write a story about squids.

Wrecked

At the time of writing this, my favourite character on one of my favourite TV shows had a reasonably noticeable lip scar that nobody would acknowledge. The show was steeped in character backstories and flashbacks and yet the actress's lip scar was continuously ignored.

"Wrecked" emerged as a tale of another forgotten lip scar on another (fictional) TV show, but otherwise bears no resemblance to the TV series that sparked it.

Candy

"Candy" is about being persecuted for who you love: about that love being seen as unnatural and wrong.

The protagonist's gender is never mentioned and "Candy" was originally published in *Postscripts to Darkness* with a linocut of said protagonist with a moustache, but for allegorical reasons I personally consider the protagonist to be female.

From Strangers

Another fairy tale combination story, "From Strangers" is a mix of "Alice in Wonderland" and "Allerleirauh," along with a heaping of our contemporary world, some magical sweets and a hedge maze.

When I was about sixteen years old, my friends and I used to purchase Chinese packets of White Rabbit lollies and eat them in a park after school. I remember them as being hard and rectangular as opposed to soft and rabbit-shaped, but fantasy can transform the mundane into miraculous things.

Honey in the Blood

"Honey in the Blood" came from a single mental image of a thylacine swimming in a river of honey. Despite becoming extinct before my lifetime, thylacines have always been one of my favourite animals.

Little Freedoms

I adore the genre of women's prison stories, and yet happened to write "Little Freedoms" before seeing Wentworth, Orange is the New Black, Bad Girls or Prisoner.

Wentworth is the first and only TV show that reflects my experience of the world: queer and Australian and women-centric with strictly-enforced rules and a strong potential for danger. It makes me sad that the fictional world I identify with most strongly is that of a women's prison, but I am nevertheless immensely happy that these stories exist.

Cavorts with Foxes

After the election of Donald Trump I could not write for several weeks. I was consumed by thoughts of nuclear war, climate change, and a dozen other apocalypses.

When I finally started to write again, I wrote this piece of flash fiction.

The Light Princess

"The Light Princess" is another story that exists because the original did not match my assumptions from the title. The traditional fairy tale of the same name is about a princess who weighs very little and literally floats away, while I wanted a story about a princess who was very bright.

Experience

This story was my very first "professional" sale, which is defined in the speculative fiction community as one paying above a certain rate. I sold it to *Daily Science Fiction* and felt elated by that sale for days.

"Experience" itself stems from being invited to job interviews at age twenty-one or twenty-two based on my qualifications, but then (upon meeting me) being told by potential employers that I was simply too young.

Morning Sickness

When I was sixteen I wrote a movie trailer for a horror/comedy film I'd dreamt up called "The Period." In "The Period," blood-attracted aliens had come to earth – think invisible air-piranhas – and if you bled, even for a second, they would appear and gobble you up.

The image I remember best from the trailer was a calendar, almost full with red Xs, and a single red marker rolling across a counter in slow motion to drop slowly, slowly to the tiles with a drawn-out clang.

"Morning Sickness" borrows this concept but is no longer a comedy.

Five Tales of the Rose Palace

Once I noticed how frequently roses (or other similar red flowers) appeared in our most famous fairy tales, my brain quickly started knitting them together into "Five Tales of the Rose Palace."

I hadn't seen a Sapphic retelling of "Beauty and the Beast" before, so I was particularly pleased to be able to contribute that to the genre.

Magnets

"Magnets" was originally going to be a play script, but it never quite managed it. I think this story captures the concept perfectly well, but I still would have loved to see the finished set; it's clear in my mind as one of the most beautiful theatre sets I can imagine.

One More Time

This story was written quite near to the predicted "end of the world" in December 2012.

I really enjoy a well-done time loop story, but I hadn't found one before where *everybody* experienced the loop instead of just one person. That sounded arguably like the end of the world to me.

Everybody Knows

One of the most overused speculative fiction plots is "the monster under the bed is actually real." For "Everybody Knows" I wanted to take this tired trope and flip it completely on its head.

And the Queen was Vein

This piece is very much about playing with the words one traditionally associates with "Snow White" as a fairy tale and shifting how we understand those words.

I love the mother-daughter relationship in "And the Queen was Vein," which is not something I explore in much of my work, but is still a theme I care deeply for.

Strange Dancemates

"Strange Dancemates" reminds me of "A Christmas Carol," where the protagonist is visited by several supernatural entities overnight in order to grow. The initial image of Lara Jane climbing upstairs to discover a mermaid in her bed came to me without prompting, and then the rest of the story developed naturally from there.

I wrote the first several hundred words of this story while temping as a corporate receptionist. Once I had finished all of my other tasks, and in between assisting visitors, I wrote the beginning of "Strange Dancemates" in tiny handwriting on one side of an A4 sheet.

Easy Like Arsenic

"Easy Like Arsenic" stands out from the rest of my writing in a couple of ways. Firstly, at about 16,000 words it is the longest piece of prose I've ever published. Secondly, it is one of my only stories written with a particular audience (beyond "general adult") in mind: a New Adult audience of approximately sixteen to twenty-three year olds.

Above all else, this story is about the dangers of believing in false things, and about how those things can shape our understanding of reality and our roles and relationships within it. It's a story that has been with me, in one form or another, for many years, but I think it's more relevant now than ever.

All the First Born Children

I have never received a satisfactory explanation for why children are taken by fairy creatures in either fairy tales or folklore. Why do the fae take human children and replace them with changelings? Why would Rumpelstiltskin even want the queen's first born child? Surely not to eat – that's an awful lot of trouble to go to for a very small amount of meat.

The Secret Death of Lane Islington

There are several popular conspiracy theories that involve a celebrity dying and being replaced by their doppelganger. As a speculative fiction author, my brain decided to run with this and extend the doppelganger character into an identical lookalike from a parallel universe.

I haven't written any musicals for quite a while, so it was especially enjoyable to write the songs for this story.

FINALLY, IN CONCLUSION

I think of this collection as me standing in front of an audience and trying to make some pictures appear on the wall behind me. We don't yet have the technology that allows me to project my imagination out through my eyes, so I have to make do with words and shadow puppets and hope you see the pictures anyway.

My immense thanks to everyone who has ever read any of my pieces, and has thus granted me their audience. And my undying love to my brilliant wife, who explained several years ago that one can actually *sell* short stories, and that published shorts weren't the exclusive domain of literary fiction.

These stories say, "This is how I see the world. Do you see it, too?"

- Ephiny Gale, 2018

IN THE BEGINNING, ALL OUR
HANDS ARE COLD

Everyone in the village is born without hands; the children get along just fine with elbows and teeth and toes.

Sally likes holding her paintbrush in her mouth, because it lets her get right up close to the canvas and add in tiny details like fingernails and leaf-veins and dress-threads. When her friends are particularly pleased to see each other, they bite each other on their shoulders. All of the doors in the village have levers. Sally can always dress herself alone unless she picks something with an awkward zipper or shoes with laces. At school she drinks her lunch, or throws her bite-sized food into the air with her teeth and catches it on her tongue. Her friends lie in a circle, and Sally stretches out on their feet and pretends she's flying.

They're too young for plenty of things, but there are also lots of things the adults are too old for. There's a children-only climbing frame down the street with polyethylene foam wrapped around the bars; Sally can reach the top with just her elbows and legs, and if you fall off the dome you drop into a huge foam pit at the bottom, which is even better than swimming. They get wooden swords strapped to their arms to duel with, and they can tumble down hills, and stick their wrists into the fittings of caster wheels like the wheelers in The Wizard of Oz. Sally's never seen an adult roll down a hill unless it was by accident. Sometimes Sally's father will try to play video games with her, but he's used to operating things with his fingers and not the facial twitches needed for kids' games and their expression analysis software, so there's never any contest.

She's only been into The Forest of Hands twice: first when her grandfather died of heart failure and then a year or so later when her grandmother joined him. When the eulogies had finished and Sally had laid an armful of daffodils on their chests, her mother had done the honours of cutting off the corpse's hands just above the wrists. The funeral director had cleaned the wrists and tied the severed hands together with ribbons – emerald for her grandmother and fox pelt– orange for her grandfather – and their little immediate family had walked through the crowd to enter the forest by themselves.

Now that she is old enough, Sally and her four other eleven-year-old friends get to enter the forest again. No adults will come with them. Sally's mother has curled her hair, and her older sister Leonie has sewn periwinkle-blue pearls along the neck and hem of Sally's new dress. Sally's father buckles her shoes, and looks so proud when Sally says she'll keep them on until she can unbuckle them herself.

The five friends enter the forest when the sun is still high, but the light is dim and beautifully speckled under the canopy. Sally watches Michael's broad grin and Fiona's bulging backpack, how Harriet darts back and forth over the path to gaze at cinnamon-coloured mushrooms and preening ravens and beetles half the size of her foot. She can smell Nicholas chewing a piece of liquorice gum, which isn't very proper, but Sally won't tell.

The path is overgrown, but over the years the village has driven thousands of sharp pebbles into the dirt with their boots, and the children never get lost. It takes them about an hour to reach the grove. Sally has been here before, but she still feels mesmerised. Hundreds of pairs of severed hands, tied with every colour of ribbon around the branches of the trees. Hands of every size and shape, hanging down from their wooden bones. Sally looks for the hands of her grandparents, but none of the hands look withered or sickly. All of the hands are in their prime.

For a minute Sally feels overwhelmed with choice, but then she remembers her parents' advice: that she'll know the right hands when she finds them. On her second loop around the grove she picks a lonely, pale pair on a lower branch. She has to kneel in the thick leaf litter to get to them, and brushes her cheek tentatively against the cold flesh. She unties the periwinkle ribbon with her teeth and catches the hands in her skirt. They're one of the smallest pairs she's seen, built for delicate precision: for minute brush strokes and tiny stitches and all the subtle twitches she's used to making with her face and can learn to transfer to her fingers. There are traces of oil paints under the nails. When she sticks her wrists inside and cradles the hands to her chest, they're cold and feel like triumph.

The hands Fiona chooses are some of the largest, and they're at head height, so Sally stands on her tiptoes and bites Fiona's hands free so Fiona can catch them. Sally's new hands only look a little too big for her, but Fiona's are comically oversized, like you could fit three of her wrists inside one of the openings. Fiona's one of the shortest in their class and has been struggling with her backpack all day, but Sally doesn't think the owner of these gigantic hands would struggle with anything. When they get home, their parents will wrap their hands and wrists in gauze until they warm up and start to mould to their arms. In the meantime, Fiona holds her hands vertically so they don't fall off.

Harriet – who acquired the nickname "Magpie" for her love of the shiny, the beautiful and curious – selects a long-fingered pair with a dozen shining rings around their fingers. They're on the end of a branch, where she can simply bite a palm and pull the hands off without untying the yellow ribbon. Sally spots a silver wolf's head ring, sapphires and topazes, and a simple golden wedding band. She wonders if Harriet has noticed.

Michael wants some hands too high to reach, so the rest of them bend over and let him climb over their backs. Michael tugs down a medium-sized pair tied with red and blue, and they fall next to his feet, in the valley where four children's bottoms are pressed together. He jumps off, surrounded by laughter, retrieves the hands, and shows off the large compass tattoo under the left forefinger. Sally's reminded of whenever she's met up with him over school holidays: he's always had a pair of binoculars slung around his neck and smelled of sea salt.

Nicholas chooses last, and Sally's starting to shiver by the time he's done. He chooses a calloused, scarred pair that is low enough for him to get all alone. *I-don't-need-anyone hands*, thinks Sally, and wonders what's happened that he'd settle on those above all others.

Afterward, he's calmer than he was. As they all grow into their hands, Nicholas grows apart from the rest of the group. At sixteen, he leaves the village to be a soldier, and Sally never sees him again.

But that's years away. Right now, Sally adores her new hands. For a few months, she only wears lace-up shoes, and she ties them in seven different knots, one for every day of the week. She learns how to use chopsticks. She could put on lipstick before, with her toes, but it hurt her back and the muscles inside her leg, and now she wears it easily. She practices signing her name, again and again and again. She pilfers small, insignificant items like hair clips and coin-sized photos and wrapped candies, and pats them inside her pockets. She learns how to floss her teeth.

She paints every day, sometimes with her mouth and sometimes with her fingers. A few of her canvases hang in hotels and pubs and hairdressers around the village. At eighteen, she eventually accepts she can't support herself solely with her painting, and reluctantly sets her sights on becoming a surgeon.

Fiona grows into the body that goes with her hands, which is the body of a handsome, six-foot young man. As a child, all she wanted was to be able to lift up her younger siblings, and now she can lift almost anyone. Fiona mostly goes by Finn these days. Sally and Finn dated for a while, but Finn wanted five kids, so a while wasn't that long. Finn builds Sally's first house and marries a nice girl with magenta nail polish. They go dancing every week, so he gets to lift her all the time, and you should see the way she looks at him.

Following the acquisition of her hands, Harriet falls in love with astronomy and spends her nights fiddling with telescopes and measurements, pens and mathematics. During the day, she designs avant-garde clothes, and opens a boutique in the attic of a delicatessen when she's twenty-three. She marries the village mayor at thirty, and when he's diagnosed with cancer a few years later, Sally operates on him to remove two tumours. He still dies. Harriet wears a gown of black feathers to his funeral, and because she has no immediate family, Sally accompanies her into the forest to hang up her husband's hands with a ribbon of deep purple. Harriet is elected mayor after her husband, a position she retains for the next thirty-nine years.

Michael's family leaves the village soon after Michael gets his hands, and Sally doesn't see or hear of him for more than a decade. He's always been obsessed with boats, with the ocean and fishing and anything nautical, so it's no surprise when he docks at the village as an adult in a sailor's uniform. The surprise is that his boyish grin now belongs to a female face. "Who knew?" he says, about the woman's hands he accidentally chose. He has his hair back in a long braid, and Sally thinks he looks beautiful.

Sally and Finn broke up a year ago, and when Sally asks Michael his preferred name and pronouns, Michael says he doesn't care, so long as she'll go out with him. Michael sneaks her onto the creaking deck of the ship he's working on, and Sally paints him stretched out on the couch in her overstuffed living room. They make a lot of jokes about the Titanic.

Michael becomes a ship's captain, and Sally stays on land, cutting bodies and sewing them back up again, but they know they belong to each other. Later, when they've both had their fill of work, they take a boat, just the two of them, and go exploring. They discover a pack of thylacines, and write six books between them, and once Sally has to extract a piece of shrapnel from Michael's leg. They sleep in treetops and behind waterfalls and below the deck of three different boats. Sally collects a necklace of bones, and Michael collects a body of tattoos: pictures of animals out of scientific journals, and nautical pin-ups and a set of Sally's fingerprints, just above his hip. Many years pass, and many sunsets, and they're still holding hands.

They're still holding hands when Michael wakes one day and Sally doesn't. They're not too far from the village they were born in, so Michael steers the boat back there where Harriet and Finn wait on the dock.

After the funeral, and after Michael severs Sally's hands and they're tied with a periwinkle ribbon, four aging adults cross the threshold to the forest. It's not quite proper, having more than their immediate family, but all of Michael's surviving family is far away down the coast. He's brought Leonie, who sewed delicate pearls to the last ribbon Sally will ever wear, and who needs a walking cane to come but still assures them she can make it. He's brought Finn, who carries a much larger backpack than the one Michael remembers, and who can carry Leonie home if needed. He's brought Harriet in her gown of black feathers, she who guides them to the grove by the position of the stars. Michael has that skill, too, but right now he doesn't want to do anything except walk and hold their hands.

When they reach the grove, Finn pulls a stepladder out of his backpack, and Michael ties Sally's cold hands to the tallest branch he can reach. He kisses each of Sally's fingers, with their prints he still wears above his hipbone. There are still traces of oil paint under their nails. He looks down at each of the faces below him, at their grey hair and wrinkles, and can almost remember how it felt to be young and handless and choosing the rest of his life. He remembers Fiona with her plaited pigtails. Harriet's fingers are still covered in rings. Leonie offers him her hand, which is sweet and impractical, and Michael thanks her and takes it and steps down.

They stay in the forest longer than any of them have stayed before. They stay for hours, with blankets and yoga mats and thermoses of liquorice tea, until they see Sally's hands puff out slightly, turning young and subtle and life-coloured, the way they were when Michael first fell in love with her.

Michael bites his friends gently on their shoulders and, having declared everything to be good, walks out of the grove.

SICKLY SWEET

One fine day behind the mill, my father chops off my hands. He does it with an axe, on a tree stump. He says the devil is coming. That he promised the devil my hands, in exchange for his life.

I do not believe in the devil. My father has been hearing voices for some time.

There is a lot of blood, but no pain. I have heard stories of soldiers, those with their arms sliced off who screamed, not because it hurt but because of the shock of seeing their shoulder and limb separated. The pain is so great that your body snuffs it out. For a little while.

I yell, too. I shriek. I clutch my bloody wrists to my dress and back away, sprinting, stumbling into the forest. My father does not pursue me; the devil can find me anywhere, if I am still wanted.

I curl up at the base of a tree, nesting in its roots. The pain arrives like a delayed traveller. I think I am going to die.

I do not die. I wake with my wrists attached to my dress, the brown of dried blood mixing with the brown of the fabric. They stick, knitting with the cotton, where I'd pressed them tightly to stem the blood flow.

I shift my torso and feel the dried blood cracking on my stomach.

My wrists are swollen, ballooning, fiery things, far more vicious than the worst burn I have experienced. I am loath to upset them further. With effort, I push myself up the tree trunk by my feet, and the bark scrapes sharp against my back.

I begin to walk.

It is a long walk. Several seasons change. My wrists heal, as much could be expected, turning into knots of scar like the knots on an old tree. I take pleasure in small, animalistic activities; biting into a sun-warmed peach and letting the juice run down my chin, diving to the muddy bottom of a river and propelling myself up with jack-knifed legs.

In spring, blood appears between my legs and again, I think I will die.

I do not die.

Later, it comes again, many times.

I don't die then, either.

In the heart of the second autumn, I stumble through a pile of leaves into a clearing. Low, golden sunshine illuminates the charred ruins of a house. And within the ruins, beneath the powdery ash and grey, brittle wood and occasional brick, something glints, metallic and inviting.

I step gingerly over the rubble and peer at my treasure. Nestled safely and perfectly, impossibly intact: a pair of silver hands.

I drop to my knees.

With infinite care and precision, I wipe each hand along my tired, tattered brown dress until the dirt disappears.

The joints in the fingers swing back and forth, more or less like a real hand. There is no rust, no squeaking. When I slip the metal cuffs of the hands onto my wrists, they fit exactly, as if they have been made especially for me.

I have avoided people, for the most part, since my hands were stolen. Now I feel buoyed, lighter; I jog to the nearest town, contented simply by the burbles of conversation, the currents of humans flowing past each other in the shopping district.

So many man-made shapes and colours make my head spin. I wander past shops selling thick, salty-looking ink in glass flasks; stalls with glazed hams suspended from ceilings; doorways with silk jackets, the colour of morning dew and encrusted with dozens of precious stones.

"You!" A booming masculine voice hits me in the ear, not three paces away. I stop, glance around. He is looking directly at me. "Are you going to pay for that?"

My heart hammers in my chest. I look down and see a large bag of flour, and a slightly smaller bag of brown sugar clutched in a silver hand. Adrenaline pours into my veins. I am a criminal. I am mortified. I feel about to faint.

The other silver hand curls, reaches into my pocket and pulls out three gold coins. I stare. I have never had any money of my own, and this does not feel like mine, either.

The merchant huffs and holds out his own sweaty hand.

"I'm sorry," I whisper in my rusty voice, dropping the coins down into his palm. He nods like he doesn't believe me.

I take off along the cobblestones, down the streets into the forest. I make a nest in some tree roots, place down the flour and the sweet, caramel-smelling sugar and examine the silver hands.

They do not feel like my hands. I cannot move the fingers of my own free will, and yet they have moved. They have curled and grasped and extended without my consent.

I shake, pressing one hand between my knees, pulling back my arm to wrench the hand away like an unwanted glove. I grunt. But no matter how hard I press or pull, the hand stays a part of me. It slips out between my knees like it's melded to my skin.

I try again with the other hand to no avail.

When my tears fall, I let them fall on the silver, and I wish fervently that it will rust.

I take the flour and sugar to the clearing, to the ruins of the house. I remember a formation of low bricks, sticking out amongst the wreckage, which gave me the impression of an oven.

I search through the rubble for any other bricks, stacking them together, interlocking them with the remnants of the old oven. The silver hands grab everything easily, nimbly, more skilled at construction than I was ever with my own flesh. They are clever, these hands. They fit the oven together like an expert puzzle.

At the end, the finished oven sits there, red and swollen, and reminds me of my bleeding wrists.

I am ashamed to say I go back to the town. More than anything – food, love, justice – I feel I am starved of opportunity.

The hands have made me ravenous.

From the stalls they pick jars of cinnamon, towers of sea salt, butter wrapped in golden cloth, cloves and ginger in wooden boxes, eggs in woven baskets... And each time, a silver hand dips into my pocket and fishes out gold coins. I never see the coins fall in, but I learn to recognise the slight weight in my pocket, the almost imperceptible clink as the silver hands pilfer someone else's pockets or bags.

I return to the clearing laden with parcels.

I sit in the rubble and press the cinnamon and ginger to my nose, inhaling deeply. I rub the exquisite, perfectly smooth egg against my arms, face and neck. I tip a little of the salt onto my tongue and revel in it, my eyes sliding shut.

And then the hands really get to work.

Deep in the woods, though not that deep, stands a house made entirely of gingerbread. The walls and roof and floors are gingerbread, as are the chimney and single iced door. If you licked the windows you would know them to be sugar, and if you bit into the windowsills you would know them to be thick, fresh marzipan.

The house does not age, or rot, or melt. Encrusted in the gingerbread are hard candies of every flavour and colour, liquorices which seem to sparkle, candy-covered chocolates in the shapes of hearts and stars and clovers.

Inside the house there lives a woman, though she was only recently a girl. They say idle hands are the devil's work, but how fervently I wish that mine would stop.

The silver hands are always moving, like mechanical spiders desperate to get out of the rain. Sometimes they clean and scrub and tidy. Sometimes they play over my body, prying open my mouth and feeling my tongue, the ridges of my teeth. Sometimes they crawl between my legs and play me like an instrument, running their intelligent fingers inside me and warming with my body heat.

Sometimes I don't mind.

Mostly, they like to cook. They like sugar. They like ever more elaborate desserts, which never seem to go off and pile in towers, gathering on most surfaces of the house and in ever-expanding nooks and crannies. They cook shelves and cupboards for more cooked treats.

They cook another room for the house.

Often, at night, I suffocate the hands beneath my mattress and feel them struggle, twisting, beneath my body weight. After a little while they give up. Alone, unmoving, quiet washes over me. Bliss.

There are usually scars from this ritual when the hands break free; long scratch marks across my torso, legs or back, one or two or five in a row, but they're always worth it.

And then, one day, a gap in my wall appears, and on the other side a chewing child.

They freeze when I open the door; a boy with his mouth stuffed with gingerbread, and a girl with her lips wrapped around my windowsill. They are short, sickly pale and bony, their wide blue eyes protruding too far out of their skulls. I suspect they're not much younger than I am.

The boy swallows hastily, the girl detaches her lips.

"You must be very hungry," I say.

The girl smiles and digs her fingernails into her other arm. "We've walked for three days," she says, "with very little food, and are lost in these woods, and our parents can't feed us anymore."

A dozen competing emotions swim inside me like a school of fish.

Eventually, I say, "If you believe you shall starve if you don't come in... You may."

The children's faces relax with joy. A silver hand pushes the door fully open, and with barely restrained hunger, they dart inside.

I feed the children like they've never eaten in their lives.

I bring them sticky date puddings drenched in hot fudge; towering chocolate cakes with sparkling shards of sugary caramel, raspberry and mint strewn in three layers; macaroons in twelve different flavours; cupcakes containing huge chunks of cookie dough; scones with jams and the fluffiest creams and melted chocolates.

When they've eaten their fill, groaning with pleasure on my wooden benches, I make them a bed of marshmallows in the corner of my living room. They curl up on the soft, rubbery pillows and are asleep within minutes.

I clean for some time to delay my own sleep. The hands have been delighted all evening, practically dancing off my wrists, and the guilt eats at me like acid. I should send the children on their way after breakfast tomorrow.

Later, under my blankets, the hands do not want me to rest. They want to play.

I decide I won't put them under the mattress tonight, won't make them angry with the children in the house.

I will send the children away tomorrow.

I am still half asleep when a third hand appears on my shoulder. I pay it no more attention than my own breathing.

"Are you alright?" asks a female voice.

My eyes snap open. The girl's blonde hair, inches away, is almost iridescent white in such early dawn. Unaccustomed to either company or shame, I throw my arms to either side of me.

"You were making noises."

I try to control my breathing, try to restrict the bile rising up my throat. "Noises?" I whisper.

"Murmurs, mutterings in your sleep... You were having a nightmare?"

I consider the girl's open face. A small glob of melted marshmallow is stuck to the side of her forehead.

"Always," I say.

We pad through the front door and around to my back garden, little more than two fruit trees and a small hill of seeded soil. The girl stares at every fruit and every leaf, cataloguing and greedy.

I hold out my arms. "You're very welcome."

She falls to her knees before a dozen strawberries, shovelling them into her mouth with dazzling efficiency. I sit nearby, my hands drawing meaningless patterns in the damp dirt. In the end she leaves three on their stems, wiping the crimson juice from her lips. Her hunger seems to still.

I suspect it's rude to ask, but the children will be gone in a matter of mouthfuls. I ask, "Do you despise your parents, for letting you down?"

The girl's eyes widen. "Why would I despise them? They did their best."

"They almost killed you."

"They sent us away because they couldn't bear to see us starve before their eyes. I can't hate them for that." She picks a fat lemon from the tree and peels the skin with a combination of fingernails and teeth. "We aren't starving anymore, thanks to you."

She comes and sits next to me, too close; my hands may damage her. I scoot back. In the dull light I'm uncertain, but I think her face falls.

"It's not personal," I say. "I lost my hands a long time ago."

She studies the patterns on the ground. "They seem to work well enough."

"They're not..." I'm afraid, suddenly, that the hands can hear me. "They're not really mine." The last word morphs into a gasp as a sharp silver finger digs into the flesh of my side. A tiny darker patch appears on my brown dress.

Perhaps the hands can hear; perhaps they simply sense intention.

The girl is up on her feet. She hesitates for a moment, rocking back on her heels, and then kicks the offending hand away from my side. With her right knee, she pushes my shoulder to the ground and pins the hand with her left boot. It convulses like a dying spider.

My other hand is blessedly still.

The wind has been knocked out of me. I lie with my head in the dewy grass, staring up at the frightened girl.

Her shin is warm along the side of my torso. I can't remember the last time I touched someone.

"Do you need bandages?" she asks. "Something else?"

I shake my head against the grass. "I don't think it's deep. It will heal like the others."

"Others?"

The hand stops its convulsions after one last spasm, but the girl doesn't move away.

"There's a town to the east of here," I say. "A bit less than half a day's walk away. You should head there. Take as much food as you want, I insist."

She doesn't respond. Instead, she looks over her shoulder at an empty wire cage. "Is that for meat?"

"Chickens," I confirm. "But years ago." I'm struck by old memories of the hands snapping their necks.

She nods. "Are we safe to go to breakfast?"

I take several moments considering the frozen hands. They are playacting, surely, but I suspect they'll behave until their next calculated moment of rebellion. "If we behave," I say. "Though they shan't like you leaving."

"I'm not planning to leave," says the girl.

Breakfast passes in relative silence. At one point the boy reaches over and scratches the marshmallow off the girl's forehead. She smiles at him and crinkles her nose, and I feel a stab of jealousy for that kind of easy companionship. This morning, the hands have refused me any liquid but melted chocolate in a mug. I take tiny sips; sickly sweet.

With a couple of short, insistent gestures the girl directs the boy to my back garden. She follows, announcing she'll be back in a minute, and either I believe her or the silver hands do, because they make no move to cease scratching patterns into the wooden sides of my mug.

The girl does return shortly, without her brother but with a strange sort of smile. She tosses a second lemon in the air between alternating palms. "We should do it," she says. "What you were talking about in your sleep."

I feel instantly naked.

"We should eat the boy," she says. "Cook him."

The only sound is the lemon thumping in her hands.

She presses on: "I mean, not even chicken for years. You must be starved for meat. I've locked him in the cage."

She points needlessly to the garden. "Go and see."

I hear the blood beating in my ears. I step outside; the cage has not moved. The boy is curled against its far corner, one blue eye open and fixed warily on me.

I take another step and he cries out. I am speechless.

"Not any closer!" he yells. "I know what those hands can do!"

I hold them up, clear in front of me. The silver fingers wriggle.

"You put them away!"

The venom in his voice makes my throat constrict. I tuck my hands tight behind my back, which is the best I can do. I venture another step.

Like a well-practised magic trick, he reveals a rusty key – the key to the cage – and winks. It disappears again.

I take out the silver hands.

"Are you going to eat me?"

I realise with relief that the hands can't reach him while he's caged.

"Not now," I say, to buy some time. "I have to fatten you up first. You're so thin; it would hardly be worth cooking you now."

His tears come right on cue, and when I return inside to his sister, she's sitting cross-legged on my dining table and squeezing lemon juice onto her tongue.

"Do you have an axe?"

My hands pause in the middle of kneading lemon-scented cookie dough. "No," I tell her, and the hands start up again.

"How do you chop firewood, then?"

"No firewood." I push a lock of hair out of my face with my shoulder. "I use oil."

The girl's mouth cracks open.

"It never seems to run out," I confess, and find I can't meet her eyes any longer.

Her footsteps retreat towards the front door. "It's just – I've been looking at your knives. We'll need something hardier to chop up a boy. A cleaver? I'll go to the town you talked about. Be back just after nightfall if I leave now."

I nod, not entirely sure what I'm agreeing to. "There's some money in the cupboard to your left, the one with..."

The silver hands have raced across the table and are climbing up my torso, digging painfully into my flesh as they crawl. I try and wrench them away, but my arm muscles are weak from this angle and the fingers sink into my stomach and breasts too deep.

Within two seconds the cold metal is wrapped around my neck, still covered in traces of cookie dough.

The thumbs are pressed tight into my oesophagus. My lips open in a continuous gasp. I struggle, bashing the hands against the edge of the table, but they hold fast. My vision blurs.

The last thing I see is the girl, her arms prying at my wrists. She calls my name like she means it.

#

When I wake, it is surreal. Under any other circumstances I would freeze completely. At this very moment I am too wrung out to care.

I am lying on top of the bed, the woollen blanket scratching against my naked back. My arms are wrenched to either side of the mattress. The silver hands are out of sight, and tugging confirms that they are both tied securely under the bed.

The girl has removed my dress and is straddling my hips, wiping my cuts with a rag soaked in green liquid. The rag stings like being sliced up all over again.

Absinthe, then.

There are perhaps two dozen cuts staggered over my torso. The girl attends to one just next to my nipple and my chest shudders. She glances up, registers I'm awake and immediately averts her gaze.

"Apologies. There was..."

"You don't have to apologise." My voice comes out hoarse and scratchy, followed by a minor coughing fit.

The girl leaves to fetch a glass of water. As she goes, her thigh brushes over my hip. My mind feels ill and unanchored, like I've come down with a fever, but I don't think I have. Thoughts arrive as if through a fog.

Sipping is awkward, with her hand behind my head and the cup at my lips. I take tiny, restricted swallows and trails of water run down the sides of my mouth. She wipes them aside with her thumb.

"What did you tie them up with?"

"I found rope in a kitchen cupboard," she says.

"It won't hold them for much longer. An hour or two, maybe. They'll slice through it. They've hollowed out chunks of my mattress."

Her face falls, her hand holding the cup shakes. A couple of drops escape, falling onto my skin and running down the cleft between my breasts. She turns away to gather her composure.

Three long, fresh scabs run down her forearm.

Eventually, she says, "Well, what else will hold them? Anything here?"

"Chains would," I say. "I have none. The mattress might for another hour, longer if they thought that wasn't going to be permanent."

She plays with her fingernails while she considers this. Glances under the bed, then climbs on and reclaims her position over my hips. "I was going to..." She leans forward, biting her lip and touches my elbows, making a sawing motion with her fingers. "But there's no time."

I nod. The axe. The cleaver. "How did you tie them up at all?"

"Oh. I wasn't planning to. But once you passed out, they went limp for a while. I don't think they want you dead." Her blue eyes bore into mine. "Really dead."

When she doesn't get a response, the girl picks up the rag and the absinthe again. "I know it seems a bit redundant. But may I?"

My mouth feels too dry. "Alright."

Her wipes with the rag are gentle and precise. She rests her other hand on my arm, my shoulder, my ribs for balance. Her skin feels twice as soft and warm as my own. Sometimes, she traces my many scars with an absent fingertip.

Despite myself, my tears start to fall.

She kisses them from the sides of my face, her lips like velvet. The light fabric of her dress grazes my stomach, my breasts, my nipples. My skin breaks out in goosebumps. My breath comes out in tiny sighs and shudders.

She kisses my forehead, my cheeks, my lips. I feel like I'm floating up out of my body, and the stinging fades to background noise. There is no mattress, no rope, no silver hands.

Then her own tears fall onto my collarbone.

"Is there anything we can do for you?" she whispers. "Anything at all?"

When the words finally come, my voice is cold and composed. Not quite my own.

"We have to cook the boy," I say.

Inside the oven, the fire blazes. Flames of a million different yellows and oranges lick at the bricks. The boy has been fed and watered. The girl has prepared the lemon-scented cookie dough for baking.

The hands are largely behaving themselves, almost humming in anticipation.

I will my pulse to slow and turn to the girl. "It's time."

She looks me straight in the eyes, so blatantly that I'm worried a silver finger will impale me. "Are you sure?"

"Yes. Check that the oven is hot enough, will you?"

She tugs open the oven door. The heat is noticeable even from here. The girl peers inside, the flames playing over her lovely face. "I don't know how to," she lies.

I blurt out the first curse I can think of. "Let me, then." I shuffle over and take her place, my heart inside my mouth.

I stick my head clear inside the oven. Farther than necessary. So close that the fire sparks in my hair and I can feel my face beginning to burn.

"It's ready," I call.

And she shoves me inside, where the world is white hot.

My last thoughts are a series of cluttered imaginings: that the girl and her brother run home, their arms full of candies and treasures and coins.

That they leave the remains of the gingerbread house behind them, a smoking pile of powdery ash.

That they arrive, safe, to loving parents.

And that somewhere, the devil appears to a father who bargains a daughter he forgets could be, behind his mill.

It's a small comfort. To know I'm not the only one.

And the silver hands don't burn at all.

EMELIA AND THE UNDROWNED

Clarice falls out of the canoe when she is five and a half. She has two siblings, older and louder than she is, so it takes ninety-four seconds for the remaining occupants of the canoe to realise she has gone. Her father dives valiantly after her, but by then it makes no difference. She has sunk too deep, and three protective tentacles reach out to claim her. A fourth tentacle pries between her lips and tinkers around like a mechanic inside a bonnet. When it withdraws, the water rushes in, and Clarice can breathe two dozen metres beneath the sea.

Emelia sleeps inside a working aquarium with three squids the size of large dogs. They hang suspended in the middle of the tank, the squids curled around her like she's the leg of a pier. She owns a penthouse near the beach, and the squids are more than capable of removing themselves from the aquarium, so Emelia can only presume they enjoy her company.

Some of her children choose to sleep in their own, smaller glass tanks, half for their own comfort and half, she suspects, because they enjoy emulating her. There are still plenty of children who prefer more traditional beds. They are not her biological children: almost every morning she swims down to the sea bottom to meet with more of the squids. Occasionally there is an undrowned child wrapped in their arms, and Emelia takes her new charge from them with reverence. Rarer still: their arms are empty, but they'll move their tentacles in the way that means: *there was a child but it went away*. Then Emelia loses half a day searching the shoreline for dripping scavengers or toddlers with imminent tantrums.

So Emelia is the one to retrieve Clarice from a cocoon of gentle tentacles, and sits her on the edge of the pier with a Picnic chocolate bar and a beach towel around her small shoulders. She tells Clarice, "Those squids saved you. They gave you a gift. But there are people who would want to hurt you, and other children like you, for that gift. They would run tests on you and make you do things you don't want to do. They might take you and other children away. So you can never tell anyone else what happened to you down under the sea. Not even your parents."

Emelia would never encourage Clarice to stay with her. She doesn't even suggest it. For some of the children, she drops them back near their homes and they return to their regular lives. But most of them have changed, after breathing seawater for hours with tentacles draped around them like a royal cloak. Most of them beg her to let them stay, to join the others who have stared long into the ocean with nothing between their faces and the deep. She's only just started Grade One, and she's wet and hungry and disoriented, but Clarice asks. So Emelia listens.

A long time ago, when Emelia was seventeen and only recently undrowned herself, another missing girl washed up on the beach with grand stories of squids and underwater adventures. It was in multiple newspapers. Emelia ripped the skin off her lips with worry, waiting for the next child with a similar report, and wondering how many more before adults would take them seriously and life would start to fall apart.

The penthouse apartment was bought when she was eighteen. There are not a tremendous amount of jobs which lend themselves to breathing underwater, but some of her children are underwater photographers. Some of them fish; some of them hunt for debris which has fallen to the ocean floor. Some of them are professional mermaids, who largely sit in the shallows with fake tails and pose for pictures. When she was eighteen, Emelia was a different sort of professional mermaid, in a largely-underwater porn film. She does not tell the children that this is how she paid for their home, or the bedrock of how she continues to support them. She wears sunglasses on the street in case anyone still recognises "Melissa Harrington" and tells the children she has sensitive eyes.

Emelia brings Clarice up to the penthouse, and the other children run to embrace her and stroke her wet hair. They all trade origin stories in the sunroom, and Emelia makes everyone pancakes with extra maple syrup and choc-chip ice-cream. In the afternoon, Emelia puts together Clarice's new bed and tucks it into a corner next to Reagan's and Elodie's. The older children start to teach Clarice the basics of squids and the maps of the beaches and nearby ocean. For dinner, they have freshly-caught fish and chips and sit around in a circle, and after she's finished eating Clarice is allowed to stand on a chair inside Emelia's sleeping tank, so she can listen and pat the squids at the same time.

Emelia hasn't had a boyfriend since she was seventeen, because it was dating or squids and the squids won. But she's proud of the undrowned family they've built, child by saved child. She feels her heart grow three times when she sees Clarice's head duck underwater, blow bubbles around the squids, and grin straight at her.

Emelia still wishes she'd met the squids under less traumatic circumstances. She wishes she didn't have to be bound, weighed with concrete and tossed into the ocean to end up here. But now at least "here" is very good.

She tucks Clarice in with a "Goodnight, squidling," and sinks down into her own watery bed, where it is silent and safe.

WRECKED

I.

They think I have the mirror for vanity reasons, but that's not really the case. I have it to examine the distinct scar above my lip, next to the right corner of my mouth. Despite all the other issues on the island, this one keeps niggling at me. I can't remember where or how I got it. It makes me feel as though I'm missing something.

Something big.

II.

The winds pick up that night, worse than we've seen them in all five years. They blow the beach up into a sandstorm. They blow our wooden shacks into the forest where they shatter on the trees. They blow our bonfire into the undergrowth and set the island ablaze.

Members of my tribe struggle along the beach, trying to preserve precious objects and provisions, but they're fighting a losing battle. "Leave it," I bellow, squinting through the wind and sand and gesturing wildly towards the ocean. "Get into the water!"

They look at me with horrified, wind-whipped faces. Everything will be gone – we'll have even less than we started with, straight after the wreck.

I manage to corral most people into the icy water before wading in behind them. A few stragglers are still on the beach, or have disappeared into the forest in search of loved ones. I submerge myself in the inky ocean up to my eyes. The salt burns where my skin is bare and ravaged by the sand, but at least the sand can't tear at me underwater.

Ray and Thelia find me and each take one of my hands. Their eyes glow amber in the firelight. I squeeze their hands and pull them closer for warmth, and together we watch the island burn.

III.

I'm woken at sunrise by the blast of a horn. The entire time we've been here, we've never seen a boat or plane of any kind. My body stings and burns, and my mouth is paper dry. I force myself up out of the tangle of Ray and Thelia's limbs.

There's a boat, perhaps half a kilometre away. A big boat. A boat heading straight for us.

Its crew are two dozen grinning people in buttercup-yellow rain jackets, armed with enough blankets, soup and hot tea for all of us. After being certain last night that we would all starve in a matter of days, it seems ridiculously perfect. I wonder if this is all a glorious, last-ditch hallucination.

I sit on the sun-warmed deck, huddled under a woollen blanket in my damp leathers, sipping lemon tea and believing it's a nice way to go.

IV.

There must have been something in the tea.

I wake to fluorescent lights, clinical whites and greys, and a middle-aged woman in front of me, staring.

"She'll be disoriented," says a man in an oversized lab coat. "Take it slow."

The woman smiles. "Hello, Kerry," she says. "Don't you recognise your mother?"

IV.

When I fully comprehend the situation I burst into tears. Between the sobs I ask to be alone, and they put me in a "private" room with one-way glass so they can monitor my state. Truthfully, I don't know what I'm crying about. Is it the hardships of the last five years, trapped on the island? The people who disappeared and assumed dead, when I understand now that they were simply evacuated? The time I lost with my mother, time from my real life. And perhaps most damning: that I chose all of these things?

Vivian wouldn't cry. She led her tribe with such confidence and wisdom, with such fire in her belly. These toned arms of mine are Vivian's arms. This hard stomach is Vivian's stomach. The only thing that's not hers is this lip scar, obvious to me because I've lived with this face for thirty-two years. I can understand how the people creating Vivian's fake memories could've missed it.

After an hour or so, my mother – my real mother, not Vivian's – walks in with some chocolate chip cookies and an orange juice box. She says, "Sweetheart, sweetheart, please don't cry. You're home and safe and you have more money than you'll know what to do with. The show was a tremendous hit, especially Vivian. You never have to worry about anything again."

I allow her to hug me, burying my head into her cardigan, which smells vaguely of lavender and fresh dirt.

I don't miss the dangers of the island, the lack of medical care, or the lack of technology. But I do miss a lot of other things. Kerry doesn't have a tribe, or any power here, or people in love with her. Kerry doesn't have a lover. Kerry doesn't have a sense of doing something meaningful with her life.

I break the hug to wipe my face with a wad of tissues. "Yes," I say. "You're right. Everything's just fine now."

V.

I have dinner with Michael, who played Ray, at an exclusive restaurant that offers us hot face towels on arrival. The other patrons take surreptitious photos with their smart-phones. To my relief, we're ushered into a more private booth towards the back, where two glasses of sparkling wine and a vase of purple roses wait.

Before we sit down, I embrace him and smell his familiar, intoxicating scent that made Vivian's abdomen tighten. Our bodies are the same, even if our minds aren't. I feel mildly giddy.

"How are you finding things?" I ask, after we've both ordered from the small selection of things on the menu that we actually understand.

"Strange," he says. "Like I always know what Ray would do, even though I'm acting different."

I nod, sipping my bubbles.

"It's weird having Ray's memories – both from before and on the island – and knowing they're not real. They felt so...final."

"But it *was* real on the island," I say. "That was the whole point. We didn't know it was a show. That was our reality for five years, even if they did alter our personalities and memories to their liking. That doesn't make it fake."

Michael's eyebrows knit together. We sit in silence until a slow smile breaks across his face.

He says, "You know what Ray really enjoyed? Kissing you."

I smile despite myself. "Vivian enjoyed that, too."

It had never gone farther than kissing because Vivian had flat-out refused to risk getting pregnant on the island. In fact, I had gotten my tubes tied before the show, but of course Vivian hadn't known that.

Michael stares at me expectantly. "Do you think we might be able to do that again?"

I leave the dinner knowing Michael is not Ray. Ray was sexier in every way, from his name to his voice, to his smile and how he ran his fingers over his stubble. Ray was a creation, and I doubt I'll be dining with Michael again.

VI.

I buy a small, beautiful house in a leafy suburb, a house with high walls and discreet security. I buy the first four seasons of Wrecked, the extended editions (the fifth season hasn't reached DVD yet), and lie in my enormous bed watching the highlights of the survivors' first four years.

I watch them fight, and learn, and build a new home for themselves. I watch them adapt, and cry, and form new families. I watch them discover luxurious debris, like Vivian's mirror, at strategic points throughout the show, cleverly placed by the production team.

I watch some of them get sick, or injured, and vanish overnight. I watch the tribe arm themselves over new threats, and watch conflicts as they come to a head. I watch the tribe split into three halfway through season two. Vivian rises up to lead the original tribe, and she looks like a queen.

She looks like Vivian, in her cloak of leather and teeth and fur, and not at all like Kerry.

I watch Vivian and Ray's simmering, largely non-physical romance build for weeks until Vivian ends it. I watch Vivian discover a very different romance with Thelia – Thelia, who was gentle and flexible where Vivian could be cruel and rigid. Thelia, who could never knock up Vivian.

This is the part of the show that I struggle with the most. Vivian is not me – is not even me playing a character, in the traditional sense – and she's done dozens of things that I would never do. Because of her, my body has killed and skinned animals, has knocked out someone's tooth with its fist, has sewn up a cut with a bone needle and strands of hair. But Thelia is different. Because I feel like my body, rather than just Vivian's mind, must be at least slightly responsible for that.

It's not something I ever considered before the show.

VII.

I know exactly what kind of life I could be living, because Michael is living it.

Two and a half months later he's still a hot topic, appearing on all of the talk shows and posing for photo-shoots in a litany of glossy magazines. I flick through a six-page spread of him shirtless, riding a white horse along the shoreline with a sword slung across his back. I spot him in an ad for expensive coffee on the side of a bus shelter, emblazoned with the slogan *"for the man you want to be."*

I know the same opportunities are available to me, but I can't bring myself to say "yes" to a single one.

Who they really want is Vivian. Not me, the poor substitute who can barely get out of bed in the morning.

VIII.

The men are half shell-shocked in their swivel chairs, glancing at each other a few times a minute and then back to me.

"So," says the one with the eyebrow ring, "did you want to change your memories as well, or just the personality?"

"Just personality," I say. "No need to confuse myself."

The other one steeples his fingers — the one with the ballpoint pen leaking through his shirt pocket. "Well, it's usually prohibitively expensive, but you're Kerry fucking Kingsley."

"Yes," I say flatly. "I'm Kerry fucking Kingsley."

"Usually you also have to get a specialist to design the personality blueprint and then we fit that to your brain, but we've still got the one for Vivian in our files. You're aware of the possible complications of the surgery?" Eyebrow Ring rifles through his filing cabinet until I interrupt.

"I'm aware."

"'Cos this is brain surgery. And it's not like the production company is going to shell out billions of dollars to your family this time if something fucks up."

I cross my arms under my breasts, over the chest of my woollen reindeer jumper. "I've already spoken to the company. They're thrilled that I'm considering this, especially out of my own pocket. Don't worry about it."

They glance at each other again, wide-eyed. Ink Stain hands me a stark white business card with a single name and phone number.

"Whenever you're ready," he says.

IX.

Two weeks before the auction of my childhood home, I stand in my old bedroom, feeling like a giant in the small space. It's only been partially refurbished – my former presence here is a selling point, complete with the ballet-printed bedclothes and framed photos of my teenage self in early stage productions.

I touch the frames with a dulled mixture of shame and reverence: here is Kerry cast as Nora Helmer in *A Doll's House*; here is Kerry portraying a figurative blackbird; here is Kerry with her head sticking out of an urn in Beckett's *Play*.

The house smells of my mother's roast potatoes and pricey orchid air freshener.

I feel half-asleep. When I shift, I can only just sense the stiff cardboard of the business card through the back pocket of my jeans.

X.

I'll schedule the surgery tomorrow.

Today I'm having coffee with Mary-Anne.

Mary-Anne has three shelves of china vases, two whippets and not a single red hair out of place. Watching her bring out the cappuccinos on a silver tray, hazy images of Thelia flash unbidden to my mind. Vivian has seen Thelia naked.

Vivian has seen Thelia naked a lot.

I dig my nails into my palms. "I didn't mean this as a date or anything," I say.

She smiles at me, wrapping her perfectly manicured nails around the mug. "I know," she says.

"I just wanted to meet you."

She nods politely. "Lots of memories."

I nod, too. With a deep breath and considerable coffee-gazing, I explain to her my thoughts on the surgery, thoughts I've not previously revealed outside of the lab.

"Vivian was pretty amazing," she says. "But I won't be Thelia."

"Yes." My eyes widen. "Of course."

"You could just be Vivian anyway," she offers. "You don't actually need the surgery."

I snort. "Just because I know what she'd do in theory, doesn't mean I can really do that."

"Doesn't it?" One of the whippets trots over and perches on Mary-Anne's foot, flicking its tail against her ankle. She massages its temple with her fingertips, and says, "You're an actress."

I freeze with my coffee halfway to the table.

"Do you really want to be Vivian?" she asks.

The hand with the coffee is shaking now. I place the mug down as gently as possible, but it still clinks too loudly against the table. "I think so," I say quickly. "Most of her."

"Then do it."

"It's not that simple."

Mary-Anne just watches me for a while, both of us silent. She picks up one of the after-dinner mints on the silver tray, tears it open and sucks on it for a good minute.

Finally, she says, "You're ashamed of her."

My anxiety, which had started to dissipate, returns in full force. "Who?" I ask.

"Vivian."

I try to focus on my breathing.

"Probably best that you don't have the surgery, because she'd remember. Vivian would remember you were so ashamed of her."

My face is burning up. I feel the familiar pressure behind my eyes, which pre-empts tears, feel myself curling further into myself. Breathe.

Mary-Anne must notice, because she dislodges the whippet and disappears into the kitchen, before returning with a glass of water for me.

I sip it slowly, glancing up at her warm brown eyes, the colour of her after-dinner mints. I wish she was Thelia.

"Vivian's well loved," she says. "I promise. You can relax."

I try and relax. I close my eyes and try and find the woman I left on the ship, bent over her lemon tea in a polystyrene mug.

I know what she would do.

"Thanks, Mary-Anne," I say. I grin and stretch my spine, working all the knots out of my neck. This body is stiff but familiar. My voice sounds a little deeper, down from somewhere satisfyingly low in my gut.

I brush a finger over the tiny indentation in my lip, acquired when I was ten years old by falling over a farm's barbed wire fence. "Now I know where I got that damn lip-scar."

CANDY

They take us there in an air-conditioned van. The cell is air-conditioned.

And at the end of the second day when they have given us water but no food she says they have made their intentions clear.

"No," I say. "I'd rather starve."

"If you do, they'll turn the heating on. I want one of us to walk out of here."

"You can't know that."

"Why else are we here?"

We stare at each other. Her hard, pink body is almost transparent in the fluorescent light. She stretches out a hand to where I'm collapsed on the floor and touches my lips.

I recoil. Even that light touch is slightly sticky. I fight the urge to lick my lips.

"It would be a good way to die," she says. "Better than melting."

I refuse wholeheartedly, but when I wake my mouth tastes sweet and she's missing her little finger.

"Does it hurt?"

"No," she says, "it just feels like losing something."

I feel like crying but can't summon the energy.

"I'd like it if you were awake next time." This is almost a demand. "I liked your mouth on my hand. No sense wasting it."

I'd never touched her before, not without special gloves on. Certainly not with my lips. Humans are warm, messy creatures, with sweat and spit. "I don't want to do it this way."

"Too bad," she says.

"They could release us in an hour."

"Too bad." She straddles my jeans with no concern for my body warmth and sticks her ring finger into my mouth. "Don't you dare feel guilty."

So I don't.

We take the rest of it methodically, with as much discussion and planning as my sugar-addled brain can muster.

When I've eaten the fingers of her right hand but not the palm, I strip and she runs her hand-and-a-half over my entire body, once, twice. I shiver in the air-conditioning. She says, "I'll miss you," and that she'd like to taste me, but we've decided that her mouth is off-limits until the very end.

When I put my clothes back on I'm a little sticky everywhere, and she has a little less of her hands than she did before.

She's been relatively quiet so far, but when I start licking her wrists she starts to moan. All the guilt I've been suppressing comes racing back. I stop. But when she opens her eyes, all I see in them is hunger.

"Keep going," she says. "It doesn't hurt. You have such a clever tongue."

I'd cry if crying wasn't such a waste.

"I love you," I whisper, and lick her wrist away while she throws her head back.

I have trouble sleeping, shaky from sugar and her ecstasy and the reality of what I'm doing. She lies next to me, not touching, with no hands and half an arm, and sings me to sleep all night.

In the breaks she tells me stories, both true and fictional, and spins elaborate tales of the life I'll have after this.

Once her arms are gone I prop her up against the wall.

She giggles when I eat her toes. Once her legs are gone I have to prop her up much better.

"They could release us in an hour," I whisper.

"Don't you dare feel guilty."

But I do.

Bit by bit, she vanishes. When she is barely more than a head, I rest her carefully on my lap while I sleep. I trace her features with my fingertips.

I feel like I am rotting from inside.

When the time comes, I ask her for her last words.

"What is there to say?" she replies. And then, "Kiss me."

So I do.

I think the door swings open less than ten minutes later.

A man stands there, neutral. I stand with difficulty. He leads me down the hall.

"It's not natural," he says. "Humans with things we're supposed to eat."

On the way back, the van is stifling hot.

FROM STRANGERS

Several years ago, the mansion and its grounds were at the peak of their splendour. Now the girl is nine or ten, and forbidden from entering the garden due to its disrepair.

Tonight is the first night she has been left to her own devices, unattended while her parents sit by lamplight at the other end of the house. If she ties a knot at the end of her white dress, she can slip out through the broken window overlooking the abandoned koi pond.

Between the flowers and the weeds, picking her way across the stones half-buried in the mud, the girl makes her way towards the topiary maze. She has a vague memory of being younger and running through the sunlit, manicured hedges when life was clean and simple.

The girl halts at the maze's entry, poised on tiptoes, and slowly lets her heels sink to the ground.

Before her, a strange young woman perches on a stone column. The woman's legs are pale as moonlight, and above them her dress looks like the star-spangled sky, like the night itself has flowed down to wrap around her skin. But it's the woman's neck that the girl's eyes settle on, where approximately four dozen teeth are strung on a silver chain.

Some of them look like the girl's baby teeth.

"No need to be frightened of me," says the woman. When she opens her mouth, the teeth inside it are largely pointy and assorted, like they've been picked at random from a variety of omnivorous and carnivorous animals. "It's wise to be frightened of other things; the world is a generally frightening place to live. But you needn't waste your fright on me specifically."

Once upon a time, a princess married a king, and they lived happily ever-

#

"Your dress," says the girl.

"You like it?"

"I've never... I've never seen anything like it."

The woman smiles gently, keeping her lips pressed closed. "A present from my father," she says. She uncrosses her moonlit legs and reaches into a hidden pocket at her waist. Her arm disappears to the elbow before resurfacing, and clutched in her hand are a variety of wrapped candies.

The girl watches, unblinking. The woman's free hand sorts through the wrappers: shiny, glossy, circles and rectangles and cylinders, striped and checked, ruby reds and royal purples and liquid-looking golds. Her fingers stop at a small, aquamarine wrapper. She drops the rest of the candies back into her pocket and pulls the aquamarine foil off with a single tug of both hands.

"Want to try?" asks the woman. She tears the crimson, sugar-coated candy in half and pops one part past her lips. A slight wind whips up, and instantly the twigs in her hair and the mud encrusted on her shoes drop away.

The girl reaches for the other half. It fizzes in her mouth like a raspberry soda. It melts over her tongue like butter in a pan. She feels the fizz race through every inch of her body, cleaning her thoroughly inside and out.

When she gasps, the grass stains on her dress are gone, the mud flecks on her stockings have disappeared. The girl is spotless.

"Be more careful on your way back," says the woman. "You wouldn't want your parents to know."

She drops down from the column, graceful as a cat, and vanishes inside the maze.

Once upon a time, a king married the most beautiful maiden in the land. And when she died young, she made him promise to never marry anyone less beautiful.

And they had a daughter.

The second time the girl sneaks away, her parents are sitting back-to-back in front of the fire, clutching glasses of brandy. Her mother has fallen asleep and is starting to drool, and her father dares not move for fear of waking his wife. The girl is safe.

She races through the garden, full-to-bursting with joy and anticipation, and cannot remember the last time running was so exhilarating. She has chosen a brown dress and brown shoes, deliberately, so that the weeds and twigs leave minimal marks.

But there is no strange woman waiting for her at the start of the maze. So she steps inside.

Inside the maze, the weeds are thicker than ever, and flowers and vines blossom in colours and shapes she's never seen before. Beetles, metallic and luminous, dart over moonlit lilies, their bodies shining topaz, lime and sapphire under their flickering wings. They remind her of the candies in the woman's palm. She fights the urge to pluck a beetle from the air and see if it tastes as sugary as it looks.

She finds the woman half-way through the maze on the edge of a dried-up well. The woman's dress is so silver, the girl feels as if the moon itself has fallen down to Earth.

The girl wants to leap into its arms and have her hair stroked and eat candy until it seeps out her pores.

Once upon a time, a princess was courted by an unwanted suitor, so she made the following impossible demands:

Three dresses: one as gold as the sun; one as silver as the moon; one as sparkling as the stars. And a heavy fur coat, made from the fur of a thousand different animals.

But her suitor sent out all the king's men, and they brought her the impossible dresses, and they brought her the impossible coat...

So she ran far, far away.

"There are many sorts of candy," says the woman. "Candy to heal wounds, candy to keep you awake, to make you big, small, hideous, pretty... Let me know the sort that you would like, and if it is in my power, I will give it to you."

The girl is silent for a few moments. "Candy to fix things?"

"What sorts of things?"

"To fix the house, the garden. To make the sun come out again. To make my parents happy."

The woman smiles with just a hint of teeth. "Ah," she says. "That last one I can do." She ferrets around in her pockets for a spherical candy wrapped in orange and gold silk. The silk is tied at either end with tiny purple ribbons.

The girl moves to take it, and immediately a small cloud of gem-coloured beetles fly off her clothes. She laughs, and the woman takes her free hand through the last of their dissipating wings.

"Have them each eat half," says the woman, her teeth entirely too close. "It won't last as long as you want it to, but happiness never does.

The girl, feeling brave, asks, "What happened to…" She gestures to the woman's morbid necklace.

"That's the result of my favourite kind of candy: the kind that pulls your teeth." The woman grins, and then turns serious. "And while I wear them, no-one can ever touch me again if I don't want them to."

Once upon a time, a princess was found sleeping in a tree hollow in a coat of a thousand furs. The king's men threw her over their shoulders and took her back to their castle, where she was still just as beautiful as the king's dead wife.

They were married in the fall.

When the girl's parents eat the candy, everything changes. Her mother sells all of her jewellery, even her wedding ring, and they stock the cupboards with food, and the girl and her mother read together, tucked into bed with full stomachs. Her father comes home from work and hoists the girl onto his shoulders, kisses his wife, and they begin to fix the house – the draft under the front door, the leak in the kitchen roof, the rotting floorboards in the study. The girl makes sure the broken window is fixed last.

But they never get that far. The candy wears off after a week and a half, and her mother cries for three days over her wedding ring, and her father loses the job he's just been promoted to. And soon after, when her parents just can't get out of bed anymore, the girl ducks back through the broken glass and into the garden.

She's distracted, and takes the wrong path, and runs into the half-decomposed corpse of her once-white cat. It's covered with several flies and one single gem-coloured beetle.

After that, she finds the woman easily: in the very centre of the maze, standing in a dress of sunshine and honey and spun gold.

"How are you always here?" asks the girl.

"I'm only here when I'm expecting you," says the woman, and opens her arms to bathe the girl in sunlight.

Once upon a time, after her brief honeymoon, a young queen was locked in her room at sunrise. She cried no tears. She'd had the choice between posing as an anonymous, soot-covered scullery maid and becoming an unnatural queen, and she'd chosen the latter.

The day was warm and stifling. She took the mirror off the wall and laid it on the carpet. She reclined on the cold, finger-smudged glass in her dress of silver moonlight.

The mirror rippled.
And she passed straight through.

"I'm not here much anymore," says the woman. "There's another world. A better world. Time is different there. I experience the future there more than the present. And in the future..." She pauses to kiss the girl on the forehead. "You're already there."

The girl's eyes widen comically. "I'm there?"

"You are. You can come back with me now, if you like." She fishes in her pocket for a candy wrapped in white. "All you have to do is swallow this."

Once upon a time, a queen fell through a mirror onto a chessboard, and the white knights and bishops and pawns had been waiting for her. They offered her candy to dissolve the base of her teeth, which came out with a firm tug, and helped to string them around her neck like armour.

The girl examines the candy thoroughly. The outer wrapper is clear and shiny, and the inner wrapper is a dull milky white.

"You can think about it," says the woman, "and you don't have to come at all. But I know life can get miserable for girls your age, and in my experience it doesn't get much better. So you have this," she closes the girl's hand around the candy, "if you decide you want to leave."

Once upon a time, the white queen climbed back through the looking glass, walked through her bedroom door (now unlocked), and descended into the basement to the room where her father's men had slaughtered a thousand breeds of animal.

She picked thirty-two teeth from where they lay scattered in the dried blood of the palace floor. There would be a candy to make them stick in her mouth – a candy to make them her own.

The woman wraps the coat of a thousand furs around the girl's shoulders. "I wouldn't want you to get cold," she says.

"Will it be cold there?"

"Not especially. But the short trip to get there might be."

The girl unwraps the candy carefully, methodically, like opening a present. Inside, the candy is in the shape of a bunny rabbit, and when she squeezes its tiny white body it bounces back into shape like rubber.

"Go on," says the woman, pulling another white candy from her pocket. "I'll be right behind you."

The girl places it onto her tongue, experiencing an instant sense of vertigo. The ground beneath her rumbles gently, and then there is nothing under her feet but air.

More than falling, she has the sensation of being propelled down the hole. The smell of wet soil invades her nostrils. Fleshy worms and plant roots protrude from all sides.

Before the maze slips completely from view, she watches the woman swallow her own piece of candy, and she follows her down into the earth.

Once upon a time, the queen spied a child – a child who looked so much like herself as a girl, when her mother had died.

She went home to her chess pieces, and mourned because her future did not contain this child. This child that she could shelter and save, as she herself had not been sheltered.

But she wanted it so badly, she felt the future change. Her reality shifted. She saw herself on the chessboard, embracing the girl, who was warm in the coat of a thousand furs.

She saw the girl in a thousand places in this world, exploring and having a childhood.

And the queen grinned with her thirty-two teeth.

HONEY IN THE BLOOD

As we all know, thylacines (or Tasmanian tigers) became extinct because they swam in rivers of honey, and were delicious. When they came back, it wasn't as part of a conservation effort. It was because we wanted to eat them.

I grew up on a thylacine farm. My mother was in charge of creating the environment there, because it has to be specific. The rivers were four to seven metres wide. There were hundreds of beehives, maybe thousands, and she chose the genetics of each bee colony herself. She could have gotten rid of the bees entirely, but thylacines taste different when they've been soaking in honey for half their lives – it gets into the skin – and just changing the thylacine's genes to taste more honey-like doesn't produce the same result.

So I grew up amongst shadowy ferns and sticky paw-prints and thylacines plump with dodos and bandicoots and genetic descendants of platypuses who learned to swim in golden rivers. Thylacines are perfectly gentle to humans as long as they're well fed, and these ones were always well fed. As for me, Sunday lunch was always gravy-roast thylacine, and sometimes I'd cry, but I'd eat it anyway.

I like to think this was because my mum made me, but as I said: they're delicious.

One of the government restrictions on the thylacine farm was that it could only kill animals that were no longer fertile (it wasn't quite so straightforward for the males, but they used the average female age). This often offered me comfort, as it meant each thylacine had several years to frolic and dive and nip at each other's ears. Sometimes I imagined doomsday clocks poised over each of their heads. Once I smuggled out two thylacine pups, their furry bodies tucked into the front pocket of my hoodie. Mum was very conflicted about that, but she couldn't let me keep them, legally. So I named them Astra and Artefact and visited them behind fences instead.

Not long after the thylacines officially went extinct, the larger bees went, too. By "larger" I mean anything bigger than your thumb. But they brought them back so they could make the rivers of honey, and when I was ten the bees could grow up to half my size.

Now, not many living people have seen the hives of bees that huge, but they come in two varieties. There are the kind that stretch suspended under the forest canopy, attached to dozens of trees and blocking out the sun. And there are the kind in underground caves, hollowing out the earth for kilometres and filling it with buzzing and honeycombs. My mother and I were never especially concerned with the hives above us, but I was never supposed to go within fifty metres of an entrance to the cave system below. She had me memorise a map of the whole farm and drew large red circles around the offending areas. If I broke my promises, I wasn't allowed back inside the farm for three whole months.

But of course, when I was ten a new entrance was formed, one that hadn't been recorded on the map. I was rolling down a hill after Astra and Artefact when the ground opened up beneath me. It was a long fall, somewhat slowed by honeycomb shells, twists in the tunnel and viscous honey. At the bottom my back hit the base of a shallow, underground honey river littered with shards of shattered honeycomb. Badly bruised, but not broken.

I don't know if any of you have ever been enveloped in honey, but it felt like suffocating. Like being entombed. But I forced my back to the surface and clawed the honey from my mouth. If it had been any deeper than my waist, that river, I don't think I could have managed.

There was a small army of bees around me, once I'd wiped off my eyes. The smallest about the size of my forearm, and all with deep black eyes and glossy stingers. That's where I got this scar in my thigh, see; it went right through, like a spear.

But at that point, the bees had started to disperse, and I saw Astra leaping across the river and snapping at their wings. Artefact's jaws clamped around the bee who'd stung me and ripped its body off the stinger. The honey had started to seep out of my ears by then, and I could hear the cacophony of buzzing. Astra and Artefact picked me up in their teeth – by the back of my t-shirt and the belt of my pants – and off we went: bounding through the caves and into the river – down, down into the river – and up again until we emerged in the open air and they deposited me on the grassy riverbank into safety.

So after that several things happened. The first was that the honey had gotten under my skin, had mixed with my blood like it had with Astra and Artefact. And the second is that it is awfully hard, once something or someone has saved your life, to forget that someone else is going to kill them and feed them to you for lunch. So once my leg was stitched and bandaged and my swellings had gone down and as much honey had been soaked out of my crevices as possible, I decided that I would save them, too.

By fourteen I'd enrolled in an online, tertiary-level biology course. I had parental permission. And it made sense for me to have a lab in our garage. I didn't need a lot more than that, and it seems a bit much that they labelled my efforts "bioterrorism." I mean, humans are living to one hundred and fifty, easy, and are fertile 'til at least ninety. It wasn't that hard to adjust those advances for thylacines, and insert them into the farmed population in the form of an always-dominant self-replicating gene.

The farm became unprofitable not long after its management realised something was awry. My mother bought it, partially because she wanted to, and partially because she felt guilty about my behaviour. It's not a farm anymore: it's a park. Tourists can explore inside caged walkways and see the thylacines and bees going about their business. I think mum still sells the occasional thylacine meat to those paying a premium, but only from animals who have died natural deaths; it helps offset the park's other expenses.

No more Sunday thylacine roast for me, or almost anyone.

I'm only locked up another eighteen months. I mean, I was only sixteen when it happened, and we can get away with a lot 'cause we're young. I'll walk through the park with all the tourists, and mum says she'll even let me back into the staff-only parts. Astra and Artefact will still be alive, if I'm lucky. If I haven't been away too long. So no regrets.

Their children will live a long, long time.

LITTLE FREEDOMS

The room is cylindrical, metal, no doors or windows. Nine of us stand in a circle, not touching, but spread your arms and you'd hit someone. I think I could lie flat in here without brushing the walls, but not by much.

The ceiling hatch above us locks shut with a scrape. We examine faces, muscles, body fat. I've seen six of these women before; two are complete strangers. We do not trade names or origin stories. We go around the circle and we say what we miss most from the outside:

Chocolate, Music, Flowers, Cigarettes, Hot Chips, Internet, Guns, Privacy.

I am Hot Chips. Privacy says hers while staring mournfully at the circular grate in the floor, and I think *oh, she must be new.*

When I was brand new I'd said "My Dog," thinking that was safe, and someone had laughed – not unkindly – and said, "Jeez, at least say your bitch."

The girl to my right asks, "So where are we going?" and there's a flurry of overconfident suggestions from those I assume got in through the physical trials. On the metal floor, every little step sounds like the smack of a frying pan. None of these women can know which terrain we're headed to. We've been told *YOU MUST NOT ASSAULT ONE ANOTHER*, otherwise their disagreement may have turned violent.

Four of us are keeping our mouths shut, including me. I assume we're the four who got in the other way – "The Lottery" – though it's not random at all. How much can you give up in a month? Food, sleep, shelter, dignity?

When there's a lull in the argument, Privacy points out a dollar-sized hole in the centre of the ceiling, releasing a single drop of water every two seconds, which falls through the middle of our tiny room and down through the floor grate. "Maybe we're not going anywhere," she says.

This is met with the obligatory smirks and laughter. Still, what feels like about twenty minutes has passed and nothing has happened, and many of us are fiddling with our shirt buttons, our fingernails, with the black bracelets locked on each of our wrists (WIN YOUR FREEDOM printed in Helvetica, light grey).

Once about thirty minutes have passed, there's an ascending chime like *the 7:15 train has been delayed* and a strip around the top of the cylinder hisses into pixelated life: *YOU MUST NOT FIDGET.* It's lit up for a couple of seconds, and then the same chime plays in descending order and it's gone.

There is laughter again, the most there's been, but now everyone's hands are motionless at their sides, or on their hips, or clasped in front of them. "This the big endurance test?" calls someone with muscles. "What a fucking piece of piss!"

Of course, when you're not allowed to do something you instantly need to do it a hundred times as much. My scalp, which felt fine seconds ago, prickles as if covered in lice. Itches blister down the sides of my neck, my wrist, above my eye. I trap my hands between the wall and my bottom and try to distract myself.

The others are arguing over whether this is the real challenge or not. I can see them flinching and wriggling every so often, as if to shrug off a troublesome insect. I am concentrating on my breathing.

My newfound desire to scratch my nose is shocking. If someone else raked their nails down my face, that wouldn't break the rules, would it? I am not desperate enough to share this secret yet.

The bug-eyed blonde on the floor – Flowers, I think, and maybe Melinda – starts complaining quietly about how much it feels like spiders are crawling over her skin. She knows a lot about spiders, too; she mentions several different breeds and the technical terms for the different segments of their legs. The others keep telling her to shut up, but Flowers keeps going, staring catatonically and moaning about rubbing her whole body against tree bark.

Eventually a girl with orange dreadlocks looks acutely nauseous, hauls Flowers up by the collar and raises her free hand in a fist. Flowers gasps and her eyes bug out like one of those goldfish.

At the last moment the fist uncurls and morphs into a middle finger salute instead.

Released, Flowers sinks back into the wall and smiles bashfully – "I'm sorry, Chocolate, did I upset you?" – but then her eyes darken and there's no confusion as to her innocence. When Chocolate turns her back, Flowers is up like a shot, parting the orange dreadlocks and blowing a single definitive breath on the back of Chocolate's neck.

It's more than enough. Chocolate leaps a foot in the air, scratching her neck with her fingernails like she's trying to rip the skin off. A pitch-black, translucent arm reaches through the metal wall and closes around Chocolate's wristband, and the whole 5'10" of her is yanked out of the room before the floor has even stopped vibrating from her jump.

Silence from the eight of us in the slightly-more-spacious cylinder. My eyes float slowly across from where Chocolate disappeared to the grate where Flowers is standing.

She looks completely serious. "Piece of piss, right?" she says.

YOU MUST NOT STAND.

There is no doubt anymore. This is our endurance test, and it will get easier and easier to lose, and we will be in here for as long as it takes.

When the second instruction flashes up, accompanied by the chime, we all sink to the ground almost in unison. There's not enough room for everyone to stretch out their legs at once, which is cause for some squabbling, but a rough hierarchy soon establishes itself.

With their legs out: Guns, the pretty Asian with the high-pony, the first to pee over the grate; Music, an athletic black woman with a chin scar; Cigarettes, a white girl who looks almost plump compared to the rest of us; and Flowers, with her legs half-over all the others'.

It's not like you can get far away from Flowers in here, but I'm pleased she's not *right* next to me.

Privacy asks Flowers why she's so desperate to get out – does she have children outside? And there's less laughter than I'm expecting, but all I can think is *new, new, God, you're so new*. Flowers says it's none of their business, but isn't that so stereotypical, that a woman needs to be a mother to throw someone else under the bus. Can't she just want to free herself more than some strangers?

The room actually seems to warm to Flowers after that. Privacy climbs carefully over the outstretched legs and crouches over the grate, tilting her head to catch the ceiling drips on her tongue. I glance around and see a few women silently calculating whether to stop her – if they can hold her down until she's no longer a threat of any kind – but no-one moves.

We take it in turns to crouch under the drip and almost drink enough. While I'm sitting there, hurting my neck and seizing up my limbs, someone yells, "No camels!" which means I'm done for now.

Two or three hours have passed and it must be dark outside. The girl to my right, Internet, who's said barely more than I have, presses her lips to my ear and says, "Help me with something and I'll make it worth your while." I study her bony face, dark eyes, freckles... And nod.

She smiles and holds up the shoelaces she's pulled free. We're all in new uniforms for this and I feel stupid for not registering the laces earlier. "I want to sleep," she whispers. "But I'm afraid I'll itch. Can you tie up my fingers?"

I thread the laces between her digits and knot them so her fingers stay apart, then tie her hands together with the excess length. Some of the other women make bondage jokes, and though I think a couple understand the actual purpose they're not sharing out loud.

"You'll scratch my nose?" I ask, and she does, one long, firm scratch down both sides with her awkward bundle of hands.

"That's the bonus," she says, but doesn't elaborate.

Internet props herself against me, back to back, hands in lap, and might be napping as far as I know. The others aren't yelling, exactly, but there's a lively discussion about whether it's like this every year. The losers aren't allowed to mention the competition afterwards, and the winner never comes back, of course.

I couldn't sleep with all that noise.

At one point Flowers unbuttons her shirt, folds it neatly and tucks it under her bottom. Everyone stares at her bare chest with various degrees of subtlety, because there are *actual* flowers there – tattoos of orchids stretching from her waist to the top of one breast, purple and yellow like permanent bruises.

It should make her more vulnerable, but Flowers wears it like armour and the group seems to treat it as such.

In the wake of this, Guns leans over and sticks her tongue inside Privacy's ear, and Privacy lets out a horrified gasp but doesn't jump to her feet like Guns obviously wants her to. I wait to see if The Powers That Be consider this assault, but apparently not, and thankfully Guns doesn't follow it with anything more extreme.

A couple more hours pass without incident and the group seems to conclude that now, in the early stages, is a useful time to get some sleep. I've agreed since Internet slumped against my back, but I can't let my eyes close. I'm a violent sleeper, the kind that steals the covers and kicks shins and tosses like a suffocating fish.

Some of the other women get shoelaces tied around their fingers. One by one, threats are issued or goodnights whispered and eyelids shut around the circle. Then there's only Music, Flowers and me awake and staring at one another.

My legs are aching by now, and one of them has suffered pins and needles for the last half hour. I twist carefully on the floor and stretch my legs into the air in the middle of the circle, careful not to touch the sleepers. While I massage the feeling back into my calves, I can see Flowers grinning at me from the corner of my eye.

Flowers is making hand puppets at me. I can't tell what they are, exactly, but they change rapidly and are surprisingly animate. I force my face to stay blank, impassive. Eventually she cocks her head like *poor dumb bitch* and opens her mouth as if to scream.

Silence. She shuts her mouth again, then opens it and takes a deep breath.

More silence. She does this a third time, and it really looks like she's going to screw up her face and shriek, but Music shoves her own shirt in Flowers' mouth and ties it firmly behind her blonde head.

Flowers jerks against the wall and reaches up for the ties, picking at the knot for a second before realising that's an awful lot like fidgeting.

She glares at Music for a straight hour after that, and Music stares back for a lot of it. Allowing your competition to sleep seems a strange tactic to me, but perhaps Music just hates Flowers. Or loves the silence. Or has a tiny, fragile alliance, like mine with Internet.

We sit there for a while longer until Flowers gradually retrieves her legs from the middle of the circle and picks her way, hunched and Gollum-like, over to me. She unfolds something navy and red-brown between us – her shirt, wet with menstrual blood – and manages to grin at me around her gag.

I open my mouth to protest, but she pivots to the girl on my left instead.

I realise I don't know this girl, and I don't remember the thing she misses most – I don't think I even heard it in the first place. And now Flowers is draping the bloody shirt over her head, and the wet part's all over her sleeping face.

Flowers sits back down and I'm frozen to the wall, and it's not like this is the worst thing I've ever seen, far from it, but it's so *silent* and *cold* and *easy* when getting here in the first place was so damn *hard*.

The ascending chime goes off, and it is *loud*.

Several things happen at once. No-name next to me wakes up with a face full of cotton and blood, and kind of a half-sob and staggers to her feet and gets dragged through the wall.

The rest are frantically blinking themselves awake and trying to focus on their new instructions, which, incidentally, read *YOU MUST NOT SLEEP*.

And Internet is struggling towards the grate, pulling down her pants awkwardly with her tied hands, and rocking back too far at the last moment...

She pees on everyone but me.

Internet sits back down and doesn't apologise, because what is there to say, and women don't generally pee in a 180-degree arc by accident.

There are shouts of outrage and swearing and clearly suppressed wriggling from the other prisoners. Privacy looks like she's going to throw up, and I expect her to throw in the towel at this point but she doesn't move.

Instead, Cigarettes is the one flailing and shaking her legs to try and get the piss off them, and bounding to her feet and the urine's running down her ankles and then there's a translucent hand around her bracelet and she's gone.

Guns, Privacy, Music and Flowers are all taking off their soiled shoes and trousers and I think I had better, too, so I don't draw attention to my relative cleanliness. They toss their trousers at Internet, who is soon sitting in a pile of dirty cotton, and their shoes in a cluster over the grate so they're not eliminated for actually battering the woman. Music mimes several different ways of ending Internet's life, including slicing her jugular, wrists, hanging, stabbed in the guts... Music has her thumbs in her underwear and I think she might go and return Internet's "favour" but Guns mouths "Later" and the room is silent for a bit.

Privacy has started crying in that way where the tears drop but the rest of your face looks normal. Guns leans over and licks them off her cheeks with some comment about water conservation. Through her makeshift gag, Flowers starts humming a familiar tune that I haven't heard for years and can't quite put my finger on. It's a children's song, one of those ones that keeps repeating over and over.

"It's that bear song," says Internet, slowly shifting the peed-on trousers away from her and onto the grate. And of course it is, that song about a bunch of bears in a bed and they all roll over and fall out one by one until it's just the little bear left and I've forgotten what happens then, if anything. Flowers is still humming and Guns calls her a sociopath.

And then there are six of us, and there's almost enough space to be comfortable, and there's wakefulness stretching before us like the desert – all the way to the horizon.

The cylinder is truly unpleasant now. The smell of drying urine is impossible to ignore, as is the hunger gnawing at my stomach. It's easy to imagine the hunger as a seventh person, expanding around us until she fills all the empty space. It's going to be one of us Lottery girls next, I'm sure, quitting just for the relief of a proper meal.

When the chime sounds again, the pile of trousers has moved and Privacy is squatting tenuously under the drip. Flowers scuttles along the floor and drags Privacy back towards the wall by her biceps, where Privacy flails and collides with Music in a muddle of limbs. Flowers claims the spot over the grate just as *YOU MUST NOT TOUCH* blinks to life above us.

I watch the conflict flash desperately over Music's face. There's barely time to extract herself, so instead she throws Privacy aside. Privacy's a tall woman so it has to be a big push, but the force slams Privacy's arms and forehead against the metal floor and there's no doubt about the pain involved.

The descending tone finishes and Music's bottom lip quivers. Then there's a hand around her wrist, and she sinks back into the wall like it's liquid and disappears.

Flowers is kneeling on the grate, head tipped back and catching the water happily on her gag. The ramifications of this slowly register: as long as we're not allowed to touch her, and as long as Flowers doesn't move, she's effectively cut off our water supply. None of us can reach it without standing or risking touching her.

"Fuck you, Melinda," says Guns, and we watch Privacy pick herself up like reassembling a doll. She isn't bleeding or crying, but there's a hardness to her face I haven't seen before. I suppose she might have a concussion.

"No-one would blame you for leaving," Guns tells her. "*That* kind of hurt – it's not part of the rules."

Privacy leans herself gingerly against the wall and doesn't answer.

"Alright," says Guns, now addressing everyone. "Just remember that this could be a lot worse. Forgotten what it's like outside? If you can't survive in here you'll have trouble out there. You can't die in prison."

Internet tucks her hands between her thighs. "You can die anywhere," she says.

And it's tempting. It's so tempting. How much I want to scratch, stand and stretch, drink and eat my fill, sleep and feel someone's hands on me. To recover those little freedoms. I have lost all sense of time in this place. *How long how long how long.*

My tired eyes rest on Flowers and an idea sparks.

For the first time since we were locked in here, I shift from my designated spot in the circle and crawl around to the opposite wall. Guns and Internet swing their legs over to accommodate me.

I peel a couple of pair of trousers from the soiled pile, trying to ignore their dampness, and tie both right legs together at the ankles; they'll stretch out to almost four legs' worth of length now. The knot is as secure as I can make it.

I keep hold of one end of the trouser-rope and slide the other end in Guns and Internet's direction. They both eye it for a second, and then Guns gives me the ghost of a smirk and picks up the cotton ankle I've offered. We pull the rope almost tight and it stretches neatly across the diameter of the circle.

Flowers still has her face to the sky and looks oblivious. I feel a delirious burst of satisfaction at the back of my skull.

Guns mouths *one, two, three* and then we swing the rope in an arc over Flower's head. It catches her mid-thigh and we hook it under her arms before she can retaliate. We jerk the rope backwards and up, and in a deliciously similar manner to what she did to Privacy, Flowers is yanked off the grate and pinned up against the wall.

For a moment Flowers seems frozen with terror, but I know her stillness is simply profound control of the game. She doesn't bash her feet against the floor. She doesn't try and untangle her arms; she will touch us if she does, and she will be disqualified. She contents herself by swivelling her head between Guns and myself, administering some of the most withering looks I've seen.

Internet and Privacy tie the last pairs of trousers together – Internet has to remove her own pair for an even number – and between the four of us we manage to tie Flowers' arms to her sides and her knees together. Then we take grateful turns under the drip. One of us could easily monopolise the water again, but there are still several shirts we can tie in knots, and no-one else wants to end up like Flowers.

A little while later, Privacy comes and leans next to me while Guns is drinking. "Tell me," she says. "Why no names? No back-stories? Just this one thing you miss. No-one explains properly."

I feel sweaty and self-conscious and exhausted. "I don't know," I mumble. "I guess because those first two don't matter in here. We're never getting the past back. But maybe it's not too much to ask, that one small thing you miss most. Maybe you can get that back, in another life."

I see her nod from the corner of my eye. "Like hot chips?"

I shrug. "It seems a reasonable thing to want."

We smile at each other, just a little, and for a moment the competition is a fraction easier.

Then Guns rocks back onto her ass. She stares at the ceiling – the dry ceiling, the ceiling that is no longer dripping – and we are plunged into the next phase with no ceremony whatsoever.

If time had seemed unwieldy before, now it feels utterly amorphous. Logically, we can't really have been stuck in the cylinder for all that long, but it's suddenly difficult to imagine life outside these few cubic meters. I fight the nearly-overwhelming urge to leave just to reassure myself that other places – other situations – exist.

And even with my churning hunger and sickening exhaustion, it is so *dull* in here. No-one wants to talk without access to water, and this test seems to have reduced itself to *who can sit here the longest*. I wish I was smart enough to think of a way to eliminate the others – I could even justify it as putting them out of their misery – but I can't come up with a thing.

Finally, Flowers starts crashing her heels against the floor, causing great thumps to reverberate throughout the room. They're slow, methodical; no one could accuse her of fidgeting. The others glance amongst themselves to see if they can stop her somehow, but it's not like they can hogtie her. And I am oddly grateful for the interruption, the un-ignorable sound, the vibrations which run up my stiff legs. I feel a rush of absurd affection for Flowers.

But Flowers doesn't stop the banging. Guns and I end up curled on the floor, shirts cushioning our heads and hands muffling our exposed ears. Privacy and Internet seem happier sitting, though there's barely room for them to do otherwise. Guns has two Asian characters tattooed on the underside of her wrists, and I spend a good half hour or so trying to deduce their meaning.

I could ask, of course, but that would ruin the game.

Flowers goes on for so long her heels must be swollen with orchid-bruises. I don't know what makes her snap in the end. But one moment she's bashing the floor, the next she's rolling into Internet, whose jaw drops like Flowers has just slid a knife into her gut.

They leave silently, simultaneously.

I guess Flowers decided she couldn't win. I would've thought she'd take Guns with her, but then Internet's pee has pressed against her skin for the last few eternities. There's a half-dried bloodstain where Flowers was sitting.

I am very, very lucky.

There are just three of us left. Not at all the last three I was expecting. My brain's not working so well anymore. I have the sudden image of the cylinder as a time capsule, and someone digging up our skeletons in a hundred years.

The sign flashes *YOU MUST NOT TALK*, and clearly, no shits are given.

Something flares in my aching chest. Only two more to beat.

I could actually win.

The next part is a small lifetime. I allow myself to fantasise about my possible freedom. Will they let me sleep and wash and dress before throwing me out, or just take me directly outside, starving and thirsty and half-naked?

I will strip 'til I'm bare and stand in the sun. I will stare at an uninterrupted horizon. I will lick salt and spices from my fingers. I will never take anything for granted again.

The ascending chime, and then *YOU MUST NOT MOVE.*

Frantic movements as we all try and stretch out onto our backs without touching each other.

We succeed.

Privacy doesn't have anything between her head and the floor; Guns and I will be much more comfortable.

And for the first few minutes, this is better than the nothingness. I am concentrating on not moving. Not moving a millimetre. Of course, no-one can concentrate forever.

My shoulder blades press down against the metal.

I just have to last longer than the others.

I assume the rules are the same as Sleeping Lions or Dead Fish, those games we played as a kid when the adults wanted ten minutes of peace: breathing and blinking are still allowed. We're on our backs so we can still read the pixelated sign, though I can't imagine how our freedom could be restricted further. Our eyes have to be open for that, and so we have to be able to blink.

I think of myself as a corpse. As a mannequin. I am acutely aware of every protesting part of my body. I think of the time I needed my wisdom teeth out, but the teeth were too close to my nerves, and if I'd moved even a millimetre during surgery I would have permanently lost the feeling in my jaw.

So I didn't have that surgery, but I can do this. I am made of fucking *steel*.

There are times when I think *I want to die, I want to die*, but I don't move. I will not move. Not when I've come this far.

A small sound whistles to my right. Guns really must have been comfortable, because she's *snoring*. And then, of course, she's not there anymore.

I think of Privacy. If this was a kinder world, I would sacrifice myself for her, or she would sacrifice herself for me. And things would be hopeful and uplifting and we'd know we'd done the right thing.

But this is not that world.

The chime comes again, for the last time, and it says *YOU MUST NOT BREATHE.*

I hold my breath on the second last note.

I don't know if I can do this. I was a decent swimmer, once upon a time, but that was years ago.

I stare at the ceiling and bite my tongue.

The pressure is building in my stomach, my nose, my throat. It feels like my face is an overfilled balloon, about to burst. Heat crawls up my neck. I think I can see Privacy from the corner of one eye: I just need to hold on longer than her. Just a millisecond longer. Then I can breathe.

Privacy is still lying there. My vision is blurring.

It's involuntary. I can't- I won't-

I take a breath and cry out. It's a tiny cry. There is no energy for tears. My whole body is shaking. I have lost. I will not get to leave. All that, so much for nothing.

I keep expecting to feel a shadowy hand on my wrist, but seconds pass and it never does.

I struggle to my knees. Privacy must know she's won, but she's just lying there. Still motionless.

I can't even see her chest rising. *The head blow?*

I crawl across the room and press my fingers to her neck, hold them under her nose.

She really did stop breathing.

I slouch over the grate and stare at nothing in particular. It's awful, it's a tragedy, but mostly all I can think is *I've won, I've won by default* and laugh and laugh inside my head, and it feels like my skin's just peeled off my body and I've been given a fresh, light, clean one.

Beside me, a large panel slides open in the wall and the prison warden steps through, flanked by her usual guards.

"I won," I say, sounding like a small child and not caring.

"No," says the warden. "Geraldine won."

Is that really Privacy's name, I think, numb. *It doesn't fit her.*

I blink at them, feeling like the adults have come home to my messy playroom. "She's dead," I say. "I won."

"You took a breath before she did. You knew the rules. And she's already received her prize; she has her freedom."

The wind is knocked out of me. The guards pick me up and carry me out. I cannot move. I cannot speak. Slowly, I adjust to the world outside the cylinder.

Next year, I think. Next year I'll win.

And in the meantime, little freedoms.

CAVORTS WITH FOXES

"You're here because you think we're witches," she says through the crack in the door. "We're not, but you had better come in."

The door swings open. Inside, it's all natural light and pale wood and antique carpets. A ground covering with trumpet-shaped flowers spills over a hallway pot. The whole place looks spacious and well-maintained – not at all what I was expecting from an old house in the middle-of-nowhere woods.

I lift my camera, but the woman – she's said her name is Leona – places her hand on top of it. "No pictures, please, at least 'til the end. I'll make us some tea."

She puts the kettle on and arranges some floral teacups that wouldn't have looked out of place at my grandmother's. "You think we're witches," she says again, "because we're a group of women in a spooky-looking Queen Anne away from the rest of the world. Correct?"

And because the Queen Anne is completely black, I think. And because of the rumours of you howling at the moon and swimming naked and cavorting with foxes. "Correct," I say.

She drops a teaspoon of sugar in my cup, and none in hers, though she does suck the last few grains from the spoon before placing it in the sink. Her curly, mostly-grey hair is tied back with a pink ribbon. I think she is early-forties, but I'm unused to seeing women under sixty with their hair un-dyed.

Once our cups are steaming in front of us, she says, "We're just ordinary women, you know. All of us. There are some genuine satyrs about twenty minutes down the highway. Or some dryads near the northern edge of Hyacinth Lake. Those are actual stories."

I mark some scribbles on my notepad. "I knew about the satyrs – not the dryads."

"They've been more active lately due to global warming. They're very friendly. Don't think they'd mind the publicity." The clear subtext here is: *unlike us.*

I wait for her to continue, and she sighs, clutching her teacup with both hands even though it's a warm day. "We're separatists. Not lesbian separatists, although I do have a wife." She adjusts her hands slightly and the rose gold ring glints on her finger. "Plenty of the women here like men. We just choose not to associate with them anymore, where possible. And the rest of society in general. Basically, we want to be left alone."

I should be taking notes, but I haven't been, and I notice my writing hand shaking slightly. "But... why?"

She smiles like I'm very young, but it's not unkind. "If you don't already know, I doubt I'll be able to explain it in the ten minutes it takes to finish your drink. The more important thing is, we try and keep our existence here as quiet as possible, so we receive a minimum of nasty letters and undesired company."

"Like me?" I say.

"You're not so bad. We worry more about the people who yell, who want to set fire to the house or slash our tyres."

My hands feel steadier again. "Have those things happened?" I ask, my pen poised.

But she doesn't answer me. Instead, she says: "Would you like a tour? No taking notes, no photos, but I'll take you around, introduce you. You can take your cup."

In the sitting room, two girls who can't be older than twenty are indeed cavorting with foxes. Freya, Asian, with a leather strip woven through her braid, rubs the belly of a red fox. Camilla, with blonde pigtails and black nail-polish, is stroking the white fox slung over her shoulder. "We rescued them when they were pups," Freya says in response to my surprise. "Now they're our friends, and sleep in our beds and we sing them lullabies."

Behind the house, three women in boots, dirt-streaked t-shirts and expensive sunglasses tend to a fruit and vegetable garden larger than my apartment. One of them waves at us with a floral glove, but no introductions are made. Leona points out the solar panels on the roof, the skinny windmill, the water tanks: "We're seventy-five per cent off grid right now. Could be more if we needed to." She ushers me across the yard to where the back of the house has been interrupted by construction.

Inside the construction area, a beautiful woman a few years older than Leona is moving wooden planks. Leona introduces her as, "My wife, Alexis," and Alexis adjusts her ponytail, tool-belt, and shakes my hand.

"Every so often we run out of space here," says Alexis, "so I build another bedroom."

In the bedrooms upstairs I meet a black woman in a rainbow cardigan painting a mural, and a redhead hand-hemming an emerald-green sundress on the bed nearby. They point out a tree-frog that has jumped onto their windowsill, and they let me hold it for a minute. I watch its neck-sac inflate and deflate above my palms.

Leona leads me back to the downstairs hallway, taking my empty teacup.

"Are you sure you're not witches?" I ask, a hint of laughter in my voice. "The foxes, the plants, the frogs..."

"Many groups of non-conforming women are quickly labelled as witches. But we don't have to be magical to be extraordinary." She winks, like I'm now part of a private joke.

"So why did you show me all of that? If you don't want me to report on it?"

"Well," she says, serious now, "If you liked us, perhaps you'd care enough to have people leave us alone." She twists open the front door.

"But... If you don't advertise... If almost no-one knows you're here... How do you get new women? Who is the back room for?"

"They tend to find their way," Leona says. "Don't worry." Her eyes sparkle with mirth. "Why? Are you hoping that the new room is yours?"

THE LIGHT PRINCESS

The queen died shortly after childbirth, of internal burns. The baby princess lay crying in the corner. They knew this because of the wails; the baby was so bright that they could barely see her limbs, let alone her features. By some curious genetic match, or perhaps mutation, instead of the slight glow of her countrymen, the princess radiated light. The king could not hold her for more than three seconds without burning, and besides, looking at her hurt like staring into the sun.

As the princess grew up, the king scoured the land for potential suitors. On her sixteenth birthday he brought her the Ice Prince. His icy body reflected her light and, although she was better adjusted to her own radiance than others, this almost blinded her. She clamped her eyes closed over the starbursts in her eyelids and held his hand through his thick glove. Seven seconds later he had to pull away; his palm was melting into the glove's fingers.

On her seventeenth birthday the king brought her the Water Prince. He left slightly wet footprints on the tiles of her room. He was naked aside from a pair of damp shorts, and tiny water droplets constantly beaded on top of his skin. He took her in his arms and neither melted nor burnt. She was light as air as she savoured the feeling of his skin, his muscles under her palms, his lips on her neck.

Twelve seconds later he pushed her away.

He said she was boiling him on the inside.

The king declared that there were no other suitable men in the world. Even he, himself could not marry her. She would never bear children. He locked her in a tower at the edge of the ocean, believing the only thing she was useful for was becoming a lighthouse.

During the night, she slept, a ball of light illuminating the rocks below. During the day she cooked with the heat of her hands and the supplies in the basement, and she examined the faded world map on the wall. A corner in the south-east had been torn off. It seemed deliberate, like a jilted lover tearing a face from a painting.

Sometimes she stood at the gigantic tower window and wished she could jump. She thought she could probably reach the waves, but she'd never learned to swim; the glare in the water had always been too bright.

During the day, she dug a hole in the bottom of the tower, shovelling dirt with a silver spoon.

At dawn on her eighteenth birthday, the Light Princess escaped and rushed south-east. She took only the spoon, a knife, and as much food as she could carry. At sunset, she hid in caves or buried herself in the ground, with just enough space for her eyes, nose and mouth. And before too long, blissfully, she crossed the border into the next kingdom.

Many things in the Metal Kingdom hurt her eyes, including the Metal Prince. She could only sit on the prince's lap for twelve seconds before heating him so much that he burnt her flesh, and ended up falling backwards and almost cracked her head open. The burns took three weeks to heal. She wondered why everything she didn't burn on first contact turned painful.

After that she came to either the Earth Kingdom or the Steam Kingdom. If it was the Earth Kingdom, its ochre-coloured prince glared from under his dusty eyelashes and forbade her from coming any closer. He believed his arteries were stems, his veins were shoots and his capillaries were roots. One touch and his entire circulation system would ignite.

If it was the Steam Kingdom, she laid her hands on its prince's shoulders while his scalp steamed gently. In seven seconds wisps of steam began to seep from the rest of him. They rose to scald her on the face and arms and hands. She cried and her tears went up in steam, too.

If it was the Earth Kingdom, she cut through the curtain of vines across its border with her knife. If it was the Steam Kingdom, she reflected her own light with her silver spoon, and thus shone a pathway through the thick, suffocating clouds of steam to the other side.

Regardless, she reached the south-east corner of the map.

The palace was made of smooth, black stone that didn't shine. Inside, in the opposite way to which those in the Light Kingdom projected it, the king and queen seemed to suck the colour and light out of the air. It was a peaceful kind of darkness, and the king and queen apologised that they had never had a son, and there was no Dark Prince for her to procreate with.

She slept in a deep, deep basement in the palace and slept for a long, long time.

When she woke there was a void in the room. It was a person-shaped void, and the Light Princess believed the king and queen must have lied. She leapt towards it and flesh materialised out of the darkness in her hands.

That flesh was cold and strong and pitch, pitch black. In the presence of the void, her heat and her light had retreated to a soft glow, and the Light Princess no longer had to squint to see around her. For the first time, she could just make out the shape of her nose where it sat on her face. She could see her hands for the first time, where they clutched at the void's back. She could see the void's long black hair and short black dress.

"You're so warm," said the Dark Princess, and even the whites of her eyes were black.

The Light Princess counted to three. Seven. Twelve.

Neither let go.

EXPERIENCE

I examine the girl across the table. Well dressed, in that way that afflicts young people where the sleeves of the suit jacket have been properly tailored but it still gives the vague impression of playing dress-ups. Glasses. I wonder if they're cosmetic, to try and blend into the industry. Polite smile. She fiddles subtly with a ring on her middle finger.

I realise I've been silent too long, and perhaps that's getting a bit mean.

"When I took this job," I say, "we had a seven day handover."

The girl nods. "That must have been nice. It must have been nice to get to know each other, you know, as people."

I'm thankful I only have to spend fifteen minutes with her. At most, she is a third of my age. She has only seen three shows in this theatre.

"You got excellent test scores," I say.

She looks bashful. "Best in the country, I'm told."

With particularly high scores on "vision," which is laughable.

I slide the saucer with the pill across the desk. It sits beside her glass of water. "Well, when you're ready."

She stares at me for a moment. Takes a swig of the water and drops the pill deliberately into her mouth. It's too big to swallow comfortably. She grips the arms of the chair, her eyes snap closed and her head slumps forward, shaking slightly.

I've seen twice of these before and they still worry me.

I had the pill made yesterday, with the help of the technicians from NextGen Human Resources. I'm assured it only contains my professional memories. The nooks and crannies of each theatre, the first show I directed when I started here fourteen years ago. The latest statistics on what draws thirty to sixty-five year-olds (our key demographic) through the gilded doors. More than forty-five years' experience condensed in a single capsule.

I worry it also contains the memories of Leo and I making out in the wings, after hours on the opening night of The Merchant of Venice. The gorgeous prop that probably would've been thrown out if I hadn't rescued it and brought it home, even though I really shouldn't have. The bottles of liquor I hid in my office for a couple of years, back when I was courting a not-quite-depression. Other transgressions I have forgotten even happened, but might be in the pill regardless.

I remind myself I am retiring, and even if the girl knows and tells, very little will happen to me.

After a minute or so, she opens her eyes. There is something older and sadder in them. She clasps her hands on her lap and furrows her brow. "I'm sorry," she declares, "I didn't know."

"About what?"

"Everything you did to get here."

I feel it catch in my throat, then – the exhaustion, the bleeding fingers, the rejected social events, the men who left me because I was never home, the child I put off until it was too late – and take a long swig of my own drink. I tell myself the girl doesn't know all of this.

"Oh. Well. Not your fault," I say. "You got the best test scores. You'll do the best job."

We stand and shake hands. She says she'll take good care of the theatre. I take my box of possessions and leave my office for the last time.

I think of all the times I've been rejected due to lack of experience. And I laugh.

MORNING SICKNESS

"Karen!" I bash my fist against the bathroom door. "I had a friend who slipped in the shower and sliced his thumb off. I'm not exaggerating!"

For several seconds all I can hear is the rumble of falling water, and I worry if she's heard me, because I don't think I can yell any louder. I grapple with the locked doorknob again.

The wood muffles her eventual reply: "If I was planning to kill myself, *darling*, I would send you far away to safety first. Don't worry." Her words are laced with ice. "I'm sitting down."

I allow myself a sigh which resembles something like relief.

"I'm really sorry, love," I say.

"Don't call me that."

Now that the adrenaline is wearing off, my legs are physically shaking and I'm finding it difficult to stand. I lean my body into the doorframe for support. "I'm really sorry, Karen. It was a terrible thing I did, I don't deny that, but I can't think of a better reason to do it."

I hear several scraping, metallic sounds and the shower stops. Karen's voice is much clearer now, though it echoes off the bathroom tiles.

"Do you know what you did?" she says. "We could die at any moment now, and you *cheated on me*. You couldn't even wait 'til I was *dead*. How do you think that makes me feel?"

"Horrendous," I say. "Appalling." My breath catches. "I gave it as much thought as I could, and it ripped me apart inside..." I hear my voice breaks and feel the tears slide down my cheeks. "But it was still the better alternative. Honestly. Luke wanted to sleep with both of us. I bartered him down."

She laughs, not kindly. "You bartered him down?"

I have a pounding headache. "Well, bartered is probably the wrong word. I explained that you'd bleed. He had a right hard time believing any woman could've gotten to thirty without having had a penis, you know how men are. But eventually, he agreed he wouldn't risk it. He didn't want to die from having a shag, you know. He'd put it into a cup for you if he still got to sleep with me."

Her reply seems delayed. "This is bullshit. You don't cheat on me *for* me. Do you how insulting it is to be told you were cheated on *for your own good*?"

"The cheating itself wasn't supposed to help you, Karen. It was the result. I was trying to save our lives!"

"I might prefer to die!"

I sink down, back against the door, and wipe my wet face across my t-shirt. There's already so much snot and tears. "Fuck." I freeze. "Listen, I need to stop crying. I'll burst a capillary in my nose before long. I usually do. Then we'll be fucked."

A pause. "Go fuck off, then."

I sit completely still, trying to get my emotions under control enough to stem the tears. Deep breaths. There's a single knock on the door behind me.

A little more gently, she says, "There's an ice pack in the freezer. For your nose."

"Thank you." I clamber to my feet. "I'll be back in a minute, I promise."

Downstairs, the country house is quiet and bright. Any sharp corners or edges have been wrapped with cloth or clothes and bound with gaffer tape. Childproofing for adults. The fridge stands next to several wide, clear windows overlooking the garden and the remnants of the tool-shed. The shed's door and half a wall are collapsed on the grass. It looks like a tornado's gone through it. Tossed nearby, Luke's one remaining shoe rests in a pile of splintered wood. It's all that's left of him.

I return with the ice pressed firmly across my nose. It's so cold that it hurts my face and the hand that's holding it there, but I tell myself the pain is comforting. It means I'm still alive.

"That was a really good idea," I say through the door. "Really, thank you."

"I don't want you to die," she says.

"Thank you," I repeat.

She laughs again. "You don't thank your girlfriend for not wanting you to die."

"Well," I say, trying to keep my tears in check, "I didn't want you to die, either. And we'd gone through all the other alternatives."

"But you didn't *tell me*." Her voice is icy again. "You didn't *ask*. You didn't say, 'Sweetie, may I fuck a guy on the off chance we'll get pregnant and postpone getting eaten for nine months?' And you didn't tell me after, either. You lied. You make me feel like I'm *nothing*."

I press the ice pack into my face as hard as I can. It's such a struggle not to start crying again, and my pain comes out as a kind of howl instead. "He didn't give me a chance to ask," I force out. "It was then or never. And I thought about telling you. But things aren't how they were, you know. I was trying to save you, and I was so terrified of what you'd do if you found out."

"Well." Her voice is very close now, right on the other side of the door. "I haven't killed myself, if that's what you mean. And I haven't killed you. I'm not an infant. I'm not a psychopath. And I'll keep trying to figure out a way to keep us alive when the babies come, if you like, but I can't *love* you anymore." The door swings open behind me, and I feel myself falling through the air.

Karen catches me with her leg before my skull can hit the tiles. I look up at her, ice pack still pressed against my nose. She is naked and dripping, looking down at me with slitted eyes. "I understand what you did, but I don't agree with it," she says. "And make sure you don't crack your head open after all that. You know it only takes them a second."

She allows me to collect myself before she walks away. Her stomach has just begun to show, and with her long, curly hair trailing behind her she looks like a goddess.

I resist the urge to bite my tongue, to run my nails down my neck, to grab the scissors from the medicine cabinet and plunge the tip into my thighs. Just a pinprick of blood and they'll appear in a whirlwind of scales and teeth. Blind and deaf and fast as lighting. Like being eaten by a kitchen blender. Too fast to really hurt, I expect. Less than it hurts to be alone.

I lie on the cool tiles with my ice pack, breathing like I've just finished a marathon. I wonder if they'd find us in a vacuum. We could wear scuba gear for air. The babies would die from lack of oxygen, of course, but they'd die anyway from being covered in blood. Could we even find a vacuum? And then what, get knocked up until menopause? I'd had a pregnancy phobia as a teenager.

I plod downstairs, where it's still sunny and Karen's curled up on the couch, facing away from me. I make two strawberry milkshakes with UHT milk and listen to the blender tearing at the thick pink liquid. I sit at the counter and watch where Karen hasn't moved.

"I had all these dreams," I say quietly, "where someone would hit on me, try and pick me up, try and kiss me, and I would say no. I would say no, I have a girlfriend, I can't do that with you. Even in the dream, even contemplating cheating on you would make me want to throw up. The guilt was all-encompassing. And then I'd wake up, and be relieved, and think what an idiot I was to feel *guilty in a dream*." I sip my milkshake and feel the sugar run into my bloodstream.

There's still a tiny bit of petrol in the car. Maybe we'll last longer than a few more months.

The first stirrings of morning sickness start in my belly. "You took a couple of scuba lessons, didn't you?"

FIVE TALES OF THE ROSE PALACE

The Fifth Tale:

My father vomits when he sees the palace.

I help him wipe the last traces from his mouth with a rag. A few flecks have stained his nicest coat, which he insisted on wearing to the funeral of his favourite daughter.

There is barely a plant in the palace grounds that is not a rose. "I hope I never set eyes on another of these weeds," he says, clutching my arm for support. "Forgive me, Beauty, for I meant well."

The palace doors swing open before us.

"I know, Father. Roses are few people's most precious possessions."

"Monsters. Not people," he corrects. He guides us down the empty corridor to the sprawling dining hall. A steaming banquet waits on the table. Flaming chandeliers hang from the ceiling; spotless burgundy carpet under our feet. This hall, like the rest of the palace, is lined with deep water channels which extend about two feet into the room.

The two of us sit awkwardly at the table, sick with tension. The food cools and my father weeps into his handkerchief. I keep silent, striving not to ruin my last hours with too much misery.

Eventually, a loud splash echoes and watery reflections dance across the ceiling. From the fountain in the middle of the hall, a long creature rears up and lunges towards us, resting its hands on the stone ledge. Light ripples across its scaly green tail. Blood-red roses wrap around its hips up to its shoulders.

"Have you come of your own free will?" asks the beast.

"Yes," I say.

"Very good." It bears its teeth at my father. "Enjoy your supper, sir, and enjoy your sleep. Leave in the morning and never return." The creature disappears down the fountain with another great splash, and the palace returns to overwhelming silence.

Stunned, we help ourselves to the glistening pork, thick applesauce, roast vegetables, crisp breads and cakes atop the table. Under other circumstances, a meal fit for a princess.

My breath catches in my throat. "Father," I whisper, "did you tell me the beast was male?"

"I don't know," he says. "It said to call it 'Beast,' Beauty. I didn't check between its legs."

The next day, everywhere I walk through the palace seems recently abandoned. Warm, caramel-coloured dough waits half-kneaded in the kitchen. A spade protrudes from fresh dirt in the rose gardens. Cooling coals still smoke in a bedroom with rumpled floral sheets.

Finally, I find myself back in the dining hall. A note has been tacked to a set of adjacent double doors:

My apologies for such a performance. You are no more a prisoner here than air is a prisoner in water. If you do choose to stay, however, everything in this palace is yours. I eat supper at nine.

My heartbeat, which had begun to level out from hours alone, spikes again. I should leave: return to my very ordinary, predictable life with my father.

I tug the note off the doors, instead, and push them wide open. The room beyond is circular, with dozens of rows of books radiating from the middle. In the centre itself is the most elaborate golden harpsichord I've ever seen, with a pile of music books stacked on its seat. And at the very back, directly opposite the doors, my reflection watches me nervously in an imposing silver mirror.

I wander through the aisles, ghosting my fingertips over various titles and worrying the note in my other hand. When I reach the back, I whisper: "Mirror, mirror, should I stay? Will father die of grief that way?"

The surface flickers for a moment before rippling and running like coloured paint. It morphs into a clear, moving image of my father arriving home from his journey. My sisters kiss his cheeks and guide him inside our cottage. He is exhausted but intact.

The image runs and disappears. I bite my lip. Then I sit at the harpsichord and start to play.

At supper, the beast asks me why.

My fingers still tremble as I cut my lamb. "Curiosity," I say. "Why did you demand I come here, if not to keep or eat me? I don't understand."

She pauses, halfway through tearing her bread into bite-sized pieces. After a long moment, she says, "I wanted to know whether anyone would come. Would sacrifice themselves. It's a rare quality."

I wait for some time, but she doesn't elaborate. "That's really all?"

"I can't tell you the rest."

I place my cutlery down with a soft clink. "Can't or won't?"

The beast stares me straight in the eyes. "Can't."

I walk over to where she's settled on the fountain's edge, motioning to where the roses are coiled around her torso, and say, "Those look very painful. May I take them off?"

The beast eyes me warily. She gives a tiny nod.

I reach down to where they're hooked around her waist, fiddling gently until an end comes free. My fingers brush against her skin, which is alternately soft and ridged with dozens of tiny old scars. I unwrap the roses, layer by layer, and a few thorns dislodge from her supple flesh in the process. Blood wells in their place, tracing down her body in rivulets.

She gasps and shivers, and when I'm finally done she reaches for the pile of roses with eager hands.

All she says is, "I hope I can tell you one day."

The Fourth Tale:

Cradling my naked body on the beach, the prince informs me that his name is Sun.

My childhood in the ocean has been marked by two passions: a statue of a handsome young man, and a patch of red flowers in the shape of the sun. My late mother had loved roses, and had said my own flowers were a pleasant reminder.

Sun has a rose petal caught in his hair. I reach up to caress it between my fingertips. He is perfection.

Then he helps me climb to my feet, and I have to bite my tongue with the agony of standing.

After he chooses her over me, after I refuse to stab him, after I throw myself into the ocean, after the hallucinations, after I am certain I am dead...

I wake just below the surface of the rippling water. Strong fiery light shines down like heaven, and I surge to the surface.

"You won't drown," says a smooth, feminine voice. "No need to act like you're suffocating."

I control the last of my coughing fit and cling to the stone wall next to me. My throat feels like it's lined with spider webs, but I am otherwise well enough. I realise I am far from the middle of the ocean; I am spluttering in the fountain in Sun's dining hall, and it is unusually empty.

The green-skinned woman sitting nearby squeezes water from the end of her dress. "There are some conditions for your life," she says. "Firstly, you are not allowed outside the castle grounds. Secondly, you may speak to no-one of your life before this moment, nor are you permitted to speak about any of these conditions I am imposing on you now. However..." She uncrosses her legs. "Should a human ever fall in love with you, this curse will break. Any questions?"

"Yes," I say. "Many questions." I heave myself up onto the fountain's edge with weak arms, struggling to make my legs work. They feel like they're bound with seaweed. The strange woman drags me up onto the cold stone; water runs onto the carpet and splashes back on her dress.

I catch sight of my old, scaly tail and collapse, heaving like a dying fish.

"For goodness sake," mutters the green-skinned woman. "What a dramatic thing you are. You must get that from your mother's side of the family."

I barely register her words. "If what you say is true," I moan, "how am I to get a man to love me? He didn't even love me when I had my legs."

"That is the challenge and the point, dear. Some people put entirely too much stock in mirrors. I'm sure you'll figure it out."

"Wait... But why are you doing this?"

Her lips curl into a smile. "How about I explain the debt when you win the game?"

When I glance up again she's vanished completely, and invisible hands are pouring me a glass of red wine.

The Third Tale:

On my fourteenth birthday my father's finger falls off.

I find him twisted in the garden between our cottage and the fence, pawing through the sand with glassy eyes. Once inside, my mother cradles his injured hand and kisses his remaining fingers. They tell me they're both very sick. I must fetch them a blue rose, which they must eat within three days, or they shall literally fall to pieces.

My parents have never left our property in fourteen years, and this illness is no exception. They kiss me underneath my eyes and watch me swim out the gate with only a snakeskin satchel.

Inside the fence, everything is illuminated in the gentle glow of lantern fish. My mother catches them and ties them inside dead jellyfish sacs, securing them to the cottage by the tentacles.

Outside the fence, the sun barely pierces water this deep. I spot the faintest outlines of the polypi forest and the skeletons, driftwood, and shipwrecked treasures trapped in their arms. They strain away from their roots to stroke me when I pass. They whisper their names. They offer me wood for the fence, bones for the cottage walls, crystal goblets which have fallen like drowned angels.

"I have no use for those today," I whisper in return. "Today I am looking for a blue rose."

The forest ripples before me like seaweed. A hundred voices breathe, "There is no blue rose."

I receive a metallic egg from them instead. It blushes with golden light, illuminating the ocean floor in a small sphere around my palm. I pluck out seven strands of hair in exchange.

That night I scour all the shipwrecks I know of, catching bursts of sleep curled inside their broken hulls. I discover snapping plants which wail for my blood, and knock flowers which scatter silver powder. I do not find the blue rose.

In the morning I swim to a human village. I prop up my arms on the sun-warmed dock, leaving my tail safely submerged and out of sight. A teenage boy approaches, hands in his vest pockets and a grin stretching his wide mouth. He promises that no-one in a thousand miles has a blue rose except for him. He tells me I can have it for a kiss.

He kneels on the ground and wraps his hands in my salty hair. His mouth seems too big on my own, and his tongue too insistent. Before pulling away, he nips my bottom lip and draws pinpricks of blood.

When he stands my heart is battering like a parade. I force myself to say, "The rose?"

And he says, "I'll get it now."

He never comes back.

On the second morning, on the bank of a long, unfamiliar river, I come across a man with a deep blue beard. He eyes me like a gull may eye a fish, and calls, "Maiden! Whatever it is you seek, I can deliver it."

I tell him I am seeking a blue rose, and he swears he can supply one. Twelve gold and ruby rings adorn his fingers, and when I ask him what he wants in return, he says, "A single touch of your skin, in the hope that you may like it well enough to be my wife."

I cling to my rock in the middle of the river, knuckles flushing white and much more cautious this time. I say, "I need to take the rose to my parents, who are very sick. Bring me the blue rose and I shall return in three days' time so you may touch me."

He agrees with the click of his many rings. He stalks across the hills and through the door of a mansion with a single turret, and when he emerges he holds a rose as blue as his beard.

At his request, I leave my golden egg glowing on the riverbank; I can collect it when I return in three days. "There's a drop of blood on this," he says; it must have fallen from my first kiss.

"Is that a problem?"

He spits on the egg, rubbing at the blood with his thumb, but it won't come off. The smile grows on his face like ink spreading in water. "Not at all."

I tuck the rose into my satchel and dive away.

At sunset I pass the palace of the Sea King, extravagant in every imaginable colour of coral. Usually I would give it a wider berth, but today I am too keen to return to my parents' arms. I miss my father's cooking, hot and satisfying in the pit of my stomach, and watching my mother toiling over her projects with needles and knives.

But a commanding female voice insists I halt. I glide awkwardly through the next few feet of water, twisting my neck around to meet her eyes. The Sea King's mother calls my name again from the palace gardens. She crooks a finger.

I force my weary body to meet her, my throat dry and pupils wide. My parents have forbidden me countless times from the palace and its inhabitants, but surely I can't refuse such explicit instruction.

The Sea King's mother asks me my age, but then smiles like she already knew the answer. I catch a glimpse of greying hair as she plucks a crimson flower and tucks it behind my ear.

"And what are you doing by yourself, so far from home?"

I explain, very simply, about my search for the blue rose, and draw it out of my satchel at her request.

Except that it is undeniably a white rose. A sickly-looking white rose with traces of blue around the edges, but certainly white. I keen over the rose like a grave; like I have been elbowed in the stomach.

The Sea King's mother promises everything will work out as it should. She seems so certain.

Sometime after my parents' deaths, I wake to a song so charming I'm holding my breath. My mother used to sing, sometimes, while she sewed, but this is nothing like that. This feels like the voice is inches from my ear, but the singer is nowhere to be seen.

Alone, I have been operating largely on instinct, and it is this same instinct which draws me like a thread through the water, following the voice into a sizeable hole in the cliffs. Darkness stretches inside, and I feel blindly for craggy handholds in the rock, pulling myself along as the voice grows nearer.

I can feel the tunnel narrowing as I go, but before it becomes truly claustrophobic I spy a patch of light up ahead. The melody halts just before my head breaks the surface.

The air beyond is warm and syrupy and I hurry to wipe the water from my eyes. At the other end of the small, square pool stands a young woman, a tiara nestled in her hair and a hand over her mouth.

Her name is Talia, and she's locked in the pool every Wednesday to bathe for exactly an hour. Every Wednesday she sings for me and I rise out of the water and into her waiting arms. She devours my stories like a starving shark and drip-feeds me morsels of her own in return.

Beyond the single door, her twin babies named Sun and Moon are watched by soldiers at the gates of the palace. They are a neighbouring king's "property," Talia and her children, because that king impregnated her one day while she slept. She never even saw his face until the twins were born.

Not long after our meetings become a fixture, I arrive to find her tears mingling with the bathwater. The king has announced he will be back to claim his prizes in seven weeks.

I press my chest to hers, slip her hair behind her ears and reach for her tiara. She yelps. She parts the hair just above her ears, and I see the ends of the tiara disappear inside Talia's skin.

"It can't be removed," she says. "He had it pierced after his first wife burnt to death."

The breath catches in my throat. "Why would he do that?"

"So that I can never escape who I am," she says slowly. "Even if I could bear to leave my children, no matter where I travel on this land, I know he'll find me."

"What if it wasn't on land?"

In the first week, halfway down a familiar river I spy a pillar of smoke. This is no bonfire; this is an inferno. The mansion with the single turret is ablaze like a flaring match head.

Standing in the grassy foreground, the mansion burning behind her like a halo: a woman enveloped in feathers and tar. Bloodstains cover her hands and she clutches my golden egg between them in a death grip.

"You have my egg," I yell, before I lose my nerve.

"*Your* egg?" she says. "You demon. You witch. You may take your egg. I expect there are no pools of blood to be found in the ocean."

I catch the egg with both hands, its shell still warm on my skin from the mansion's flames. A whisper of something stirring inside knocks against my palms.

In the fourth week, growing desperate, I use the egg to light the polypi near my childhood home. They greet me in clouds of whispers like a chorus of old friends, stretching to tangle their elastic limbs in my hair. Then they circulate something from one to another until it reaches me, pressing the leather into my hip.

I steal glances at the small, leather-bound book whilst trying to extract myself. Normally, any books found at this depth are irredeemably waterlogged, a mess of swollen pulp and vanishing ink. This one is beautiful and soft, and when I flick through the pages the ink is entirely legible.

A spell-book.

I am intoxicated.

#

I return to the palace pool at an unscheduled time. Talia is absent. There are no songs. Only my eyes breach the surface, hunting for soldiers. The single door is open, but the corridor beyond it seems empty. The soldiers avoid the palace where possible, believing it haunted.

I sing a mediocre, butchered version of her own song and she flits into the room, her salmon dress floating around her calves, her face rosy with haste. She kneels by the water and cups my jaw with trembling hands.

"Do you still want to do this?" I ask.

She takes a little while to answer. Her children bind her here like stones, but she is only a little older than me and she has been a prisoner her whole life: imprisoned by her parents to protect her from spinning wheels, imprisoned in sleep through no fault of her own, imprisoned by a foreign king within her own palace. So she says yes with an edge to her voice, and kisses me like I can make her forget.

It is not a complicated spell, but it is a difficult one. We mix her blood and tears in a pot with sea water, and bind the cuts on her arms with bandages. I slice the two fins from the end of my tail. They are quick, clean cuts. We bind my tail tighter than her arm, to stem the blood flow.

I dip the severed fins in the pot of blood, bind them to her ankles with seaweed, and cut a tiny slice from the left fin to slip past her lips.

She swallows it... Convulses once, twice and collapses on the watery tiles. I lunge and capture her head as it falls. I cradle her while the blood on my tail clots, while the skin on her legs slowly knits together. While it hardens and takes on an opalescent shine.

When her tail seems complete, I draw back her long hair and find gills protruding in lines across her neck. I kiss her once, and she is all warm breath and rose-petal lips.

I say, "Let me take you home."

When I push open the door to my parents' old house, no-one comes to greet me. No corpses cuddle in the chairs. Just a layer of sand on their seats from the weeks I've been gone.

My mother's lantern fish are dead and the darkness is thick. Talia shivers at the table, though it's hardly cold and I've given her the golden egg to cradle. If I require its light elsewhere, I have to lift it from her fingers when she sleeps.

Without my fins, I am embarrassingly awkward and it takes me days to catch a single lantern fish. Talia shadows me throughout; she cringes at the polypi and speaks of whirlpools I've never noticed before.

Goosebumps prickle her skin when she lies in my arms, and no amount of rubbing seems to alleviate them.

When she doesn't come home one day, I am frantic. I finally find her at the Sea King's palace, slumped on the coral wall, golden egg cradled in her lap. She has been waiting for me.

When I approach, she stretches out the egg like a peace offering.

"You're not coming home?" I ask.

"I'm sorry," she whispers. She fiddles with the silver tiara, still locked securely to her scalp. "I'm a *princess*."

The Sea King rises out from behind the coral wall, wraps his muscled arms around her waist, and I can't spot one lone goosebump wrinkling her skin.

Now the egg twitches more regularly between my hands, and the creature inside knocks against one palm and then the other.

I am expecting a chicken. I watch over my prize on the rocks above the water, ensuring my chick doesn't drown the minute its shell cracks. But instead, two tiny sea-snakes emerge to tongue the air. They curl around my fingers like living rings.

Over the next few years, those snakes breed and thrive in the sands around my house. They wind themselves around my waist and tail and compensate for the fins I lost like extra limbs.

The polypi whisper of the Sea King's palace: those inside call me the "Sea Witch," and when Talia dies young her six mermaid daughters blame only me.

I never discover how she dies.

I am expecting Talia's youngest when she calls. She is fifteen years old and looks so much like her mother, pale and shaky from the journey. Where Talia clung to me years ago, her daughter simply eyes my snakes like a prey animal.

She is lusting after her half-brother, the prince, which draws the first laugh from my throat in many months. "A very bad idea," I say, although I won't explain why. That story is long and only mine, now that Talia has died.

Nevertheless, the girl insists on gaining her legs, and I don't refuse her. She's willing to pay the required price, plus the price for my help: I bottle her beautiful voice.

It sounds just like her mother's.

#

Talia's youngest has died and turned to sea-foam, which I have carefully scooped from the sunrise waves and stoppered in a crystal vial. Listening to her voice has become compulsive: it reverberates always in my head, calling me somewhere that doesn't exist anymore.

And from the darkest depths of my little house, a green-skinned woman emerges. She has two human-looking legs and a smooth green neck where her gills would cut. Her unfocused eyes and pinched cheeks give the impression that she is continuously drowning: drowning without dying.

When she speaks her tone is deep, strained and watery. "You have lost some of your body, most of your heart, much of your mind. Still..." Her hazy eyes settle fleetingly on the jar containing the second-most beautiful voice I've ever heard. "I believe removing that will take the rest of it."

She holds out an expectant hand. Part of me, the part that is quick and dark and very tired, is compelled to hand it over right away. But I force myself to still.

"I'll give it up," I say, "but I'd rather not just hand it to you. There's something I want to do with it."

The green-skinned woman has several conditions, none of which cause me extensive hesitation. Talia's old palace, the one surrounded by roses, has been recently abandoned. This is explained to me briskly in the cool night air, in far more relaxed tones than underwater:

When Talia fell into her extended sleep, the palace's servants were also subjected to a similar spell. They were expected to attend to the princess when she woke, but the spell was flawed and they ended up rotting. After that there was one eternal sleeping beauty and dozens of ghostly servants cleaning up their own decomposing bodies from the rooms around her bed.

Later, when Talia left with me, her twin babies were split up and the spirits eventually fell dormant. Until the day that Sun brought home his new bride and the presence of female royalty woke them up again.

The green-skinned woman announces they'll have another mistress very soon. The spirits must prepare the castle. Every room will need to be lined with water channels, two feet deep, wide enough to swim in.

Back in my own home I combine the little mermaid's sea-foam with her heavenly voice, the locks of her sisters' hair and several drops of her mother's blood, and I bring her back to life.

#

The Second Tale:

I climb through the mirror legs first, perching on the rim before dropping into the library. Already, I can feel the cut across my thighs healing.

This library is grand and the afternoon light streams through the western windows. Still, the mirror looks out of place here: a trophy on display, not something chosen to compliment the space. I feel my slow-boiling fury re-ignite in my gut.

When I throw open the doors of the palace's dining room, they bash simultaneously against the walls and all eyes twist to me: rows and rows of guests, including my twelve younger sisters in various pastel frocks. The blue fairy has a spoon of chocolate pudding dangling from her lips.

There, at the end of the room: the king and queen and a bassinet. Without taking her eyes from me, the queen reaches down and clutches her baby to her breast.

"You really didn't invite me?" I shout. "You, of all people, Snow. You think by ignoring me your daughter's life will always be perfect and pure? I thought you'd grown up."

The queen's delicate hands start to shake. She has always been pale, but now her face looks sickly white.

"Not everything is as straightforward as you believe," I continue. "I am not above teaching lessons."

"Please," she says, thrusting the baby into her husband's arms and stepping forward. "If you must punish someone, punish me. My daughter is innocent."

"Yes," I agree. "She is." A ragged black butterfly flies out of my dress, darts around the chandeliers and towards the royal family. Guests push out their seats to chase it. The king and queen shelter their daughter with their bodies, clutching towards it with desperate hands.

Too clumsy. Too slow. The butterfly soars straight into their daughter's gummy mouth.

"When she is sixteen," I announce, "she shall prick her finger on a piece of flax and die."

The king and queen bellow at me. They are crying. They have their fingers down their daughter's grimy throat, searching for the butterfly.

I see her then: the little cinder girl with her glass shoes, now with her own crown and an expression of heartbroken betrayal, staring straight at me.

I am gone in a matter of moments, cutting my fingers and knees in my scramble back through the mirror. I am counting on the blue fairy to temper my death curse into a long-term sleeping spell. My sister has never blessed anyone before finishing her dessert.

A little more than eighty-five years later, I greet the very first mermaid in the middle of the ocean. She reclines across some craggy rocks, her tail dipped in the water, watching the roses smother the palace walls. She has allowed the first traces of grey to bloom in her hair. More than anything else, that is why I have chosen this moment.

I perch next to her, the ends of my dress darkening and ballooning in the salt water. "There is still a debt to repay, old friend."

"I didn't forget." A hint of familiar mischief plays around her eyes. "And I have a proposition for you."

"Oh?"

"As you may well know, my son has come of age and declared himself the Sea King. There is no one to contest his title, so very well. But he persists in demanding a wife."

"I will not make him a wife."

She snorts. "I'm not asking for that. I would much rather choose that one." Her finger stretches towards the top of the palace, where the roses have completely enveloped the highest turret. "Wouldn't you agree?"

"So you know enough of the story to know that she sleeps, but not that she'll wake in fifteen years? Or you're planning on stealing her prematurely?"

"No, I can be patient." A slow smile breaks across the mermaid's lips, and I cross my arms to ward off the worst of it. Her beauty has yet to fade, if it ever will.

"So," I say, "continued revenge. Yes, she wakes in fifteen years, and – you have a plan?"

"I cannot enter the palace for fear of recognition. I refuse to send my son, partially out of fear for him, but mostly because he cannot pay the price the transformation will require."

She reaches for my hands, licking the flecks of dried salt from her lips. "I want your help to create a tithe," she says. "A girl of my flesh, whose only purpose will be to seek and transform the princess, and then to sacrifice her own mind, body and heart. A girl who will pay both her own creation debt and my outstanding one."

"A girl?"

"It's been eighty-nine years, my dear; grant me a little growth. And besides, she won't be living with me. I shall craft her parents out of sand.

They will be temporary. And," she adds bitterly, "I know how palace life works. It has to be a girl."

Eventually, I declare, "This is acceptable."

The first mermaid squeezes my fingers. "She will need to be drawn to the princess. Something ingrained, in the blood."

I nod. "My sisters always bless children with beautiful voices." Then I am up on my feet, and it is done with just a flick of my wrist and trace of black dust.

Seconds pass. "What are we waiting for?" asks the mermaid.

I can almost feel it, crawling on its spindly legs up the princess's throat. Prying open her lips like a cocoon. Wedging its way through the roses and out into the air, fluttering all the way down across the waves to its mistress.

I see it now. The ragged black butterfly.

"It's been sitting next to her vocal chords for over eighty-five years. It knows her voice. Explicitly."

The first mermaid watches the butterfly like a morsel of meat.

"Yes," I say. "Open up."

The First Tale:

This is the first time I've left the castle since my stepdaughter died.

Then the groom lifts the veil and it is my stepdaughter, and her skin is almost as white as her wedding dress.

The priest does not speak. There are no expressions of love. Several men lift me from my seat and carry me around the corner of the palace, where a pair of shoes glow red-hot on coals.

Not three paces away, the grave of Snow's mother is marked with its old headstone and crimson rose-bushes, the colour she wished her daughter's lips. The dirt that covers it is fresh, and I wonder how I missed its transplant from my own grounds.

Someone removes the shoes with a pair of tongs.

"Really, Snow," I say. "I only wished you out of existence for a little while. Torture was never in my plans."

No-one replies. My own shoes are unlaced and thrown into the fire. My stockings are rolled off my legs while my stepdaughter watches, her eyes like ice. The red shoes are forced clumsily onto my feet and they feel like drowning in flames.

I'm released and I can barely think. My feet dance inside the shoes, due to the excruciating pain or some enchantment, I can't tell. The grass blackens and sparks underneath me. I can feel flames licking up my legs, can feel my skin melting. Smoke rises and I smell my charred flesh. The crowd moves with me.

I leap from the cliff believing I will die. I fall backwards through the void, watching what remains of my feet still dancing hysterically, and beyond them dozens of glassy eyes staring from the cliff's edge.

My sudden plunge into the ocean is a revelation.

The sun has cooled by the time I finally open my eyes on the rocks. No-one watches from the cliff. My legs are fused together in a mess of burnt flesh from my ankles to half-way up my thighs. Some charred bits of my dress have melted in. I look like a beast has chewed on and discarded me.

Walking, and climbing out of here, will be impossible.

With trembling fingers I unlace my bodice and remove my spell-book from where it has been tucked against my breasts. The pages are soggy, but still strong, and the enchanted ink has not run. I flick through potential spells with careful hands, trying to keep my breathing steady.

And flick through again. There is nothing remotely suitable that can be made with such a lack of ingredients.

I am about to check a third time when she appears: the oldest of thirteen fairies walks to my feet, silhouetted in the sunset. She drops to one knee, and in the shadows of the cliffs I can make out her flawless skin, the colour of fresh grass, and her hair in all the colours of autumn. Her black dress flutters slightly over her chest – she took it off once, years ago, and showed me the dying raven quivering inside her ribs.

"Come to put me out of my misery?" I ask.

"Normally I would, but you are a special case."

I would laugh if there was a drop of laughter left inside me.

"The shoes are drenched in powerful magic," she whispers, slowly pulling them from my feet, and taking some skin with them. "Their effects cannot be reversed, only altered."

She leans down and wraps her long, snake-like tongue several times around my ankles. The change happens in a wave, like hair bristling along a wolf's back: the pocked and blistered skin turns smooth and scaly, and my feet stretch and flatten into translucent fins.

When she pulls her tongue away, my body ends in a crimson fish's tail, and all the pain has gone.

"Now the sea will be your mirror, and you will have three-hundred years with which to admire yourself." She smiles at me and rips bloody lines in my neck with her fingernails, which sting and heal and revise themselves into gills. "I do believe you are the fairest sea-beast I ever saw."

"What can I pay you with?" I ask, feeling drunk and light-headed. I stare at her lips as she speaks, and I think they are the same shade of red as my stepdaughter's.

"You have paid for your transformation with pain and power and your soul. There is no magical debt. For my payment, I will take these," she holds up the shoes, which have cooled to a transparent crystal. "There is a little cinder girl who will like them. Is this agreeable?"

"Yes."

She goes to stand, but I cry out for her to wait. "There is no-one else like me in the whole ocean, is there?"

She shakes her head.

"I would so love to have a child."

The oldest fairy fixes me with her beady, raven eyes. The dress over her chest flutters. "Not a daughter, I think." She stretches over me with mutterings of forthcoming debt and how she must do everything herself.

Then she tears the remnants of my dress down the middle, grips the bottom of my bellybutton with two hands, and tears a two-inch hole in my abdomen.

Her tongue plunges inside.

The Fifth Tale, Continued:

The oldest fairy pauses, her tongue darting over her lips. She tears a small strip of pork from the table and drops it into her cleavage, presumably for the raven. Everyone in the glittering dining hall holds their breath.

Silence.

I interrupt it: "Please don't just stop there! Why did she want Snow dead, after all? Why did you help her?"

The oldest fairy smirks at me. "I said I'd explain the debt. I won't keep going back and back until the beginning of time." She takes a swig of red wine. "By the way, you'll have to forgive me putting words in others' mouths, especially in that last tale. But my understanding is quite astute, I assure you."

"Wait." The mermaid shifts in my arms. Her skin has dried, and I run my fingers through the tendrils of her still-soggy hair. "I don't understand," she says. "The debt is paid. The curse has broken. I shouldn't be a beast anymore."

The fairy picks her words very deliberately. "I think you must have misunderstood me. Your *body* was never transformed by the curse. You," she gestures to the two of us, and I feel myself blushing, "have love, and still you ask for more? Have you not been listening at all?"

The mermaid shrinks back against my chest.

With a half-wave and a flutter of her dress, the oldest fairy disappears in a puff of black dust. She leaves the smell of crackling firewood and damp meadows behind her.

Silence.

One of the transparent ghosts brushes the dust off the chair.

Our wine glasses are refilled, the table tidied and the ghosts dismissed. I pull the mermaid gently off the fountain's ledge and back into the water, my arms around her naked waist and my dress billowing around her tail. The water is still freezing; I kiss the goosebumps off her spine.

I say, "Do you not believe I love you?"

"I do believe you," she says. "But I ask the mirror in the library each day, and each day it tells me I'm a monster. You deserve someone as beautiful as you. Someone who can take you dancing."

I bite my lip. "I don't think that mirror should be trusted..."

She wriggles out of my grip and dives into the fountain, disappearing into the depths in a cloud of bubbles. I watch the green of her tail dissolve into the dark; the exact shade as the oldest fairy's skin.

My dress drips all over the palace before I find her in the garden, staring at the headstones which mark the lives of her mother, her grandmother and her great-grandmother. Roses twist around the graves like lovers, embracing and strangling.

I kiss her gills with lips like rose petals. I make her shudder.

We hold hands and watch the roses bloom.

MAGNETS

Thomas is writing a play.

In the play, Rachel and Violet are underground in an electric power plant. They were there when the super-volcano erupted, so they're not dead like everyone else, but now Rachel thinks the outside air might be toxic.

Rachel is a scientist and has dreadlocks and a lot of chemistry equipment filled with bright green liquid.

Aside from the chemistry equipment, most of the room is taken up with a double bed. Violet is usually on the bed. Violet needs help to move most of her body that's not her arms, hands, neck or face.

Violet is twenty-three and used to be a runner, but she had an accident. They replaced her spine and ankles with metal parts, and because the power plant uses giant magnets to run, she's now stuck to the mattress.

Much of the conflict arises from Rachel trying to detoxify the air, Violet crying when Rachel has to help her pee, and some guy offstage implying they're fucking each other. They're not, by the way. Thomas is eighty per cent sure. He wants his play to appeal to a mainstream audience.

It's a little bit of a shame, though, because gay plays are much easier to write than gay short stories. In gay short stories, the main characters always share the same pronoun.

Thomas is single.

Thomas and his boyfriend broke up a couple of months ago. It wasn't because he stopped loving him. It was just that he was just having trouble breathing. They're better off apart, working on their stuff. Thomas thinks he thinks so.

He was pretty sick, actually. And Thomas might have had depression, a little bit.

Thomas knew another gay couple who broke up to work on their stuff, and then six months later one of them threw themselves off a bridge.

Thomas and his boyfriend are still talking. He seems really good, actually.

In the play, there's an angled mirror above the stage so you can see Violet on the bed, like one of those daytime cooking shows. Thomas is really proud of that mirror.

In the play, Rachel tells Violet she'll never leave her. A couple of years go by and there's no solution to the air outside, but there's a mask Rachel's invented that should let them breathe. It has an orange chemical inside that Thomas imagines tastes like mandarins.

There are only enough materials for one mask.

Then there's a lot of silences and crying. Rachel wants Violet to go, because once she's away from the magnets she'll be able to run again. Violet says she won't leave Rachel behind. Violet says to leave because she's dragging her down. Rachel says she said she'd never leave her.

Sometimes Thomas wants to throw up into his coffee.

Thomas isn't sure, but maybe neither of them goes. Or one of them goes for just a little while and then comes back. The important thing is that the mask has been made. And by the time they're finished arguing about it, maybe a little while later the air clears on its own, anyway.

Because of course they'd stay together; there's barely anyone else left alive on earth, as far as they know.

At the end of the play, they stumble hand in hand into the sunlight.

Thomas calls his boyfriend.

ONE MORE TIME

They say the world might end on December 16th, 2019.

I don't believe it, in a similar way that I know I'll wake from a general anaesthetic. I'm still anxious in my gut. I stay at home on the 15th, peeking through the curtains in case some crackpots decide it's the perfect day to go on a killing spree. The internet is full of bad jokes about the apocalypse. I call my mother and my ex-girlfriend, just in case.

The clock ticks over to a quarter to midnight. No burning cities, no streams of locusts and rains of toads. I allow the knot in my stomach to slowly unfurl. I curl up on the couch with a polar-fleece blanket and sleep.

In the morning I wake in my bed, Britney Spears' "Hit Me Baby One More Time" blasting from my phone's speakers. I don't remember setting the alarm.

My sleepy hand gropes for the phone and almost knocks it off the nightstand. Six missed calls in the last three hours. I stumble to the window and pull back the curtains, in case I really did sleep through the end of the world. The birds are singing in the trees. Everything looks normal.

I check my phone again. The date reads "December 16th." I stare at it until I'm sure. Then I restart my phone and boot my laptop.

Everyone on the internet is overwhelmed. Some guy's brother died yesterday and he's alive again. A girl's tattoo disappeared overnight. Some college students finished a last-minute essay which has vanished this morning, and I can't tell if they're legitimately angry or taking the piss. Everyone is writing in capitals.

My mother rings again. "Oh, thank God," she says. "You know what's going on?"

"I'm getting the idea."

"Want to come for lunch?"

I nod into the phone. "You're not going to work?"

She laughs. "Hardly. And Sam? Be careful on the roads. It's crazy out there."

The 7th day it's December 16th is the worst. Everyone's realising this is permanent but doesn't know how to deal with it yet. Almost no-one is at work. Countless numbers throw themselves in front of cars and off buildings. The radio stations play their backup playlists, interrupted occasionally with commentary from hysterical DJs.

They say it's a fresh start. They say it's the end of the world. They say we're in heaven.

Nothing is worth anything anymore. Whatever you buy or make today will be gone tomorrow. Your job is worthless. Your degrees are worthless. However young or skinny you are today will be how young and skinny you are forever. If you're eight months pregnant, we're sorry. If you've got two broken legs, we're sorry. If your lover is overseas, we're sorry. The planes don't run anymore.

There are lots of fires on the 7th day. Lots of murders. No-one can go to prison anymore, not really. The most permanent thing about your life is the bedclothes you wake up in.

I'm getting to know Friday, December 16th very well. An unusually mild twenty-three degrees. Cloud clearing with light winds, says the bureau of meteorology.

God, I hate Britney Spears.

By the 28th time it's the 16th of December, things are starting to stabilise. Money is long dead, but trade still exists. We trade in experiences, in stories, in human company. Knowledge is still worth something, to those who care. Sex is still worth something. Imagination is worth something.

We pass on new stories like folktales, posting them for a few hours' glory on the internet, yelling them from street corners and whispering them to each other under blankets. We re-watch and re-read the old books and DVDs like gospel. Sometimes people break into a TV station and there's crap on TV again. Shops are like libraries, where people can take whatever they like for a single day. After a couple of tries I learn how to smash a window without cutting myself.

I got shot in the chest once, on the 19th day. That was impressive, because it's so hard to get a gun in Australia. But no-one gives a shit anymore. And I get to say I got shot. At least it was in the chest, so it only hurt for a minute. I didn't really mind.

I knock on my ex-girlfriend's door. She answers in a black terrycloth robe and smudged eyeliner, and she looks utterly gorgeous.

"We'll never starve," I say. "We'll never worry about money or houses or having kids. We'll never fight over the dishes or doing the washing, or whether there's enough time to stay in bed this morning. I just want to be with you."

She gives me a lazy smile and reclines against the doorframe.

I pull a gigantic, canary-yellow diamond ring from my pocket. "Marry me?"

"Come on," she says. "You know it doesn't work like that anymore."

"No-one gives a shit anymore."

She takes the ring and slips it on her finger, and I kiss my wife for the first time. The carpet's slightly sticky from where she spilled her coffee this morning. I've never been happier.

I wake in my bed every morning, and it's nine A.M. and twenty-three degrees and as perfect as it's ever going to be.

They say the world ended on December 16th. They say we're finally living in the present.

God, I love Britney Spears.

EVERYBODY KNOWS

Millie saw the monsters as a child, so she knows the signs when they come for her daughter.

She sees the scratches on Sarah's arms, on her back. Sarah's dark drawings of claws and eyes and wings. The notches on the windowsill. The notches on the closet door. The subtle and not-so-subtle mutilation of Sarah's dolls and soft toys.

Sarah wets the bed for the first time in years. Sarah wants to sleep with all the lights on. Sarah has dried blood under her tiny fingernails.

Millie knows what to do. She nails everything up: the windows, the vents, the unnecessary doors. Everything but the front door. She seals all the drains, everything but the kitchen sink and the toilet. She takes the closet doors off their hinges. She dismantles the bed. Everything monsters could hide behind is dumped outside.

She can't let Sarah out of her sight, and it's not safe outside, so Millie misses work and Sarah misses school. Millie has canned groceries delivered to the front door once a week. Millie sleeps sitting up with a knife in her lap, with Sarah lodged between herself and the bedroom corner.

Even so, sometimes she wakes to Sarah's screaming, her daughter jammed against the bedroom door, one of Sarah's arms wrenched into the hallway. Millie can only hope the monsters give up sooner than later: that they leave them alone eventually like when she was a girl.

Sarah sleeps most of the time, waking only to eat cold canned spaghetti and pee and draw with a deteriorating black marker. Millie's eyes are burning. Millie's skin crawls. Millie strokes Sarah's hair and knows they are losing the rest of their minds.

When child protection services come, Sarah doesn't look back at her mother. She knows her mother has collapsed to the floor in the hallway behind her, snot dripping down her chin. Sarah just looks at the sky. Sarah is smiling.

She was so silly, her mummy. Monsters aren't real. Everybody knows that.

"I'm okay," she repeats to the adults around a mouthful of cookies and milk. Old mummy never let her have cookies. These adults keep telling her everything will be fine now, but Sarah already knows.

She'll be adopted by some kind, rich parents who'll buy her expensive clothes and a pony and take her to Build-A-Bear. Sarah dislodges a chocolate chip from one of her big-girl teeth. "Are there more cookies?" she asks.

AND THE QUEEN WAS VEIN

The queen's first child was a small, strange-shaped boy with a tumultuous spirit. When he was three, he developed an eye infection and went half-blind, and then when he was seven, by accident or design – she could never decide which – he poked out her eyes with a two-pronged fork.

The queen ordered her huntsman to steal the boy and abandon him deep in the forest. The king would throw him in the dungeon or to the firing squad, and she assured herself the forest was a kinder alternative. When her huntsman returned with the bleeding heart of a stag, the queen announced it as her son's; he was now dead as she was blind.

While the pain in the queen's face gradually lessened, the king scoured the land for something to ease the pain in her heart. At the other edge of the forest he came across a weathered cottage belonging to an old man. For a small fortune, the old man sold the king three items: a mirror, a white-gold knife and a vial of clear liquid that bubbled perpetually beneath its cork.

The king and queen hung the mirror beside their bed. It was enchanted to describe whatever it reflected, so that it could function as the queen's replacement eyes whenever the king could not. Then the queen took the knife and the vial into the snow, knelt in her thickest dress, and prayed for a child the exact opposite of her first; a girl, pure and breathtakingly beautiful as the snow beneath her gloves.

As per the old man's instructions, the queen drank the contents of the vial in one gulp, and soon after dozens of her veins protruded as thick blue ridges. She felt for the ridges on the exposed skin of her arms, cut seven different veins with the enchanted knife and let the blood fall onto the snow. She had not expected to feel so lightheaded.

When she woke in the snow minutes later, she was pregnant with her second child.

#

Most days, the queen cradled Snow White to her chest and had the mirror describe every detail of her daughter's tiny frame. Afterwards, glowing with pride, the queen would ask, "Who is the most beautiful in all the land?" And the mirror would coo, "You," directly to Snow White and add, "She grows more beautiful by the day."

For years the queen's heart swelled fat with happiness. Her daughter's tinkling laughter filled every hallway in the palace. And then Snow White's seventh birthday arrived, and her screams echoed down the hallways instead.

The adults found three dead bodies in the parlour: one beneath the window, one face-down in the birthday cake and one impaled on the spinning wheel. When the doctor later questioned Snow White, he had barely laid eyes upon her when he collapsed, knocked his head on her bedpost and promptly died.

The princess was inconsolable. She opened her door only to her mother, who brought her the sweetest of apples and braided the whitest of ribbons in her hair. And as the hours rolled on and the queen braided and braided, a hot, dark knot grew inside the queen's stomach and made her gasp.

When she could stand it no longer, the queen brought Snow White before her magic mirror and asked, "Mirror, mirror, is my daughter breathtakingly beautiful?" And the mirror said, "Yes, of course," and added, "She grows more beautiful by the day."

The king would return to the kingdom soon. The queen refused to live without her husband, or without her daughter. She had already lost one child. She would not lose another.

The queen dug deep in the earth and retrieved the enchanted knife from so many years ago. If the princess's face was not so beautiful...

Snow White woke to find the knife inches from her nose.

The princess fled, out through her bedroom window and far into the depths of the forest. The huntsman followed. With each of her daughter's steps the queen felt her own veins constrict and her heart grow tight, like a dangerous weight was multiplying on her chest.

The huntsman caught Snow White within the hour. She cried the queen had tried to kill her; she drenched his jacket with her tears. She said, "Please, don't take me back there, or she'll try again!" And the huntsman, who could only see the faintest glint of her eyes in the darkness of the new moon, killed a boar and took its heart home instead.

The queen did not believe him. Her veins told her the girl was still alive, not eaten by wild animals as the huntsman claimed. But the queen's grief was real and there was no advantage in the truth, so she lied and thanked him for finding the remains of her daughter's body. She would not send others into the forest; it was a suicide mission, for those with eyes.

When he had barely turned eight, the queen's son came across the weathered cottage belonging to the old man. "Please," howled the muddy boy, "I'm starving and I can hardly see. Won't you help me?" And the old man offered him a deal.

From deep in the basement came a pair of enchanted scissors, their blades tinged with crimson, which snipped off seven of the boy's eight fingers. Where the fingers fell on the dusty floor, seven copies of the boy grew slowly to full-size and stood naked, shivering in the evening air. Once they had been dressed in the old man's identical, oversized work shirts, the old man said, "Now you share the hunger and thirst of one boy between the eight of you. Which one is coming with me?"

They drew straws. One of the boys clambered onto a loaded wagon, the old man flickered the horses' reigns, and the remaining seven watched from the porch as an eighth of themselves rolled away.

It was dusk, years later, when Snow White stumbled upon the same cottage. She found numerous grimy, makeshift beds, seven bloodstains on the ancient wooden floor, and a trapdoor locked with the largest silver padlock she'd ever set eyes on. She was in the process of leaving when its occupants appeared silhouetted in the doorway.

The seven boys stepped inside, axes and rabbit corpses over their shoulders and streaks of mud on their chins. They stood only slightly taller than Snow White – their aging was spread between the eight of them – and they stared at the hazy, girl-shaped blur in their living room and started to whistle.

But Snow White cried that the queen had tried to kill her, and there was nothing that could have bonded them better.

The queen needed no manufactured disguise. Her veins pulled her always in the right direction, and the closer she grew to her daughter the easier the pressure on her heart. But she had nothing to navigate the step-by-step terrain, and by the time she emerged at the cottage she looked like she had fallen through the forest horizontally. This bloody, exhausted, filthy woman bore little resemblance to the queen who had first stepped out of the palace.

So much so that Snow White spied a beggar through the window, and called out, "We have nothing to spare!" And the queen unbuckled her shoulder bag, explaining she expected to be giving rather than receiving gifts, and held up her offering.

The bodice was truly beautiful, but what really drew Snow White was its shining white ribbons. As the queen laced her up, the girl thought of all the times her mother had adorned her with similar ribbons, and how warm and loved she had felt – before the deaths. The beggar's hands were wonderfully gentle, until they paused, and then the laces pulled tighter and tighter until Snow White was having trouble breathing.

With one hand, the queen held her daughter by the ends of the ribbons. With the other, she pulled the white-gold knife from her boot. And then she heard the low, dangerous whistling of a mob approaching from the hills, so she released the ribbons and fled.

Snow White fell to her knees on the blood-stained floor. The whistling turned into a stampede of small footsteps, and the many versions of her brother clawed at the bodice until she was free.

When the queen returned to the cottage the following day, she came brandishing a glittering comb which cast sunspots through the window. The lights danced along the inner wooden walls, mesmerising Snow White and beckoning the girl outside.

The queen apologised for running off during their last encounter. The whistling alarmed her, she said; could she offer this comb as compensation? And Snow White coveted the comb like a magpie and longed for those motherly fingers in her hair, so she swung open the door.

Manipulating her daughter's curls between her fingers, the queen struggled to keep from weeping fat tears down the back of the girl's neck. She wrapped Snow White's locks into a glossy roll and wielded the points of the comb like a weapon.

But the whistling came again, louder this time and instantly chilling. The comb fell to the floor with a raucous clatter, and the queen had vanished by the time it stilled by Snow White's feet.

There was no more time. The queen had advised that she may be absent for several days, but they would have dispatched an official search party by now. So she lingered closer to the cottage than was strictly safe, listened for the sound of the mob departing and crept to the window one final time.

She pulled a perfect, scarlet apple from her bag and set it on the windowsill. With the white-gold knife she cut a chunk of ripe apple flesh and brought it past her lips. There was no unusual tang or toxic aftertaste. She had expected something bitter, or at least abnormal, given that she'd submerged the entire apple in poison days earlier.

Snow White was smiling as she ate the rest of it, the queen could hear it in her voice.

The queen could not bring herself to smile. She murmured, "You are loved very much," and left her daughter alone to die.

Several hours later, the queen's horsemen hoisted her highness onto a black mare and returned her to the palace. She retrieved the antidote from a hole in the back of her dresser, a thick liquid stoppered in the same vial she'd used to conceive her daughter seven years earlier. Her veins were quieter than they'd ever been since Snow White's departure, and the antidote caught in her throat.

When her veins relaxed completely, the queen was hunched behind her bedroom window, cradling a length of white ribbon. Her daughter took a last, fevered breath in a nest of bloodstained blankets and expired.

The seven copies of her brother discovered her body in the morning. They locked her in the corner of the basement, inside the thick glass coffin that had been gathering dust there.

Their eighth brother had been polishing an antique lamp when he suspected his sister's death. He felt his brothers' sadness as a dull ache at the bottom of his spine, and the rumour spread whip-quick through the perfumed city streets.

Another prince, fully-grown and in search of a wife, heard the story of a princess in a locked glass box and the old man who might own it. But that same old man would disclose nothing of its location or secrets, and the strange-shaped boy beside him whispered that he could take them there if he was not bound to his master.

The older prince slit the old man's throat in one fluid motion. He held out a calloused hand to the shaking boy and said, "I am your master now."

#

The prince's men hauled the frosted glass coffin out into the sunlight. The body inside it slipped about – it only occupied about half the space – and for a moment the prince entertained second thoughts. Nonetheless, he adjusted his finest coat, turned the key until it clicked in the lock, and raised the lid.

When the prince collapsed inside the coffin, he fit perfectly.

His men locked the coffin with both bodies inside. They were to be buried together, Snow White in a white silk dress and the prince in his suit, who attained a peculiar version of the marriage he was seeking.

The queen bent over her bed, overwhelmed with memories of holding her daughter in that same place for years. She could practically feel Snow White's warm skin against her cheek. The old words slipped unbidden from her lips, and the mirror said, "You are, my queen," and broke her heart.

Eight identical boys whistled as they stepped off their front porch. They were together again, and it was time to settle an old score. The eighth boy had retrieved a particular pair of crimson shoes from the basement. He knew most of the cottage's contents from his travels, but these shoes seemed especially fitting.

Their mother must be dancing on their sister's grave.

And the queen could dance until she died.

STRANGE DANCEMATES

One August evening, in a mix of grief and hope, Lara Jane Hudson accidentally opens the portal to Hell.

It takes her two and half days to fully realise this has happened: that there is a slightly shimmery, raised-edge circle on the floor of her basement storage room, with a suspicious crust on top like the surface of an apple crumble. It stinks of air freshener, but at least she feels a little less like she's losing her mind.

FUN FACT: *Lara Jane Hudson accidentally opened the portal to Hell with her own bad dancing. She was a professional dancer once upon a time, until her right ankle was crushed under a falling set piece when she was twenty-two and she opened a children's dance studio instead. Occasionally, when everyone had gone home, she lingered in the middle of Studio A's $76,000 floor and danced the best she could.*

Aside from the vanilla-and-fresh-laundry portal in amongst her costume racks and spare gym mat, there is an additional consequence of blurring the lines between the realms. That first night, when Lara Jane climbs the stairs to her apartment above the Lara Jane Dance Studio and slips under the bed-covers, she finds a mermaid in her bed.

The mermaid does not receive a warm reception. There is ample screaming, and cursing, and Lara Jane has a loud voice honed by yelling regularly at children. The air smells strongly of oysters. Lara Jane crouches up against her padded headboard, and the mermaid curls lethargically on the crimson sheets like a bleeding fish.

When the mermaid won't exit of its own accord, Lara Jane pushes it forcibly off the bed with her wooden cane. Its long hair slides off the mattress like kelp.

It reappears back on the mattress like magic.

More screaming. Lara Jane tries pushing it out of bed again and again. Finally, she drops her human feet to the carpet, and then the mermaid truly vanishes. She feels spent, and like she might cry, which she normally only does once a year when someone dies or she feels especially humiliated.

Lara Jane slumps back onto her sweaty pillow. Instantly, the mermaid is back beside her... And the real troubleshooting begins.

FUN FACT: *Over that first week, Lara Jane Hudson tested several methods to banish the creatures from her bed. She tried sleeping on the floor, sleeping upright, sleeping with no bedding, sleeping in hotels, sleeping in a single bed – none of these worked, and the last seemed particularly cramped and frightening. Whenever she exhibited the intention to sleep, something strange and otherworldly would appear nearby.*

Eventually, she creates an enormous bed of gym mats in Studio A and lets her eyes slip shut.

The mermaid comes every Monday.

On the second Monday, Lara Jane Hudson can share a large bed of gym mats with the mermaid without screaming, cursing or sweating profusely. There have been six other creatures to visit her, and frankly the mermaid now seems safe and wholesome by comparison.

Lara Jane has not been sleeping well. Lara Jane has been taking involuntary micro-sleeps in her children's dance classes and on the toilet, and waking seconds later with her chin smooshed against the toilet paper. Lara Jane has been considering taking a mental health day, and Lara Jane *never* takes mental health days. Lara Jane is royally pissed off.

She glares at the mermaid, and the mermaid stares straight back at her with its blue-black eyes. She says, "Hello, my name is Lara Jane, and you are in my dance studio," and the mermaid says, "Hello," and this feels like the most progress since she opened that damned portal to Hell in the first place.

The faun comes every Tuesday.

At least, Lara Jane suspects that he's a faun. There are a couple of antlers growing out of his head, but a blanket's always covered his lower half, thank God, because a lot of the creatures seem to turn up naked. Point is, she doesn't know for sure what's going on past his waist, and she doesn't really care for confirmation, either.

It's the second Tuesday. Now that she's no longer trying to threaten him out of bed with a butter knife, he's nestled crossed-legged in a wad of blankets and harassing her for cigarettes.

Lara Jane laughs sharply under the dimmed fluorescent lights. "Does it look like I carry cigarettes?"

The faun grips his antlers in frustration, pulling them apart like he's about to break over-sized wishbones. "Come on, come on," he drawls. "Don't send me back there with nothing. Have a bit of compassion."

Compassion is not usually well-stocked in Lara Jane's inventory. The nearest poster declares WINNING IS THE ONLY OPTION with a picture of a tutu-clad child leaping for her life over a ravine.

"Where's 'there'?" she asks. "Where do you go when you're not here?"

"Ah." The faun taps the side of his nose with a slightly-furred finger. "Cigarettes, my darling, cigarettes. Then you'll find out."

The golem comes every Wednesday.

Lara Jane has the beginnings of a migraine. Her entire elite squad must have shot up with pixie sticks or red cordial or something before class, because this evening's lesson was shockingly unfocused. Regardless, she's in no mood to lug half a dozen gym mats and blankets into position in Studio A, and she thinks she knows who (or what) to expect beside her tonight, so she consents to the luxury of her proper, four-wooden-legs queen-sized bed.

When Lara Jane collapses under the doona, Wednesday's visitor is slumped forward like a dying battery. Lara Jane thought it was a robot the first week, because every inch of it seemed made of silver metal. But the only seam in its casing is a small square panel in its lower back, and robots don't move like this thing does – fluidly, the way real human flesh and muscle would move, despite the silver.

It turns its solemn face on Lara Jane, and two tiny candles seem to burn inside its eye sockets.

"Go to sleep," croaks Lara Jane, and so they do.

FUN FACT: *Shortly after opening the portal to Hell, Lara Jane Hudson performed several hours of internet research on magical gateways, "mythical" creatures and the afterlife. She found it comforting to learn the approximate terms for many of her night-time visitors, even if their anatomy and behaviour did not match identically with her readings. Lara Jane also attempted a few do-it-yourself exorcisms and disenchantments involving salt, chalk, holy water, a small amount of blood and some more questionable dancing. These only made her bedroom and basement storage room messier. The portal remained.*

Upon her alarm, Lara Jane rolls out of bed immediately, a habit she's developed to minimize the amount of waking hours she has to spend with her bedmates. There is a scrap of paper on the bed, torn from the notebook she keeps on the bedside table.

On one side, written in big block letters: *PLEASE LET ME STAY.*

Lara Jane turns it over. *OR HELP ME TO DIE.*

The gumby comes every Thursday.

Lara Jane calls it a gumby because of that kids' show that was on twenty years ago, with the green plasticine man who could stretch himself into an infinite number of shapes, and, she suspects, could split himself into pieces with no harm done.

The gumby that comes to visit is not green. S/he lies naked on Lara Jane's gym mats and pulls off two breasts, one penis and a ponytail's worth of strawberry-blonde hair, stacking them in a pile beside her/him. Each piece peels away neatly with a slight sucking/sealing sound, like closing up a zip-lock bag. There is only flawless skin underneath: no wounds, no scars.

"I hope you don't mind," says the gumby. S/he smiles warmly at Lara Jane. "I find it easier to sleep this way."

It is unnerving to have so much blatant nudity in her "bed," even if the gumby is sprawled a few gym mats away and is currently approaching the non-existent sexuality of a Barbie doll. Lara Jane is used to thinking of herself as something similar.

FUN FACT: *Lara Jane Hudson was always adamant that she would share the appearance of the portal and its accompanying "emissaries" with no-one. She had been single since her twenties, an only child with a deceased father and a mother in care for dementia. Her closest relationships were with the children she taught, and her reputation meant absolutely everything. Not even the portal to Hell could make her put it at risk.*

The gumby's androgynous voice reaches her from across the room: "If you could make sure I've reattached everything before you leave the bed in the morning, I'd appreciate it. I wouldn't want to risk losing a part."

"Sure," says Lara Jane, considering the gravity of the situation. "I promise."

The tentacles come every Friday.

They are, of course, attached to a man. His torso twists like a screw-top and out fold the tentacles, all six of them.

It's the second Friday evening, and Lara Jane is still horrified by last week's visit. Friday is not a bedroom night, or even a gym mats night—Lara Jane plans to sit in the Dance Centre's kitchenette and plot the choreography, set, and costume for next fortnight's competition entry in extreme detail until she falls asleep, unintentionally, drooling on the notepaper. Mugs and mugs of hot chocolate. Phone alarm in her bra set to wake her for Saturday's competition.

She hopes to avoid the tentacles almost completely.

And the new dance for her elite team is stunning; monsters emerging from the shadows of a child's bedroom. Six children covered with fur, horns, scales, glitter. One child on an artificially shortened bed – a nine-year-old, Lara Jane's best little actress. The monsters want to devour her. The girl outwits them, out-monsters them; they make her their queen. Then something goes terribly wrong, and they tear the child to pieces anyway.

Glorious.

Lara Jane knows it's a winning number.

She sees only the slightest blur of tentacles before she passes out.

The starmist comes every Saturday.

In a neighbouring state the hotel bed is sterile and fluffy, and Lara Jane is deeply pleased that one of her girls won first place with a solo today, and less pleased that both their group dance and the duet she choreographed only took second in their categories. The group number was something clean, feminine and glossy, and loosely based on the fairy tale *The Twelve Dancing Princesses*. In hindsight, rehearsing that dance had kept Lara Jane from driving a screwdriver into her neck the first week.

The starmist floats sedately beside her, a few inches off the bed-covers, and for once Lara Jane barely minds the company.

"Why do you think you're here?" she asks.

Her visitor resembles an almost-transparent teenager who swallowed the night sky.

"So you can help me," breathes the starmist.

And Lara Jane was afraid of that.

FUN FACT: *This is where the starmist was, when she wasn't with Lara Jane Hudson:*

A pine forest. Hunters, in hazmat suits and flamethrowers. It was night, and she was almost invisible. She'd watched her mother, father and brothers immolate into trickles of ash and plumes of smoke, and she should've been soaring away, far above the treetops where no flames could reach her. But her sister was down there.

A frantic search, weaving through fiery trees and umpteen hunters, and she found her sister inside a glass cage on a folding card-table. Her sister's small dark hands were pressed against the front panel. There was a Tupperware container in the dirt nearby, half-filled with water, and with a silver key at the bottom. The key to the cage.

They knew that starmists could barely interact with physical matter, if at all.

Still, she reached inside the container and tried to grasp the key, again and again. She swore the water trembled in response to her hand. She could almost feel the metal against her fingers, she was concentrating so hard. And the forest fires crept closer and closer; she was shimmering in the heat like the air above a campfire. She was starting to burn.

Finally, ecstatically, her fingers closed properly around the key. And then she heard the hunters behind her, and the whir-hiss of the flamethrower, and then there was the total immersion in fire when she caught alight.

This was where the starmist went, always, again and again.

Lara Jane does not feel qualified to help.

Lara Jane does not feel qualified to do anything but teach dancing.

Una comes every Sunday.

Lara Jane doesn't know what to call this one, except for her name, and Una doesn't have any other answers. Just curls on the bed like there are weights in her wrists and rocks in her torso.

It's the second Sunday, and Lara Jane is back home and early to bed, because she's not the kind of woman to shy away from a challenge.

Thankfully, she's also had enough forethought to bring supplies. Lara Jane wraps Una's shoulders in a knitted blanket, since Una's arms are too heavy and sore to lift into a t-shirt. They sit silently on the bed and eat red liquorice and watch a DVD of the studio's annual concert.

When the last child finishes their dancing, Lara Jane closes her laptop and attempts to start gently. "You look just like me," she says, "but all of my visitors are a little different. Can you tell me – or show me – what makes you different? Maybe then I can try to help you."

This earns her a short bout of acidic laughter. Very slowly, Una turns her naked back on Lara Jane and drags aside her long brown hair.

A thick bronze zip runs down her spine.

FUN FACT: *In preparation for Week Three, Lara Jane Hudson performed several hours of online shopping in her official trademarked Lara Jane Dance Studio fuzzy slippers. Purchases included: 1 blow-up swimming pool, child-size; 2 packets of low-end cigarettes, 12/pack; 2 fresh notebooks with waterproof-ink pens; 1 metal tub, 1.5 feet long; 1 anti-rape device (essentially a female condom with teeth); 6 silver prop keys; 3 bags of red liquorice.*

The mermaid barely says a word, but still coils up inside the plastic swimming pool like a sleepy river snake. Lara Jane has propped the pool in the middle of the bed and stripped most of the bedclothes to minimise any impact from the four inches of water. It hasn't sloshed over so far. And as Lara Jane watches over her notebook, the mermaid's green-blonde hair grows longer and longer until the mermaid can completely wrap itself in the hair like a cocoon, until only its nose and mouth are visible between thick spirals of hair.

Over the next week, Lara Jane has regular, amusing visions of grabbing the end of the mermaid's hair and tugging so it unfurls like a yo-yo string. Eventually, this morphs into a kinder, more inspiring idea wherein Lara Jane installs three dozen metal loops across the walls of her bedroom, and when the fourth Monday rolls around she explains her plan to the mermaid with gestures and sketches.

So Lara Jane balances on the mattress and threads the mermaid's hair through the metal loops, and the mermaid grows it almost as fast as Lara Jane can thread it. When they finish, the room is crisscrossed with an intricate web of thick, rope-strong hair, and Lara Jane ties it off so nothing will pull on the mermaid's scalp.

Lara Jane steps up into the web with her good foot, grabs a higher green-blonde rope and lowers herself so she's sitting in a cradle of hair. She grins at the mermaid, whose scaly tail is still dipped inside the children's swimming pool. "Come and play."

FUN FACT: *The mermaid's name was Scalion, back when the world was wet and did her bidding, and she was one of the finest jewellers in her city. The city bloomed deep, deep in a lake in the middle of a flowering desert. But this is not where the mermaid went when she wasn't with Lara Jane Hudson.*

In Scalion's 29th year, the water level started dropping rapidly. Unnaturally rapidly. There began a mass exodus from the city, slow at first and then exponentially faster. Scalion was much too content to admit that anything was wrong. She grew her hair to her knees and braided pearls and sapphires and emeralds to every second strand. Her knuckles were covered in diamonds and jewels like a queen. And then there were only two hundred mermaids left in the city.

One day, Scalion woke to bone-dry, sun-warmed sand beneath her back. No more water in sight. The lone survivor in a deep, dead pit with the skeletal remains of her ghost city. Her gradually cooking body, and the dizzying stench of rotting fish.

This is where the mermaid was, when she wasn't with Lara Jane. Barely breathing and choking on sunlight.

Later that day, Scalion grew her hair into a rope and threw it over the sign for her jewellery shop. Wrapped it around her neck, pearls and sapphires and emeralds digging into her windpipe. And hanged herself amongst the bones of her happiness.

Lara Jane watches the mermaid pull herself through the ropes of hair, sinking down through the gaps and slithering in slow, vertical circles like a needle through calico. She watches the joy of it creep up on the mermaid's face. The movements become quicker and wilder, half-eel and half-gymnastics, until Scalion runs out of hair slack and she's forced to pause and grow more.

"It's like swimming," says the mermaid, smiling and panting.

Lara Jane experimentally pokes her own head through a gap in the ropes. The hair is taut and flexible, smooth and slippery. Lara Jane hasn't felt this excited about exercising since she was twenty-two and performing front-aerials on Broadway. She climbs and slides and hangs from her knees and twists herself around. And laughs. Her weak ankle, which she can always walk on carefully but never flex, barely makes a difference here. It's not at all like dancing on a stage, but it's almost like dancing.

Lara Jane perches at the top of the web while the mermaid plays. She's there for almost half an hour while Scalion revels in the almost-swimming, and then she notices the mermaid stop in the centre of the ropes. A few tears drip into the blow-up pool. And everything vanishes—the mermaid, the metres and metres of hair, the ropes that Lara Jane is sitting on.

Lara Jane falls six feet and crashes awkwardly onto the bed, bouncing three times and splashing the water from the pool high into the air. It soaks her carpet and dresser and most of her desk chair, but presently Lara Jane is too shocked to mind. She feels like her whole body's been slapped. But she picks herself up and takes in the bedroom: that she's lying on the bed alone, perfectly alone.

Lara Jane fills the pool again the following Monday, but Scalion no longer appears on schedule. She never sees the mermaid again.

FUN FACT: *Around this time, Lara Jane Hudson choreographed a new solo piece called* Head Below Water, *where the imaginary water level dropped steadily throughout the two-minute dance, and it won first place by a landslide.*

The kids are loving the monster dance. They are being raised to be proper young ladies, and their chances to snarl and climb over each other and jump on beds are few and far between. The prop bed is already finished – a half-sized single made of lightweight wood, so that six girls can lift the bed between them, even with a seventh on top of it. A delicious game. Lara Jane has decided to put her child character in a white outfit with a big zip down the front; a homage to *Where the Wild Things Are.*

On the evening of the third Tuesday, the prop bed is stored in the corner and the gym mats are Lara Jane's bed for the night. The faun sticks a cigarette into his mouth and wiggles it with just his stubbled lips. Lara Jane has forgotten to buy a lighter. She wanders into the kitchenette to find some matches, and when she returns to Studio A the faun has vanished. She climbs back onto the gym mats and he reappears, reeling from some kind of cosmic whiplash.

The faun has Lara Jane light the cigarette for him, and then lies back and smokes with his antlers digging into the mats. Normally Lara Jane would forcibly remove anyone who lit up in her Dance Centre; everything would stop until the smoker had been ejected. But tonight this seems like a tolerable price for closing the portal: just a tiny speck of fire and brimstone.

"Are you going to tell me your story now?" she asks.

"Give me a break," he says. "I've just come back from war."

"Literal war?"

He grins at her around the cigarette filter. "Wouldn't you like to know."

Lara Jane grits her teeth. "You don't actually get to take those back with you?"

One lazy eye focuses on her. "No. I can pretend, though."

He props himself up on his elbows and surveys the studio: the floor-length mirrors, the barre, the motivational posters (Lara Jane admits that these are usually brightly-coloured threats). "You should dance for me," he says.

Lara Jane manages to blanch and cackle simultaneously. "I don't do that anymore." When the faun pushes, she explains about her ankle and that the centre's insurance only covers her children.

He laughs. "Insurance? I don't care about your insurance. Dance for me and I'll tell you."

"No! Are you kidding me? You can't keep moving the flags."

The faun pulls back his blanket and stubs the cigarette out on one shiny black hoof. Lara Jane sees that his antlers and hooves are the only parts that make him unusual and makes a small disgruntled noise at seeing more of him than she'd like.

The faun notices, and scoots over on the mats to snatch the matches. He lights a second cigarette. "Dance *with* me, and I'll tell you."

"No," says Lara Jane, and twists her back towards him. "You know I could just get up at any time. Five hundred times a night if I wanted to. So fuck off and go to sleep."

Violently, she fluffs the baby-pink pillow beneath her head. The orange poster above her says DANCE OR DIE in a large font and *(figuratively)* in a smaller font. To Lara Jane's relief, the faun keeps silent for the rest of his visit.

The fourth Tuesday, Lara Jane arranges the gym mats so that they outline a three-metre-square section of the studio floor. She drapes the blankets so that small sections of wool and faux-fur fall into the square. When the faun arrives, she dresses him in some old shorts and a beige sweater and feels immediately more comfortable and in control.

"This is the bed for today," she says. "Come put your hooves here." Lara Jane points to the square of hard floor next to where he's kneeling.

It takes a few lazy drags of his cigarette, but then each hoof makes a sharp little click on the dance floor and makes Lara Jane's lips twitch upwards. "Good," she says. "Very good. Stand up and we'll see if you warp back to the mats."

He doesn't warp anywhere. And now Lara Jane's fully in her comfort zone, staring at a lukewarm tap dancing student with her manicured hand on a portable CD player.

"If you want me to dance with you," she says, "you've got to learn how to dance first."

FUN FACT: *This is where the faun was, when he wasn't with Lara Jane:*

Concrete and spitting rain. He removed the plastic seals from the filters of the gas mask and fitted the mask to his head. Checked the attachments on his belt. The front doors were locked with chains the size of his biceps; his team were around the factory's side. Even stubble could interfere with the function of the gas mask, so he felt unusually clean-shaven.

Ironically, they entered through the air conditioning system.

Inside was a maze of rooms, doors and corridors. A mess of lights and steel and broken plastic tape, the non-stick type with warnings printed on one side. Chairs were scattered like bowling pins. The faun and his team were quickly separated; blink and they were replaced by machinery or shadows or enemy units. Not war – at least not public war. The faun's 28th mission.

It took his knife, laser gun, carabineer and screwdriver to make it to the top floor. It was almost silent when he got there, and the main corridor was brightly lit and flooding with his teammates' blood. It was shallower down his end: just a thin coating that was beginning to dry and congeal.

He started down the hall with his laser gun in one hand and his knife in the other, picking his way over the bodies of his fallen friends. He'd survived an impressive catalogue of attacks and dangers in his short life, but in that particular instance his hooves slipped, unprovoked, in the blood. The knife flew from his grasp. His masked head smashed to the floor. The blade arced down to bury itself in his chest, and he died almost instantly.

When the faun learns to tap dance from Lara Jane, he doesn't slip. Not once. Not ever.

She does dance with him, eventually. It's not traditional. He coaxes her onto his shoulders and Lara Jane wraps her candy-pink nails around the top of his antlers. Tap is one of her worst styles, these days; the only way she can tap is sitting down, one-footed. Or she can ride his shoulders like some kind of fleshy air hopper, and cling onto his bony antlers until the world comes to a stop.

He's not terrible-terrible, for a beginner, and the hooves are fun. But she can't say she enjoys being an attachment while he dances. Too much like horse riding, and Lara Jane never felt enough in control while horse riding. Just the once upon his shoulders is enough.

The faun tells her his story, and he keeps dancing, and one day his hooves leave the ground in a jump and they never come back.

FUN FACT: *The day after discovering the portal to Hell, Lara Jane Hudson hired a locksmith. She alone had possession of the resultant keys to the basement storage room, and she informed her staff that no-one else was to have access to that room for an indefinite period of time. She was working on a secret project, she claimed – which was not technically a lie.*

By the third Wednesday, Lara Jane needs to decide what her false "secret project" will be. Something she can display hints of in the office, or show the teachers the finished project (assuming the storage room is ever secular again) when it's "done." It needs to be big enough to warrant several weeks' work, and small enough to fit amongst the clothes racks. And yes, Lara Jane could be brainstorming in bed rather than in the kitchenette in her Minnie Mouse pyjamas, but she's honestly not keen to try and drag out life stories from unwilling creatures for the fourth night running.

In lieu of any better ideas, she decides on gift hampers. For her half a dozen teachers and the parents of her elite squad. She can pretend she put them together by hand, agonising over each personalised item, when she actually ordered them in bulk at the last minute and then threw in some studio merchandise and redid the ribbons. Lying makes her angry, but what can you do?

When she does end up in bed, she passes the golem a fresh notebook and pen and rolls over to sleep.

On the first page of the notebook, Lara Jane has written: *Write down where you go when you're not here. I'll try and help. Sorry I can't stay up and chat tonight. L.J.H xx PS: Sorry you're dead.*

She receives a several-page reply.

FUN FACT: *The golem was "born" into a gated community who believed the world was ending. She woke under the street in a room full of mechanical animals, some wound and some immobile, mostly birds. A mechanical fish swam in the light fitting. A middle-aged man stood in front of her and explained she existed only to take care of his daughter.*

The daughter was seven. In the event of the end of the world, the golem was to take her into their state-of-the-art panic room and care for her for the rest of her life.

Her father's other mechanical creatures had limited intelligence. Humans were subject to the end of the world and could be burnt and starved and suffocated. Much safer to use magic and write LIFE on a slip of paper and insert it into the golem's lower back panel. Much safer to use something alive-but-not-alive.

But this was where the golem went when she wasn't with Lara Jane Hudson:

Two months after the golem woke, a mob of teenagers jumped her in the backyard and pushed her into the wet grass. They wrote SADNESS and ANGER and DESPAIR onto slips of paper; everything they wanted to take out of themselves and put into someone else. They dropped a dozen paper slips into the golem alongside the one which said LIFE and melted the panel closed with a welding torch.

That night the world really did start to end. The golem peeled herself off the grass and dragged herself inside through the bitterness and hopelessness and everything else that escaped from Pandora's box. Up the stairs and grabbed the girl and into the padded panic room.

Ten years passed, and every second of them, the golem desperately wanted to die. Then the seventeen-year-old girl wrote DEATH on a scrap of paper, folded it three times and slipped it through a crack in the golem's lower back panel.

It worked, more or less.

Lara Jane is re-evaluating what it means to be in Hell.

The fourth Wednesday, she retrieves a pile of tools from the basement storage room and dumps them on the gym mats: foam earplugs, two pairs of industrial-strength ear-muffs, a saw, one pair of oversized tweezers and some plastic safety glasses. Lara Jane's props and sets are always designed by her and outsourced for construction, but they occasionally need last-minute adjustments.

Tonight's adjustments consist of burrowing the saw blade into a tiny gap in the golem's back panel. Lara Jane is very pleased that the studio's closest neighbours are more than a hundred meters away, because the screech of saw teeth on metal could easily bring the police at ten o'clock at night. But there are no interruptions.

Two hours, a bottle of lemonade and an improvised crowbar later, Lara Jane can pry up the top of the panel enough to squeeze in the extra-large tweezers, inspect the slips of paper and extract them. They stack up on the discarded saw, the ink not even faded, the paper still crisp white. Lara Jane is reminded of that cartoon surgery board game which buzzes if your tweezers slip. She carefully leaves the final slip inside–LIFE–and pulls out the crowbar.

The golem peels herself off the mats and flexes her fingers, swivels her joints and bounces experimentally on the balls of her feet. She smiles at Lara Jane. Then takes off running in circles around the edge of the mats: *thwap, thwap, thwap* across the plastic-covered foam, dimmed fluorescent lights bouncing across her silver frame.

After a dozen circles, the golem picks Lara Jane up by the waist, and Lara Jane cries out in shock and protest. She's a tall woman, and borderline chubby these days: unaccustomed to being carried like she weighs nothing at all. Thankfully the golem slows down to walking pace.

"I appreciate that you're excited," says Lara Jane, "but can you put me down?"

"I'm so grateful," says the golem. "Don't you want to run or dance and celebrate?"

Lara Jane watches the studio walls speed past her. "I don't really do that anymore."

The golem thrusts Lara Jane above her head, and Lara Jane cries out again. "You can do *this*."

"What? I can't bend my ankle. The lines will be ugly. It'll be all wrong!"

"So?" says the golem. "Who'll know?"

And Lara Jane has to admit that she's smiling a bit, and that some of the movements she might make in the early hours of that morning could be considered dancing. However questionable the technique.

When the golem tires herself out, she asks Lara Jane to pull out the last slip of paper.

The fires in her metal eye sockets snuff out. And then Lara Jane is lying next to an empty shell.

Lara Jane is having nightmares: her girls discover the creatures when she faints in class or lies down to demonstrate a piece of choreography, or when one of them barges into her hotel room. She has a gut-churning moment with a foamy toothbrush hanging out of her mouth: all those micro-sleeps. If a twelve-year-old saw a mermaid for a few seconds, mid-rehearsal, would they dismiss it as a trick of the light? Is that one of the reasons their mothers have been extra-fussy lately, complaining she's working their kids too hard?

The monster costumes arrive that third Thursday, and they are a comfort, the difference between hiding a creature in an empty room and a Halloween party. The costumed girls look strange and glamorous and wild. They swipe each other with fake tails and butt each other with furry horns.

That night, the gumby places its daytime body parts in the box Lara Jane provides, and Lara Jane props herself up on a stack of lacy pillows. She asks, "Where do you go when you're not here?" and is surprised when she receives a direct answer.

FUN FACT: *This is where the gumby went, when s/he's wasn't with Lara Jane:*

The entry gates of a labyrinth. A slow day. The gumby stood at the ticket booth, "SUPERVISOR" embroidered in gold on a navy polo shirt.

A large man approached: fake, plastic Viking hat and very real axe, blade glinting in the summer sun. There was nothing ambiguous about him. The gumby abandoned the cash box and ran, into the protection of the stone-walled labyrinth.

No time to shut the gates. The gumby raced along the concrete paths towards the centre; s/he knew the twists and turns better than anyone. A labyrinth is not a maze – there is only a single path – but s/he just needed to gain twenty seconds on the axe-man.

Five minutes down the path: a small hole at the base of the left wall, so small that no human over three feet could fit inside. So the gumby ripped off a foot at the ankle, reached inside the hole and through a subsequent smaller gap in the stones, and tossed the foot inside.

S/he tore off pieces of leg and hips and torso faster than ever. The "storage" compartment inside the hole filled with stacked flesh, and then the gumby half-pulled, half-rolled the remaining parts inside.

S/he just fit: most of a torso and two arms and neck and head. A piece of shrubbery obscured the hole to anyone on the pathway. Further down, there came the thump of heavy feet and the clang of an axe on stone corners.

With difficulty, s/he reached up and back into the storage area, feeling around discarded body parts for the phone zipped into a jeans pocket. The gumby pried it free. Fourteen per cent battery left. Not fantastic, but enough.

Calling anyone would be too loud. S/he texted family, a handful of friends and a couple of colleagues. Put the phone on silent. Waited patiently.

And waited.

The sun fell, the phone died, the gumby hadn't heard a whisper from the axe-man for the last couple of hours. S/he clawed out of the hole and started reassembling pieces of torso, hips, thighs. S/he was almost done when an evening shadow fell over the wall, and with the crack of metal-on-spine s/he felt the enormous axe-blade split her/his back in two.

Blood soaked into the navy polo shirt. The large man left the axe stuck half-into the gumby's flesh, sighed deeply and stalked away.

Blood dripped onto the path. The gumby stretched for the last body parts so s/he could die whole.

When the gumby pulls the blanket from her/his legs, Lara Jane notices for the first time that s/he's missing a right foot.

On the fourth Thursday, Lara Jane's lack of inspiration is an excuse to sleep in her proper bed. She scratches at flakes of lipstick and asks the gumby, "How do you think I can help you? Because I can't take an axe from your back."

The gumby shrinks against the bed frame. "I don't expect you to help me."

"Because I'm pretty sure I'm supposed to."

A twitch of a smile. "It's just nice to feel safe for a while."

Lara Jane takes a big breath. "Yes, but there must be something else you want. Something I can give you."

Eventually, the gumby admits that s/he would like to feel like someone cares, but that Lara Jane was the only option, and now she doesn't qualify because she just wants her bedtime solitude back.

"But I do care about your future," says Lara Jane. "I care about the future of everyone in my studio. I wouldn't teach children if I didn't care."

Evidently this is not very convincing.

So Thursday nights become a kind of quiet, platonic seduction, with Lara Jane many years out of practice at being actively likable. The two of them play checkers and Monopoly, and during the lulls the gumby juggles with four torn-off fingers. Lara Jane shows off the costume designs for the reverse-Pandora's-box group number she's choreographing. The gumby teaches her yoga. They experiment with dancing, two workable feet between them, because Lara Jane is curious whether some traditionally-solo moves are possible if shared between two.

Approximately half of these work.

One night, they're eating caramel popcorn and watching Project Runway, and the gumby says, "Don't go to sleep. Please. Stay up with me." And Lara Jane considers going into work late tomorrow, even though she's never been late for anything less than stomach surgery.

So she stays up all night: all the way to midday, when the gumby blinks out of existence.

And the next Thursday she's alone.

The third Friday, Lara Jane awkwardly inserts the anti-rape condom in one of the toilet stalls. She knows it's a snap judgment, but surely there's nothing wrong with taking precautions.

She has to face the tentacles sometime.

Lara Jane builds a pillow fort on the gym mats before climbing in, and then peeks over the fluff of the topmost pillow at the strange man beyond. The fort stinks of her signature perfume. He sits halfway across the dance studio, tentacles twitching, peering back at her.

"If they scare you," he says, "I can put them away."

Lara Jane raises an eyebrow. She weighs his offer for a moment, but then says simply, "Tell me."

FUN FACT: *His name – the man attached to the tentacles – was Chiton, back when he was known as the greatest mountain climber in at least sixty acres.*

Every day, at the base of the cliff face, he stretched his two arms and six tentacles into the eight sleeves of the jacket he spent a month sewing. Every day, he scaled the mountain, his ten limbs curling themselves into snowy crevices and propelling him upwards with superhuman grace.

Every day, he plucked the blue flowers from the top of the mountain. And was home again in time for tea.

He was driven out of his first two towns for his tentacles, so he kept them hidden entirely from the third one. The third town, where there was something in the water making the residents critically ill. Where they were too poor to move away. Where the blue flowers were an antidote. Including for him and his new wife, who still didn't know about his tentacles, but whom he loved with all his heart.

And this is where Chiton went, when he wasn't with Lara Jane:

His last day. His backpack open at the bottom of the cliff, and his special jacket with the eight sleeves completely missing. It would take him days to make another, and the blue flowers grew scarce in winter. He had to make the climb.

The regular jacket bunched up mid-torso, above his bare tentacles and bare stomach.

He died quietly of exposure, halfway up the mountain and attached to the cliff-face like a cicada shell.

So Lara Jane sends off the measurements for a similar eight-sleeved jacket to her costume maker, and it arrives in time for the fifth Friday. She's expecting the first time Chiton pulls it on to be the last time she ever sees him. And therefore she miscalculates and omits her usual bedtime pyjama shorts the following week.

Lara Jane thinks she knows what happens next. But maybe leaving the portal open would be less mortifying.

Her elite squad are less proficient in hip-hop than any other style. The few hip-hop numbers they've performed in competition have never placed highly. When Lara Jane announces she's bringing in a special guest to inspire them for an upcoming street dance number, no-one can claim it's unjustified.

Truly, it's more of a street dance/gymnastics number where the girls are soldiers/assassins, but they can already execute a dozen backhand springs with their eyes closed.

Lara Jane sends their mothers out to buy diamante-encrusted leggings and foam daggers. She's sewn Chiton's tentacles into his jacket – extra material forming six inbuilt gloves – so that it can pass as a costume.

When the time comes she feigns a sudden sickness, and all her little dancers are too busy fussing over her to notice a ninth body appear on the dance floor. Chiton slips the jacket on like a second skin. Lara Jane greets him warmly, despite the figurative portal expanding in her gut.

They see him now, all her little dancers. They see the monster in their studio.

From her position half-slumped against the wall, Lara Jane explains that their guest specialises in a new type of circus hip-hop. At least two of her girls have circus posters plastered over their bedroom walls, and juggling batons in their bookcases.

Fourteen pairs of eyes are fixed on Chiton. And then he starts to move.

No human has spun with such 360-degree ease outside of a hamster ball. He spins on his head, hands, tentacles, and legs. He spins like he's a torpedo shot from a cannon. He bounces off the floor like it's spring-loaded.

His lines are sloppy and his technique is mediocre at best, but Lara Jane can't help but smile at his passion and the sheer, strange spectacle of it all.

Just as much as she watches him, she watches her girls. The energy blazing in their wide eyes, coiled muscles and grins threatening to burst from their cheeks. They're clapping and gasping and bouncing on the balls of their feet. Two of them are squeezing each other's hands with joy.

Chiton notices their enthusiasm and his own speed and power doubles, triples. Laura Jane feels the floor vibrate as he lands. She reads the rising bliss in his body and yells, "Enough!" and he slams himself to a stop.

She watches him stand there, panting, and inflating with the girls' frantic applause.

"Girls!" she bellows. "Please thank Chiton and then close your eyes, tight."

"Thank you!" they chorus, and Lara Jane checks in the wall mirrors that their eyes are all shut.

Chiton looks so high that he could drift up to the ceiling. Lara Jane meets his gaze and gives him a smug little wave. He releases a final, satisfied sigh and blinks out of her studio.

"You can open again," says Lara Jane, and clambers to her feet. The girls search around for Chiton, and she says, "How's that for circus magic?" and they're all a mess of questions and hands clasping at her t-shirt and Lara Jane has to laugh with sheer relief.

Thank you thank you thank you is looping in her head, and she's not even sure who she's thanking. Maybe she'll take her elite squad out for ice-cream. "Good girls," she coos and hugs them to her chest. "My good, good girls."

The third Saturday: Lara Jane lies next to a row of prop keys. She's rolled them around in her fingers for hours. They're a lightweight metal: so light that a fist-sized helium balloon could lift them off the ground, but she still suspects they're too heavy.

The starmist spots them immediately and drifts up to just under the ceiling. "Come on; come on down," says Lara Jane, a little more impatiently than she intends. "I thought you wanted to try." So they spend fifteen minutes with the starmist grasping at keys like she's clawing at something under glass, and both of them finish feeling low and impotent.

Lara Jane carries the keys with her over the next week; around her neck in the shower, pinned into her pyjama short pockets at night. She polishes them and watches her reflection in their shine, but by the morning of the fourth Saturday she has to admit to no further ideas whatsoever. Maybe she was completely off-base, buying the keys in the first place.

At least she has this fortnight's state-wide competition to distract herself with.

Thankfully, her girls execute the monster dance flawlessly on stage, and Lara Jane is almost bubbling over with pride. It's one of the best pieces she's ever choreographed. Of course, it places first.

Back in their dressing room, her girls shriek with victory and thrust their trophy and glitter-covered bodies towards her. She'll never get the sparkles out of these clothes.

Their winning dance replays in Lara Jane's mind all evening. And in her cold hotel bed later that night, she tosses a key through the starmist's body like a bullet and barks, "Dance!"

On the evening of the seventh Saturday, Lara Jane takes the starmist into the forest. She's still fuming that her reverse-Pandora's-box number only took second the previous weekend, after which she requested to see the winning team's scoresheet because she was *robbed*, but even so... Everything stinks of eucalyptus. Lara Jane lays out a picnic blanket topped with a yoga mat topped with a sleeping bag, and climbs in up to her waist.

FUN FACT: *The last time Lara Jane went camping, she was twelve and woke up with a mouthful of dirt and a weeping gash on her right calf. As an adult, she had no intention of repeating the experience. She'd booked a cabin three hundred meters away, with all the modern amenities and the plump bed she would have occupied if sleeping were necessary.*

The starmist hovers tentatively on the other side of the fire she's built. Lara Jane polishes off a pair of service-station chicken and mayo sandwiches, trying to give the starmist some time to acclimatise. No words are exchanged. When she's finished, Lara Jane balances one of the keys on her nose, and that actually earns her a small, singular laugh.

Thank goodness for progress.

She's acquired a lot more keys by now – piles of them – and the starmist is familiar with dodging her aim. The keys glint over the fire with each toss. About one in six or seven hit their mark. Lara Jane mentally notes where the keys pass through: the starmist's foot, shoulder, hand...

The starmist darts through the air behind the fire, speedy but not especially agile. A burst of translucent stars before the shadows of the trees.

The starmist's hip. Scalp...

Most of the panic, the fear, has dissipated. Lara Jane can tell by the way she dances.

Lara Jane pitches the last three keys in quick succession, and one of those passes directly through the starmist's heart. No part of her tries to grasp the key, to hold on.

There is a rippling, a flickering, and then there is no-one beyond the fire anymore.

They've positioned Una diagonally across Lara Jane's mattress, and Lara Jane is braiding her hair badly as they talk.

FUN FACT: *Once, when Una was a child, her body was not quite so heavy.*

When her peers grew old enough to stop running regularly for fun, she could almost believe she was like everyone else.

Shamus was in the grade above her, and seventeen with well-kept stubble, and his friends would chant his name when he went to write something on the blackboard, or toss some crumpled paper into a bin. He seemed to notice her suddenly. He brought her a bunch of plucked daffodils and announced she was the most beautiful girl in town.

To the very best of her memory, she'd never exposed her back to anyone except her parents. But she and Shamus had been together for months, and she loved him, and he loved her, and he wanted to see her.

So she let him open the zip, just a couple of centimetres. Of course he was curious. He was gentle, but a few grains of shiny red dust scattered out, anyway.

It landed on some hay and turned it cerulean. It landed on some wood and turned it to steel. It landed on Shamus' fingers and he rose, gradually, three feet in the air.

Una pulled up her zip, tight, and kissed her boyfriend where he hovered.

Over the next few months, Shamus' sister fell terminally ill. In tiny increments, Shamus and Una convinced each other that using the red dust on her on would be the right thing to do. And within twenty-four hours of it touching her skin, his sister had fully recovered.

But such a thing is hard to keep completely secret for long.

They came in droves to Una's door: the curious, the desperate, the greedy. They offered their money and their sob stories and their business deals. Una's parents locked her in her room (from the inside) and locked the front door. She didn't go to school anymore. She barely went anywhere anymore.

Eventually, her visitors stopped offering and simply took what they wanted.

When Una's skin grew slack from lack of dust, the thieves replaced it with sand, with stones, with straw. Miracles became a regular occurrence in town: talking chickens and men with super-strength and quadriplegics who could walk again. Until there was barely any dust left at all.

She was sure she was dying, then. Shrivelling up inside her skin. She had been planning to compose orchestral scores and become a school headmistress and with some luck, the town mayor. She missed her geography lessons and her violin and Shamus' letters, which had stopped arriving a couple of weeks after she could no longer write back. Thus began a very long year of tears and shouting and bedsores, and at the end, her cold body in the sheets which wouldn't wake for anything.

"So what help can you give me?" Una snaps. "Since you can't make me better and you can't give me justice?"

Lara Jane is struck dumb for once, tying off the braid with slightly shaking hands. "I don't know," she says. "I'm sorry."

"I understand all of this far better than you."

"Yes," agrees Lara Jane. "You do." She pauses, biting the edge of her tongue. "But would you like me to try?"

Una stays the longest, out of any of them. After so much of Una's life and death has been decided by others, Lara Jane feels strongly that Una should have the satisfaction of driving any improvements by herself. Lara Jane tries to vary her Sunday night locations in order to facilitate this, but remains otherwise occupied with the rest of her visitors and preparing for rapidly-approaching Nationals.

It's only once Una's the sole remainder that Lara Jane worries they've missed opportunities. What if one of the others knew something relevant, or emitted some kind of helpful substance? Most of the dance season has passed and the two of them haven't made any progress at all.

And Lara Jane really likes Una. Respects her. She's almost come to terms with the concept of Una visiting every Sunday for the rest of her life... At which point, of course, Una offers an exit suggestion.

"What's inside that?" asks Una, eyes fixed on the translucent black balloon in the corner of the bedroom. "Is it some kind of gas?"

The balloon has wilted somewhat since its onstage debut the day before, but is still largely afloat. "Helium?" says Lara Jane. "You don't have helium where you're from?"

"If we had it," snarls Una, "don't you think we would have tried it?"

So Lara Jane gets her wish of helping Una empty the rubble from her zip, and cleaning out the remaining debris with a cloth and a vacuum cleaner. It takes a couple of hours and they bark insults at each other the entire time, but it's mostly affectionate. When they're finished, Lara Jane lodges a wad of tissues under Una's leaking eyes.

They've hired a large helium canister, with a small nozzle attached that slides into the top of Una's zip. Lara Jane releases the gas at just a trickle. She ties a ribbon around Una's waist and the other end to her bedpost. Una begins to levitate above the mattress, gradually inflating into her usual shape, and her tears fall onto the doona.

"If you don't disappear tonight," jokes Lara Jane, "I can make a bed in a limo and fly you out of the skylight."

"No. I don't want to have to relive another moment of my life if I don't have to."

So Lara Jane twists off the helium when Una's all full up, stretching her inflated limbs and rolling in circles and humming in airborne delight. Every so often, Una's body blocks out the ceiling lamp, and her shadow dances wildly around the room.

When there's a natural pause, Lara Jane clasps Una's featherlight hand inside her own heavy one. "You take care," she says.

Una smiles and says, "Cut the ribbon."

So Lara Jane does, with her free arm, and never lets go of Una's hand. But then all the dancing shadows have gone, and there's nothing to hold on to anyway.

Lara Jane finishes the hampers. Even personalises them. She distributes them to her Elite Dance Squad and their mothers in Studio A, at the end of the dance season and getting close to Christmas. Nationals: almost a clean sweep, and Lara Jane can rest easy until the next year, even if she's not entirely sure what she'll do with herself.

She stares at her line of dancers in their Lara Jane Dance Studio crop tops and booty shorts, with their teeth-braces and their knee-braces, and their little-kid manicures and big-kid muscles and giant smiles.

She stares at their mothers, with their questionable fashion choices and their botoxed faces and their painted mouths with giant smiles.

And nothing has really changed between the night a portal to Hell spread inside her costume cupboard and when it later cleared up like an obedient rash, but Lara Jane Hudson finds herself overwhelmed with affection for every single person in the room.

She taps her cane and sees her own grin blossom in the opposing mirror. "Okay, ladies. Shall we begin?"

EASY LIKE ARSENIC

"To the Witch of the North-Northeast," begins the letter. "I can offer you a large sum of money to imprison a girl in your tower – should you have a tower – for as long as it takes for her rescue. She should not be especially easy to rescue, nor terribly difficult. Nor should she be treated especially well, nor terribly harshly. This is for the ultimate good of the kingdom – I do not know whether this means you are more or less likely to accept my offer, but I assure you your fee shall be more than acceptable."

The return address is printed "care of" someone in the palace to the north. Sera re-reads the luxurious parchment in the low light of her kitchen as her water boils.

Of course she has a tower.

When the soldiers arrive, they bear the same circular crest she recognises from the envelope: a regal, violet bird curved unnaturally so that it swallows its own tail. Its beak and talons curve too, like miniature bronze scythes.

Sera ushers in two of the soldiers while the third waits, fidgeting, just outside. With a metallic thump they dump her money in the closet under the stairs, and then follow the steps up to deposit the rustling, weeping girl-sack in the tower room. Before the girl can escape, Sera locks the tower door with a click-snap and ushers the soldiers out with haste.

By the time their uniforms have vanished into the trees, she can hear the girl's panicked cries of "Help! Help!" slicing into the evening air. Sera collects a chunk of bread and a flask of cold tea from the pantry. When she finally sets eyes on her prisoner, the girl is leaning headfirst out the tower window with her toes almost airborne.

Sera sets down the flask with excessive force, and the noise makes the girl right herself.

"What do you want with me?" asks the girl. Two spots of blood dot the waist of her pink nightgown like scarlet buttons.

"Nothing," says Sera. And leaves her alone for the night.

The following morning, Sera returns with another husk of bread and another flask of tea, and the girl flings the tea directly into Sera's face. Sera flinches and ducks her head, struggling to see through the waterfall dripping over her eyelashes. She hurries to block the door with her body, but the girl doesn't move; she simply stares wide-eyed at Sera, waiting for something to happen.

The tea is mildly sticky. Sera blinks it out of her eyes, growls, "Not that kind of witch," and leaves with the rations in hand. The liquid has loosened the glue on her prosthetic nose, and she withdraws into her bedroom to fix it.

At the end of Rinaya's first day travelling, she stumbles across a char-black inn tucked into a forest clearing. Flowering vines weave up through the wood. A handful of customers cluster around freshly-lit candles on the table outside, and their collective eyes follow her through the open door.

She receives a similar welcome inside, complete with multiple snickers and a pattering of outright laughter. Rinaya fights the urge to adjust the too-large breastplate sitting awkwardly around her hips. She supposes she *would* look comical: a little girl who ran off with her father's old armour.

Which is the truth, of course. Except that she's nineteen — and tall for a woman.

She orders a large mug of goat's milk and a bowl of pork, crushed nuts and cooked apples, and trots upstairs to plonk on the last step before the landing. When she pries off her sodden boots, the swamp water squelches underfoot and rushes back between her toes, and half a dozen blisters burn and sting where the shoes have rubbed her raw. Regretfully, she leaves her wet socks around her ankles and curls against the banister with her dinner.

A few people pass in both directions, room keys clinking in their hands. Eventually, two pairs of well-polished boots pause a couple of steps below her. Two soldiers, dressed in the purple and bronze uniforms of her city, offer identical smiles that don't reach their eyes.

They block the entire staircase.

The one with the moustache grunts, "Trying to give us a laugh, girl, or you really fancy yourself a hero?"

Rinaya shrugs, pulling her damp shoes back onto aching feet. "I guess so."

"Because we've got real heroes for that."

"Usually," she says. "But he injured himself, didn't he? That's why you're out here."

The soldiers share a loaded glance. Rinaya struggles to keep her eyes on them while fumbling with her laces.

"Have you saved her yet?" she asks. A secret part of her feels validated that they're out here: Rinaya's journey into the forest had been a gamble – a statistically probable gamble, given that most kidnapped princesses in the tales are taken into the forest – but a gamble nonetheless.

"Only been out a day," says the younger soldier, his hair flopping over his eye. "Let's take you home."

Her blood pummels like a woodpecker in her ears. "No, thank you. I'm probably the city's best able-bodied hero now."

Moustache laughs, a deep belly laugh where his stomach inflates like a fabric balloon. "Never even heard of a girl hero." He grins. "I thought George refused to train apprentices." He's humouring her.

Rinaya shrugs again. "He had a competition when I was twelve. If someone could retrieve the head of a minotaur, break a curse on an innocent, and sing about one of those, he'd train them. But no-one could." All that had achieved was a few dead townsmen.

More importantly, her boots are securely tied to her feet again.

"Enough of this," snaps the younger soldier. He lunges towards Rinaya's arm and she jumps backwards onto the landing. Moustache knocks over the remains of her dinner; crushed nuts go flying through a gap in the banister. She races down the upstairs corridor as fast as her tender muscles will allow.

With no obvious exit, Rinaya ducks into a room with a half-open door and skulks across the floorboards towards the window. She could hide under the single bed, perhaps, or behind the dresser. But the door crashes open too soon.

"Why are you running?" asks the younger soldier. "We just want to take you home."

Rinaya backs up against the windowsill. With every breath, her chest expands against the solidity of the breastplate. She knows they're being truthful: they'll just take her home. The End. She can't understand why that terrifies her.

The evening breeze teases the calico curtains by her sides. She grabs the window frame behind her and launches herself up onto the sill, crouching like an animal.

Moustache reaches instinctively for his sword hilt. "Come on," he says. "No need for anything rash."

He makes a tentative move forward. Her heart in her mouth, Rinaya twists on the sill and leaps from the second-floor window. Her legs swing wildly through the air, and the ground approaches like a blow.

In the hours following the tea incident, Sera feels like her nose is always slightly loose. When she skins a rabbit she nicks her forefinger with a knife, a mistake she hasn't made since childhood, and sucks the blood from her fingertip. In the middle of planting tomato seeds she finds herself kneeling immobile in the dirt, her legs wracked with pins and needles when she shifts. She avoids cooking entirely; it wouldn't do to get the quantities wrong, to start any fires.

Her skin practically *crawls*.

The girl is not a usual job. "Rescue" is not a usual goal. She cannot deal with the girl in the usual manner, by pretending to kill her, or pretending to turn her into one of many winged or furry creatures. There have been other long-term prisoners in the tower, especially when Sera's mother was still alive, but none have ever inspired guilt before.

The summer sun swallows the cottage whole. The girl will have consumed very little liquid in the last twenty-four hours. At the same time, the witch can't return to the tower room yet; can't reward the girl's outrageous behaviour with additional rations.

When Sera tops up her animals' cages, her water jug shakes like the cottage is tearing in two.

Finally, when the sun has set and she can't quench the persistent dryness in her mouth, Sera stalks to her bedroom. She brushes the tangles from her long, ash-black hair, soaks off her nose and scrubs her face. She even applies a slight lip stain. Lastly, she unbuttons her patchwork dress in favour of a brown calico slip.

In the mirror, she sees someone she hasn't laid eyes on since her mother died.

Sera peers through the keyhole at the girl sprawled over the straw mattress, her leaf-matted blonde hair spilling out of a woollen blanket. The lock, the tower door open soundlessly.

The girl is groggy when woken and her bloodshot eyes are slow to focus. She props herself up with effort, and Sera helps her lift the pot of beer, laced with sleeping draught, to her lips. The girl takes incrementally larger sips until Sera tugs it away.

"Don't want to throw it up," Sera whispers, and fishes several gingerbread biscuits from her pocket with deliberate showmanship. The girl's enormous blue eyes travel from the biscuits to Sera and back again, and then she sets to work devouring them.

"Who are you?" the girl asks around bites, and a few crumbs fall from the corner of her lips.

It's a real struggle to form the word. "Sera."

"Are you helping to rescue me?"

"No."

"More drink, please." The girl stretches her arms out, gulps it down. "Do you work for her?"

"I don't." Sera assesses the pale skin, un-calloused hands, expensive nightgown. "Who are you?"

The girl pauses mid-sip and stares, mouth open, her puffy face suggestive of a dead fish. "You don't know who I am?"

Silence.

The girl hisses, "I'm the princess," and attempts to finish her meal as fast as possible.

She does not quite get that far. Before long she slumps back against the wall like a discarded doll, her arms droop, her eyelids fall.

Sera's hands tremble when she lowers the princess's body back into bed. It's been more than five years since she's touched another human being, and the girl's compact shoulders feel unnaturally warm. Still, Sera tucks the blanket around her inch by painstaking inch.

After collecting all evidence of the beer and gingerbread, Sera unlaces her own shoes and collapses barefoot on her kitchen counter, one hand draped over her eyes and one over her heart. Her world spins like a whirlpool in a cauldron, and her own sleep is far off and hard-won.

At midday the witch provides a bland but ample lunch, and at midnight Sera brings a bowl of salted meat and apple juice laced with sleeping draught. The princess wakes easier this time. If she notices Sera has the same faint scarring around her mouth as the witch, she hides it effortlessly.

"I thought you were a dream," says the princess, and shovels the possum meat into her mouth with grubby hands.

"Yes. Almost."

Sera had not intended to return to her this way; it is indulgent, it is wicked in all the wrong ways. But she has been made to remember her loneliness.

When she finishes her meal, the princess runs her finger around the bowl and licks the salt from her fingertips. "What are you, then?"

"A spirit, of sorts," Sera whispers. "I was trapped here years ago, and I sliced my neck open on an icicle growing from the windowsill. So the witch cursed my soul to stay on."

"Sliced... Sliced it open?" She stretches out, inch by quivering inch, towards the hard bone above Sera's breasts. "You feel real."

"Just for a little while, at night."

Her eyes rarely leave Sera after that. This princess is not an especially stupid girl, but she has grown up fed on fairy tales. That is sometimes worse.

"Why were you kidnapped?" Sera asks, but the princess cannot say. Everyone loves her, she says. She's to be crowned queen before the month is out. Her parents are dying, she says; she must return to spend their final weeks by their bedside.

Sera's own private memories flood the tower room. Instead of attempting comfort, she murmurs, "My parents are dead. Probably. My father was a magician, and my mother was a scientist. One day, my father failed to re-appear from his vanishing act. They blamed my mother." She picks at a loose thread on her slip, intoxicated by this small feat of honesty, like unwrapping ribbons from a ring box. "He never came back."

Princess Penelope has taken to performing a series of stretches and vocal exercises after lunch, and to massaging the sluggishness out of her arms and legs. Mid-afternoon seems to be the optimal time; her movements are persistently groggy in the mornings.

No matter how she scrubs and itches, her skin seems permanently caked with dried sweat and filthy tower dust. She wonders what she might do when she starts to bleed, should rescue have failed to arrive by then; she does not suppose she can sit on the chamber pot for four days.

Perhaps Sera can bring her a bath. The woman seems peculiar for a ghost, but then Penelope has never met one in person before, and the tales are surprisingly quiet on the subject of spirits. She wonders if they all smell like this; powdery and sugar-coated, like rose-flavoured Turkish delight. The previous summer, she'd eaten pyramids of the stuff at high tea with her parents and half-brother, Henry, their twenty-four fingers sticky with gelatine and snow-white sugar.

Metal scrapes on stone behind her; Penelope jerks herself out of a stretch. A grappling hook secures itself to the lower lip of the tower window. She rushes over just as the rope attached to the hook pulls taught, and with it the universe seems to right itself.

The colours look brighter, the details are clearer. Penelope feels joyously aware of the stones beneath her feet, the air currents on the back of her legs, the soiled nightgown over her breasts – even the dirt between her toes. She's waited for this her entire life.

The rope disappears into the trees several metres away, and she spies the gratifying flash of silver armour between the undergrowth. She feels too overcome to even smile. And then she is struck in the chest by something small and hard, and stumbles backwards.

A second, thick piece of rope has bounced off her sternum and onto the floor; slightly shorter than her arm and with hand-sized loops tied on either end. She stoops to pick it up, still recovering her breath, and tests the knots for strength. They hold fast.

She'd always imagined her gorgeous knight vaulting through the window, the breeze in his hair and sun glinting off his chainmail, but yes, this will do.

Penelope swings one leg from the tower and then the other. At least three stories up, the fall will surely kill her if she drops.

But that is not how the stories go.

There is an abrupt drop before the rope catches her. The larger rope stretches between the tower and the trees at quite an angle, but the two ropes still snag on each other and her journey down is made in fits and starts. Jagged leaves rush towards her face. With a final jolt and airborne twist, Penelope is caught from behind by her armoured rescuer.

The slam against his breastplate will leave a slight bruise, but the iron feels pleasantly sunlit-warm through her nightgown.

Once Penelope finds her footing, his arms leave her waist to untie the rope, and she scrambles to grab a nearby branch. In her periphery, her rescuer tugs to release the grappling hook, but it seems stuck fast. He abandons it and scrambles down the tree within moments, his arms appearing through the thick leaves to help her to the ground.

Penelope swallows and rests her foot in his hands. Her final descent is quick and awkward, and then she comes face to face with the knight, and thinks her heart must stop.

He stands only slightly taller than she does, with a delicate face, and thin arms, and hips and...

"You're a girl."

The girl nods, grasps Penelope's hand, and pulls her away into the forest.

Then Penelope can't quite get her balance back. The forest floor is littered with sticks, thorns and a variety of debris which jab her bare feet and dig into her soles. She's certain she must be bleeding into the soil, and the girl pulls her along so severely she fears her arm might dislocate.

"Wait!" she cries between breaths. The girl glances behind her, slows, but does not stop.

Penelope repeats herself, louder this time. The girl grinds to an abrupt halt, tugs them both behind a tree trunk, and Penelope almost crashes into her.

"You'll need to keep your voice down," says the girl. "My father was supposed to come for you, but he was injured. We're probably being followed."

And Penelope is dragged through the forest again, feeling the bile rise in her throat and tears prick the corners of her eyes. "You don't understand," she calls as they walk. "You're supposed to be my husband! This was my last chance!"

Not one princess in the storybooks ever married past the age of eighteen.

The girl's jaw drops. She hesitates between the trees, and the two of them gape at each other until Penelope gasps and squeezes the girl's hand between her own.

"Oh, it's fine!" Penelope feels blessedly certain now. "Almost perfect. I mean, you're not a monster or a frog or anything in the books, but..." Her smile could envelop her whole face. "You certainly are my prince. I'll kiss you soundly, and then you'll change into your true form: manly and handsome, like all the enchanted ones. Oh, I know it!"

And Penelope darts forward and kisses her right on the lips.

The girl staggers back. "Are you mad?" Her face is calm, her eyes wild.

Penelope waits, but any bodily changes must be hidden by slightly rusty armour. "I'll have to do it again."

"I'm not..." The girl wipes absently at her lips with her thumb. "I'm not cursed."

"Well, you might not know it! But I know how these things go. No such thing as a lady knight, and whoever rescues the princess just must marry her, and they live happily ever after and have plenty of babies and..."

The girl grabs Penelope gently around the forearms. "You're hysterical. Please, let's get you home. It's not safe."

"Let me try again!"

"Nothing will happen."

"So nothing happens. Let me try."

Penelope places two work-calloused hands onto her own stained hips. She threads her own fingers into the girl's dark hair and along her jaw, just like the hand-drawn pictures in the storybooks.

She kisses her long, and thoroughly, while the taller girl freezes like a startled animal. She kisses her like she's drawing out another being, coaxing up a prince from the girl's throat and out between their lips.

Penelope eventually withdraws, her mouth slightly swollen. "I think that was long enough," she breathes, and watches patiently for a metamorphosis that does not come. "Maybe I have to do it after dark, or at dawn, or maybe I don't love you enough..."

And then she feels an abrupt sting in the left side of her neck, and brings her hand up to feel where a feathered dart has lodged itself in her flesh. She tugs it from her skin and examines it lying dormant in her palm, but she already feels lightheaded. The forest blurs and spins around her. There sounds a distant thunk as her skull hits the earth.

Above her, the girl has drawn her sword, and that is the last thing Penelope sees for some time.

A knock at the door, and the princess is returned in a motionless calico sack. Sera fights the urge to tug it open and press her fingers to the princess's pulse point, to hold them under her nose and check for breath.

Again, the soldiers deposit the sack in the tower room, and Sera spots the small grappling hook lodged firmly in her window ledge. As they descend the stairs, she asks, "Something went awry?"

"Something like that."

"I fulfilled my obligations."

The soldiers' jaws and shoulders visibly tense. "Nothing you did wrong..." They struggle for an appropriate honorific for her, and then abort this anxiously when none presents itself. "Just circumstances. Continue as normal."

After concluding the princess's health satisfactory, Sera throws herself into her work. In addition to the regular running of the cottage, there have been broader tasks she has neglected lately: trapdoor hinges to oil, pulleys to test; vast vats of liquids to concoct; crimson apples to paint with a sticky, concentrated dose of sleeping draught; "enchanted" trinkets to prepare for distribution or display.

If she can only be a shadow of Sera – the girl who whispers to the princess every night, muffling their laughter so as not to wake the crone downstairs – then she will be a truly exceptional witch.

#

Rinaya wakes to the soft scraping of her father's quill. He hunches near the end of her bed, bathed in sun from the window. Her head feels thick and cottony, her tongue like a dry, foreign body in her mouth. Her eyes drift around the loft – to the folded-paper horse dangling above her pillow, the faded maps tacked to the walls, the violet snapdragons creeping through a crack in the wood – before interrupting him.

"Papa?"

George's crumpled face relaxes instantly. He sets his parchment aside and drags his chair forward, steepling his fingers by his chin. "You worried me, silly thing. You've been asleep nearly a day."

Rinaya gapes at him. "A day?" She attempts to lift herself from the pillows, but her elbows, upper back and abdomen all burn with old bruises, and she sinks back into the sheets, panting. "How am I home? I was a week's walk away."

"Some soldiers found you at a nearby inn, brought you back. You'd fallen out a window there. You don't remember?"

Rinaya winces at the thought. Her memories come in still pictures and snatches; the inn, soldiers, fall, pain. "I think so," she says, though so much time seems unaccounted for.

Her father scratches at greying stubble. "You'll take time to heal. And you'll promise not to leave the city again."

She scowls at him instinctively.

George scowls back. "Don't look at me like that. I know you thought it was unfair, always staying home while I left for my work... But you go and leave anyway, and you end up half dead. The forest is a dangerous place for anyone, *especially* young girls." He pinches the bridge of his nose, violently, as if to ward off a headache. "Thank goodness you didn't lose a limb in a bear trap, get skewered by a troll or cooked by a witch. I couldn't save you, do you understand? I still have to hop up the stairs like a bloody invalid."

He looks her right in the eyes, and she says, "I'm sorry," because she is – that he's injured, at least. "Did you find out what happened to your ankle?"

"What, that I snapped a tendon? They don't think it's broken, at least. I'm more concerned with the ditch that caused it, that appeared magically hours before I went to leave that night."

Rinaya suspects his eyesight is just fading.

Her fingers close gingerly around the glass ring between her breasts, still strung around her neck on a leather cord. She'd dug it out of the leaf litter on her first day travelling, and now it warms slightly in her palm. "I'm so confused, Papa... I thought I was doing well."

"No." He pulls his chair even closer and leans over her, gripping her shoulders. "You're not safe outside, my darling." His wrinkles crease deeper than she remembers, and an ink stain streaks over his right cheek. "You break your father's heart, play-acting at something that isn't your role. I need you to promise me."

Rinaya struggles to force air into her lungs. The terror, the claustrophobia has returned, of having only two choices in life: as a wife or as a servant, and she cannot even see much difference between the two. She has attempted a third choice and found herself incapacitated.

George squeezes her aching shoulders. "Promise me," he commands, and she feels something inside of her break.

She closes her eyes. "I promise, Papa." And clutches for sleep.

In the early hours of the morning, while the princess lies under the spell of her daily drugged sleep, Sera empties Penelope's chamber pot onto the lemon trees and wipes it clean with a rag. And on this particular morning, while she climbs the stairs to return it to the tower room, she hears a thump.

She hurries up the last few stairs and presses a wide brown eye against the keyhole. The cool metal digs into her forehead and cheek, and what she spies inside the tower makes her breath catch.

A man, a young man, in the most expensive clothes she's ever seen. He saunters over to where Penelope sprawls on the dirty mattress, his ultra-white shirt shining lavishly in the moonlight. He crouches before the princess and brushes the golden locks from her face. He dips his head, his hair the colour of fox pelt, and he kisses her.

Sera's free hand settles against her heart.

The man smiles and draws himself up on one knee. He waits for the princess to wake from her enchanted slumber. He shakes her gently, then harder. He draws her eyelids open with his finger, closes them. Checks for signs of life. He kisses her again and again.

Sera stands frozen behind the door. She has no plans for this. If she was still dressed as the witch she could burst in there with some tripe about sleeping spells. As the girl in the plain brown slip, she holds no cards at all.

And then he takes the bottom of the princess's nightgown, and he draws it upwards.

Sera sweeps into the room like a fiend, crosses the floor and swings the chamber pot. It connects with the man's head with a crack, and he drops like a sack of flour. It happens in a heartbeat.

She watches his eyes, his fingers: neither twitches. Blood pools on the floor beneath his skull, mingling its deep purple-red with the orange of his hair. Sera fumbles for his pulse, knees weak as putty, but she already knows he's dead.

They think she has killed dozens; truly this is her first. She can't shift her eyes from his clean-shaven face, the blood soaking through his shirt, the way his arm twists beneath him at an unnatural angle.

There must be a way to fix this. There is a way to fix everything.

Sera focuses on settling her breathing and her traitorous, riotous thoughts. He cannot be here when the princess wakes, that is a certainty, so she grips him by his calves and drags him across the tiny room. A big man, but not so big that she cannot move him with all her panic and horror in the world.

He leaves a smear of blood on the floor in their wake. Her knuckles flare white around the fabric of his pants. Her arms blaze, and with every step she pushes her boots against the stones as if dragging a body from a well.

It gets easier on the stairs. She has the advantage of gravity there, plus the musical accompaniment of his head thumping with every step. She pauses at the window halfway down: two more men outside, observing from the tree line. Soldiers again – bronze and purple uniforms. She swears internally with every curse word she knows.

The soldiers will be waiting for him. Little time, and so much more to explain. No time for guilt. Save herself. Save the princess.

She keeps dragging the body. Pull, thud, step. Pull, thud, step. By the time she reaches the bottom of the stairs, she has the essence of a plan, and Sera can feel the stars aligning above her once again.

In the candlelight on her kitchen floor, Sera plunges a knife deep into the man's motionless chest. And she cuts out his heart.

The heart is wrapped in a towel in the wicker basket on the bench. The rest of the body smoulders in the oven. The kitchen walls flicker like the inside of a lantern, like a phoenix reflected on dark water. Smoke will be billowing out of her chimney in bulging streams, and Sera wishes fervently that the night is too thick, or the soldiers too dim to notice.

It was fiddly cramming the man's body through the oven door; a heavy puzzle of flesh and bone. More difficult than fitting her mother inside. She does not have the luxury of watching the flames lick him into oblivion; she rushes from room to room as fast as her boots can carry her.

From her bedroom she collects her mother's witch's hat, which she has worn most middays when visiting the princess. Oh, she is glad of that now.

From the living room she collects the pottery jars above the window, two of the few relics she's inherited from her grandmother. They are identically sized, but one weighs much more than the other.

Finally, from the cupboard under the steps she collects a pile of fresh rags and a small tub of river water. She tucks each item into the basket next to the cooling heart, and she rushes upstairs.

The tower room looks just as she left it, with the princess dishevelled on the bed and the trail of blood smeared out to the landing. The initial blood pool in the middle of the room is essential, but she spends several precious seconds debating whether the trail needs cleaning immediately.

No, she decides. Screw it.

She empties the two jars of ashes in a miniature, cindery mountain near the blood pool, waving the dust from her face to prevent her breathing in dead relatives. She gives quick, silent thanks to her mother and infant sister for their assistance. She drops the witch's hat on top, where it makes a small indentation in the ash.

Sera crouches next to the princess, tugs the nightgown back into place and shakes her more harshly than intended.

It's several hours since midnight: the princess does wake this time. Her bloodshot eyes take several seconds to focus. "Sera?" she murmurs. "But it's daylight."

Sera hadn't even noticed. She curses internally, viciously. The window suggests early dawn.

Sera says, "Yes, the spell is broken. Witch is dead. A prince came in the night and killed the witch with a potion, but he slipped on the potion and cracked his head open." She moves a little to the side, revealing the pile of ash, the pointed hat and the blood congealing between the stones. Then she leans forward until her face dominates Penelope's view.

"Listen to me very carefully. Before the prince died, he told me that someone from your palace ordered you to be locked up here. You can't go home. If you leave, you'll only be locked up elsewhere." Her voice comes low, intense and breathy. Sera pauses to let that sink in. "The only way you'll be free is if we fake your death. So we're going to use the prince's heart and say it's yours. That you're dead. Understand?"

The princess's eyes shine wide and liquid, like sapphires beneath the surface of a lake. "I... Not fully," Penelope says.

"Okay, I need you to give me your nightgown."

The princess just sits there.

Sera feels her tension headache tighten. "Please!" she hisses. "Give me your nightgown or you might die!"

Between the two of them, they peel the soiled nightgown from the princess's body and leave her shivering in her underwear. Sera unwraps the heart from the towel and re-wraps it in the nightgown. The princess just gawks at her. Sera unloads the rags and water tub and directs Penelope to clean up the blood.

Then Sera takes the heart and basket downstairs.

She really does feel like a storybook witch now, floating down into her cottage with the embers of a body in her oven. She must look quite a sight.

As she opens the cottage door she allows the trauma of the night to sink into her bones, and the release is like opening a dam. She feels her face contort with tears, feels her entire body weak and trembling. And so when she stumbles to the soldiers, bloodstained and weeping, she looks much younger than her twenty-four years. She looks like a mess. She looks like a victim.

"They're all dead," she cries, and lets a corner of the nightgown fall away to expose the heart. "All of them. The nice man, the witch, the princess." She struggles to keep eye contact with the soldiers through her tears. "The witch took Penelope's heart before she died. You want it, don't you?" She thrusts it at them.

They grasp the nightgown parcel with horrified faces.

"Go," she mutters. "Tell them. They need to know."

The soldiers hold the parcel at arm's length, gaping at the blood which seeps out onto their gloves in drips and rivulets.

"Go!" she sobs. And to her immense and incalculable relief, they do.

Henry has tried many ways to bring his half-sister back to life. All the usual remedies, then the more unusual ones: his tears, direct from his eyes or bottled over several days and administered over the heart; his blood, cut from his palm. He has submerged the heart in holy water, and placed it in various locations around her bedroom: pillow, window, piano. He has even kissed the heart once or twice. But eventually he exhausts all possible avenues, and must accept that Penelope is gone.

He has the heart locked in a glass jewellery case under his bed. He has the nightgown cleaned, but the bloodstains never come out.

He will be a remarkable king. He will give his citizens something to smile about.

Over the span of two and a half weeks, Rinaya's bruises have faded from a sickly violet to a more sedate mottling of blue and yellow. She has rarely left her bed, let alone the house, and its permanent stench of wood-smoke and horses has been making her dizzy.

Tonight, the only sounds in the loft are the faint gasps and crackles of the dying fire. She has the distinct sensation of being a live cricket pinned to a board, and her father has fallen asleep in front of the embers, so there is no-one to bar her way.

Rinaya finishes lacing her boots and tiptoes downstairs. Her muscles have atrophied considerably since her travels, and her movements are stiff and clumsy; she feels like a marionette being pulled by a drunk. As is customary, various offerings have been left for her father on the bottom steps; three jars of plum jam, a freshly-knitted woollen jumper, a couple of quills, some kindling tied with an orange ribbon. Fewer offerings than usual. George's fortnightly palace stipends have shrunk since he hurt his ankle, too.

The scholars have been visiting more frequently, recording his knowledge in books like *Techniques for Slaying Gorgons* and *Common Curses and the Kisses Which Break Them*. He used to be more stingy with his trade secrets. His injury has been healing painfully slowly, and Rinaya can't remember the last time he fell asleep so soon after sunset.

The open air renders her mind blissfully quiet. She shuts her eyes to the summer wind, the gentle shuffle of the horses and the laughter echoing through the city streets. And then there is a soft hand sliding into hers.

Rinaya blinks. "Fern!"

Her godmother smiles affectionately and squeezes her fingers. "I was just on my way to see you when you stepped out. I hope you don't mind I haven't visited much; I wanted to give you plenty of recovery time before I imposed."

Rinaya shakes her head as much as her stiff neck will permit. "No, of course. Whenever you like. And thank you for the paper horse."

"I have another surprise for you." Fern's curls are secured with an elaborate series of tiny metal chains and jewelled pins. She winks and tugs on Rinaya's fingers. "Come on."

The walk to Fern's door takes mere minutes, but Rinaya still finds herself winded and sweating. She tries to concentrate instead on Fern's bright, melodic voice, the burble of the owls, the scrambling of the possums. On arrival, Fern sits her down and pulls a sky-blue dress from the back of a chair.

"You're wearing this tonight," her godmother declares.

"To what? The Ball of the Bruised and Beaten?"

"Oh, it's not that bad."

Rinaya wipes her sweaty palms on her cotton tunic. "Really, I have a welt the size of my fist over my cheekbone. We do own mirrors."

Fern beckons her to her feet once again, and before Rinaya can protest her tunic has been lifted over her head and discarded onto the table. It sprawls there amongst piles of fabric, half a dozen sewing needles and several folded paper animals. "So," says Fern, "you are aware of the ball, then?"

"I'm aware that it's happening," Rinaya mutters, vaguely uncomfortable with Fern's deft fingers making short work of her shirt buttons. Her godmother had attempted to teach her dressmaking once, but Rinaya had neither the talent nor the patience for it. "I didn't know it was tonight. I don't think I'll be going."

With a couple of swift jerks the shirt is on the table, and Fern is lifting up her arms to pull the dress over her head.

"You will," says Fern. She adjusts the dress around Rinaya's shoulders and hips before moving behind her to the laces. "He's expecting you."

"You're having me on."

"He likes his women in blue."

Fern cinches in the waist and Rinaya groans, doubling over. The soft silk pulls like rope burn against her bruises. Rinaya rests her palm against the table for support, and Fern releases the laces.

"I'm sorry," her godmother murmurs. "I'll do it loosely."

Fern laces the dress with Rinaya still bent over the table. She brushes Rinaya's hair, braids it and secures it to the crown of her head in a bun. She drags long white gloves up Rinaya's arms to conceal marks. She powders Rinaya's cheeks, though it does little to hide the flowering wound there. This all happens in silence.

The one thing Fern does comment on is Rinaya's ring, glowing faintly on its string at the top of her cleavage. "This is nice," she says, slipping a finger into the glass hole. "I'm glad you're wearing it."

Then Fern buttons up her own ball-gown, takes Rinaya's gloved hand in her own, and escorts her through the streets – through the clouds of flitting chocolate moths and sidestepping mounds of horse manure – towards the palace.

#

The honeyed ballroom light shines like hot candle wax. Fern has insisted Rinaya walk in alone, and Rinaya finds herself wavering at the top of the staircase, absorbing the swish of gowns and the sparkle of chandeliers as if assessing a combat arena. The dancers' eyes seem oddly drawn to her awkwardness. She feels the colour rising in her cheeks, hikes her skirt and escapes down into the glittering crowd.

Rinaya pounces on a chair at the edge of the ballroom, considering unpinning her hair so she can hide behind it. She spends several minutes studying the marble floor before a perfectly-shined black shoe falls into her vision.

King Henry kneels before her on the white tiles. She glances around for who he's really propositioning, but he reaches for her hand with a welcoming grin. "May I have this dance?"

She can't seem to summon an appropriate reply, but he pulls her onto the dance floor regardless. She wills her exhausted body to behave; for her feet not to trip, for her back to stay straight, for her arms not to flail and make a greater fool of herself. Henry places her left hand onto his shoulders and laces his fingers with her right one. They feel toasty through her gloves, and he smells of cinnamon, cracked chestnuts and chilli powder.

He leads her in a simple but enthusiastic waltz, and Rinaya can't meet his eyes for the first minute or so. The hand on her waist sometimes presses too hard on her bruises, and the act of dancing at all feels like sunburn blistering across her body. When she glances up he's still grinning like she's the only thing that matters. She almost feels embarrassed for him.

"I noticed you as soon as you walked in," he says as they change direction. "You're the most beautiful woman in the room."

Rinaya opens her mouth to disagree, and then decides it would be rude to correct the king so publicly. She curls her lips into a polite smile instead. She wonders whether he likes his women beaten.

He is a very good-looking man, as far as she can tell. She finds no fault with any of his features, excluding the arrogance of his smile. He dances proficiently – much better than she does, especially through the pain. He chuckles kindly at her like the kings in the storybooks.

"Witch stole your voice?" he asks.

"I'm just surprised," she says. "And I'm sorry about the princess."

His face darkens and then bounces back into its original smile. "Thank you. I threw this ball to find a queen, did you know that?"

Rinaya blushes despite herself. "Not entirely," she says.

Henry twirls her, and the aches across her body intensify. She knows she can't keep this up much longer; she will throw up on his shoes, collapse on the tiles, or both. In one of her father's tales, the princess can't even sleep on twelve mattresses... Before she can rethink it, she extracts herself from Henry's arms.

"I'm sorry," she says. "It must be getting close to midnight, and my father will wonder where I am."

"I hardly think it's that late."

"Regardless. I'm sorry, I haven't been well; I don't want to embarrass you at your own party."

He sighs and brushes a strand of hair behind her ear. "Very well. I'll take something to remember you by." His grin is back in full force, and his fingers close around the ring between her breasts. With a sharp tug he breaks the string at the back of her neck. She almost gasps with the pain.

Henry lifts the glass ring towards the chandeliers and beams at the rainbows. "If we're meant to be together, I'll find you again. The girl with the finger it fits."

Rinaya blinks at him. "I'm sure it fits plenty of fingers."

He slides his thumb along her jawbone. "I also know your face." She sees he's trying not to laugh.

He scoops her into a kiss before she can retreat upstairs. He is a good kisser, at least compared to the few ruffled boys she's kissed over the years. She expects an insistent tongue to invade her mouth but it never does.

Still, she has never quite understood the appeal of kissing. It's supposed to be magical, isn't it? When Henry pulls back he looks appropriately enchanted. She must be defective somehow.

She abandons him with minimal ceremony. He pockets the ring and waves her goodnight, rooted to the dance-floor amongst a swirl of tuxedo tails and peacock feathers.

In the weeks following the witch's death, Sera feels adrift in her new, mundane role. The spirit version of herself from the tower room has minimal context downstairs. All of the witch's knowledge – the locations of objects, awkward tower lock, the proper care of the cottage's flora and fauna – must be stumbled upon. The gold under the stairs will eventually run dry.

The princess seems washed out, on edge, like the very act of waiting in the tower was putting blood in her cheeks. She flits about the cottage and can be of occasional use, if given the right task and appropriate direction. Sera can pass her a knife and carrot to peel, or a sewing needle and possum skins to merge into blankets.

If left unattended, the princess tends to drift back to the tower room, though Sera has cautioned her against being seen in the window. Regardless, she never leaves Sera's mind for more than a moment; everything smells like her, like apples dipped in caramel and salt. They share the same clothes, they share her mother's old double bed. It is a warped wish, having the princess living with her like this, but it has been granted nonetheless.

"Sera," says the princess one autumn evening. She has fastened her hair with a couple of forks and looks somewhat ridiculous. "Can you turn my hair golden? Like they do at the palace?"

"But it's golden already," Sera says gently. Her fingers tighten around her mug of tea. That was unnecessarily cruel.

The princess crumples her sweaty fists into her dress. "Not all of it," she whispers. "The new bits aren't yet."

So Sera nods and checks the cupboards. Maybe this will be the thing to turn Penelope's skittish, fleeting smiles into something solid.

Roses haven't worked.

Desserts haven't worked.

It takes her almost a day to walk to the nearest road, flag down the appropriate merchant, return and prepare the necessary components. The last step is to mix the powder into a paste, which must be applied soon after. She goes to check on the princess in the next room. "Are you almost ready? I don't want to make this up again."

Sera stiffens in the doorway. She knows the princess has been boiling water. She expected a small bucket to rinse the chemicals off when they were finished. But there, in her entryway, sits a steaming wooden bath.

Penelope twists around in the water, completely naked and doe-eyed and says, "I'm ready."

Sera's brain threatens to shut down. She swallows quickly and makes a show of turning away. "You went to the river," she says. "I told you not to go outside. It's not safe. You'll be captured again, locked up somewhere else. Last time you were taken before the sun even moved across the sky."

A loud swish of bathwater. She must not have been as convincing as usual, as the princess asks, "Are you unwell?"

The urge to laugh is overwhelming. Sera brings a hand to her throat and says, "I'm fine. Just get under the water and drape your hair over the edge." She stumbles to the kitchen to finish the paste, the image of the princess's dripping body flaring before her eyes.

When it's ready, Sera kneels beside the bath with the mixture and a paintbrush. The tip of Penelope's hair dribbles water onto Sera's knees and dampens her slip. Her mind swims with the princess's curves, all too visible under the bath's surface, but her application is still expert, efficient. Sera bites her own lip so hard she's afraid she'll break the skin.

"You should wait a while," says Sera, and it comes out hoarse. "At least until the water's cooler. Before you wash it out."

The princess twists in the bath and a handful of water sloshes over the side. She folds her arms over the rim and stares at Sera, and the hunger must be all over Sera's face, because Penelope's cherry-red mouth falls open and nothing comes out.

Sera scoots back across the floor. Though she has no more breath, she says, "It's just that I've been alone a long time, and you're so perfect, and I know it's a big mess for you, being here, but for me it's a gift and..." She climbs to her feet, wiping off the bathwater which hasn't yet soaked into her dress. She glances at the princess, whose face has morphed into an expression of pity – pity! "I'll leave you alone."

Sera catalogues the ways throughout the cottage that she might kill herself.

The princess does not sleep in the bed with her that night.

The odour of fresh baking penetrates all the way up into the tower, and Penelope stirs on her lumpy mattress. She's been counting down the days against scratches on the wall, but she doesn't bother to mark off this last one; she knows very well what day it is.

Downstairs, Sera licks a smear of pink icing from her thumb. Eight flawless cupcakes sit steaming on the counter. "Happy birthday," mutters Sera, and her tone is significantly frostier.

"Oh." Penelope wishes her dress had pockets to bury hands in. "Thank you."

"You thought I'd forget?"

"No," Penelope blurts. "I just... Don't really feel like celebrating."

Sera barely looks at her; just throws the doughy utensils into the sink and returns the remaining ingredients to the pantry. Ever since the bleaching, Penelope has been – avoiding isn't quite the right word, more like failing to actively seek out – the older woman, and she suspects Sera of the same. Penelope worries the cotton dress between her fingers; she should stay, try and re-establish where they stand with one another.

"I'll sit with you a bit," Penelope offers. "Have an apple instead." She reaches towards the bowl of crimson fruit on a nearby shelf, but Sera swats her hand away.

"Honestly! You don't each a witch's apples. They're poisoned. Everyone knows that."

"Poisoned?"

Sera catches her eye. "Sleeping spells," she says definitively. "You never wake up."

"And everyone knows that?" Penelope traces some hearts in a patch of spilled flour. "So really, I could go outside and pretend to have bitten one, and fallen asleep..." Her voice rises in anticipation. "And I wouldn't be dead, just sleeping... And a prince could come along and kiss me, and then I'd be alive again!"

But her excitement feels so forced this morning, so habitual. She wonders if Sera can recognize the difference. It seems not, as Sera's expression suggests an animal just peed on her carpet.

"But your heart is missing," Sera says.

"That could be part of the sleeping curse." They're a knee-jerk reaction, these words; like she's following a script.

Sera snatches up a damp towel and wipes the flour from Penelope's hands. "You really want to get locked in some other tower," she says, and Penelope can hear the hurt in her voice now, "then be my guest."

Penelope doesn't know what to say to that. There's a part of her that wants to embrace this strange, prickly woman, but she doesn't dare. She stares at the glossy apples instead, and glimpses something gold peeking out from underneath the bowl.

When Penelope grasps the golden book, the real life she's supposed to have rushes back like a vision: regal-sweet and true-love and happily-ever-after. She feels faint, like her arms are too weak to even hold the book. And when she peers up again, the dusty cottage – with its cupboards too warped to close properly, the bloodstained living room floor, the rows of coloured poisons and herbs and animal teeth – looks like living in a nightmare.

"God," she breathes. "Sera. It's the third copy of the book. I have to go home. Just to look. Just to set eyes on my parents before they die. To check on my brother. Please." Penelope reaches for Sera's shoulder, and Sera flinches but doesn't move away.

"You know I can't allow that."

"Please. I'll go in disguise!"

"Absolutely not."

"Do you not understand that I'm eighteen now?"

"That doesn't make the slightest bit of difference!"

Penelope bursts with manic laughter. She cradles the golden book to her chest and strolls away, calling, "Oh, it makes all the difference."

She perches before the piano in the entryway, setting the book open on the stand like she used to at the palace. She'd wiped off the piano with a damp cloth a week earlier; clearly Sera never played, given the layer of grime and how out of tune it was.

The melody comes easily. From the residue of her departed dreams: her husband who never arrived, like he was delayed at the tailor's and faltered there forever; the children who blinked out of possibility before they sparked in her womb. The roar of the crowd as she is crowned queen; their smiles as she rules with wisdom and benevolence. The epic romance of orange-juiced mornings and gradual, daily discoveries with a lover – what his stubble feels like against her palm at six o'clock, what it feels like at nine. The slipping of booties onto tiny feet, which will have that distinctive baby-smell but also something only hers, only theirs. The ring on her finger as it swells fat with age and happiness, until she dies an elderly woman surrounded by a vast family who might cry enough tears to revive her again.

It is made from her existence here: the isolation, like a figure in a distorted dollhouse, like a butterfly in a glass vial with the oxygen running out. The circle of strangling trees, ensuring she can't even see the sky while keeping a safe distance from the windows. The deadly apples, the mysterious lever, the spiders crafting their own stringy palace in the witch's menagerie. It has stripped her of everything, this place: now she's supposed to be dead at eighteen.

There are great wet patches on the front of her dress. Her cheeks drip, her fingers throb, her face twists in unearthly sobs. And Sera stands beside her, crying too, and holding out the witch's hat.

Penelope reaches for it like the condemned reach for a last meal.

Sera says, "My dear, my dear," and "we leave next week."

King Henry knocks on Rinaya's door, a gilded carriage stationary behind him and the glass ring dangling from his fist. He beams at her and slips it onto her finger, a moment she will later recall as *when I got engaged without realising it.*

The offerings immediately multiply upon her staircase. Everyone she passes wants to know the tiny details of their courtship: *Wearing? Kisses? Dancing? Are you constantly swooning? I would be constantly swooning.*

They go on three dates; the customary number. He brings her three dozen bouquets, and despite her cinder-covered clothes he is generous with compliments, childhood stories and the mechanics of his kingdom. They ride horses through the sprawling palace gardens; Henry proficient, Rinaya capable but unpractised. They explore the palace underbelly in fits and starts. They feast on an elaborate picnic by a lake in the city outskirts, where he keeps filling her glass and she becomes quite drunk.

On the carriage ride back home, Henry says, "You know our wedding's in a week and a half?"

He says it as a fact, as he brushes some clinging grass seeds from his tailored pants.

In the couple of seconds that follow Rinaya might have objected, but she says nothing and he starts describing the venue, the entertainment, the guest list. It's all very fairy tale and proper. Her head still feels fuzzy from the wine, and though she does not love Henry she can think of no better alternative to marrying him. He kisses her soundly and cups her breast over the silk dress he's given her.

"Very good," he says, and his grin echoes all the princes in the storybooks.

From the edge of the forest, the princess sneaks them into the palace gardens with nothing more than a boot knife. She knows exactly which wall stones can be manipulated. The first stone was naturally loose, she explains, and then she spent many childhood days chipping around the other two.

When questioned, Penelope says, "Bad things happen to princesses. I might need a secret exit, or my daughter might."

"I thought your knights would always save you."

Penelope hesitates, but keeps burrowing her knife between the bluestones, chipping away at the silt and flowering mosses. "They usually do. But only from things you can't save yourself from. You save yourself first, if you can."

And the princess slams the last stone through and slithers through the hole like a black and gold snake. Sera, taller and bustier, has to squeeze through on her back.

With newfound respect, Sera helps the princess wipe away the worst of the dirt, pulls the brim of the witch's hat over Penelope's face, and declares, "No more than half an hour. Then home."

Sera waits amongst the undergrowth, secreted under her patchwork crimson cloak. She'd worn a fraction of it as a small child, and her mother had sewn on additional pieces as she'd grown. The gardens seem strangely deserted. Nevertheless, she expects guards to apprehend them at any moment.

Penelope returns at a sprint, the witch's dress tied in a knot at her thighs.

"I didn't see my family," the princess pants, "but everyone's preparing for something. You can hear crowds outside the gates."

Sera hasn't heard anything. "We can't wait," she says. "I'm sorry. We won't be this lucky for long."

"I was snatched from my bed." Penelope's eyes are slitted, her tone the least polite Sera's heard. "You were expecting impressive security?"

Before Sera can properly process this, the princess darts away into the trees. In the opposite direction to where they entered from. Sera grimaces, adjusts her cloak and follows the smear of black through the leaves.

After a minute, the princess lets herself through a small cast iron gate in the bluestone wall. The crowd is clearly audible now. Sera glances through the iron bars and sees the edge of the assembly – so many bodies, so many buildings – and experiences a feeling not unlike vertigo. She clutches the gate for support.

The princess looks truly diminutive compared to most of these people. Penelope backs further and further away from the edge of the crowd, seeking an uninterrupted view from higher ground. The anxiety Sera felt watching her sneak around the palace windows is swiftly replaced with a wordless, dull panic.

For now, everyone's attention is focused away from them. The gates open with a simple tug – blissfully silent – and Sera steps into the city square. She hears a click as it shuts behind her. She pulls the gate again, and pushes it, but it's shut fast. There are not enough swears in the world.

And then Penelope reaches a high enough point on the hill, and lets out a scream.

Sera rushes across the square while the citizens are still busy twisting their necks. She tugs the princess into stirring. "Run!"

Several people have already broken away from the group and are struggling towards them, hurdling potted hedges and slipping over scattered paper hearts. Footfalls slap like heavy rain. The wind knocks free the witch's hat, and the two women sprint into the catacomb of city streets.

Neither of them are runners. Sera has secured a vial of acid around Penelope's neck and her own pockets are lined with fire paper, but these precautions seem useless now. They must find a place to hide immediately, or soon hands will clasp around their dresses, cloak, hair. But this city is alien to Sera, and no hiding place presents itself.

Over the sounds of her own blood and burning breath, she hears, "Take my hand," and follows the sound into an open stable. From a hole in the ceiling drops a retractable staircase, and an arm and the top of a man's head strain towards them. She makes a snap decision and pulls Penelope inside.

Between Sera and the stranger, they hoist the princess through the hole in the ceiling in an almost-continuous thrust, and then Sera clambers up behind her. The retractable staircase follows, allowing less and less natural light inside until it snaps closed, and the tiny room plunges into darkness.

Penelope fumbles blindly for Sera's hand.

They hear a match being struck, and then a flame hisses into life. The man lights two sconces on opposite walls and sinks onto a crate. Sera spots a cane beside the door.

He follows her gaze. "Locked it from the inside," he says, "and I can padlock the trapdoor, too, if you'd like. But they won't look here." When she looks no less concerned, his lips twitch upwards: "I'm the hero."

"*That* kind of hero?" Sera asks, though the room itself answers. Stacks of containers line every inch of wall except the door, and atop them pile bottles, trinkets, fabrics and weaponry, in various states of disrepair. More are nailed into the walls, plus several lifeless, fleshy things which resemble monstrous body parts – a stinging emerald tail; the head of a mythical beast; a claw halfway between man and wolf. Many, many items Sera recognises from her own cottage.

"That kind of hero," the man confirms. Like their kind of witch.

Sera examines him properly; dark skin, dark eyes, greying stubble. She's seen so few human beings in her life. This one, she thinks she remembers sitting at the kitchen table with her mother, or being brought upstairs to the tower room. Her mother had never indicated that he knew more than any other client. Sera had understood, theoretically, that there were others in on the deception, but she'd never knowingly communicated with any of them.

The man shakes off his own thoughts and stands with the assistance of his cane. "I promised my daughter I'd watch her wedding from the window. You'd best leave when it's safe."

Sera nods, and he closes the door behind him.

She realises the princess has been immobile for the last minute. She lifts Penelope's chin with her free hand, and waits until blue eyes settle on her own.

"Why did you scream?" Sera keeps her voice gentle.

The princess laughs, sounding quite unhinged. "It's all wrong," she says. "My half-brother can't marry him. He certainly can't marry my half-brother. And did you see the crowns they were getting?" Penelope hyperventilates, and Sera feels the quick breaths blow over her palm. "They were my parents'. My parents are dead."

When the princess cries she does so soundlessly, and the tears pool gradually in Sera's cupped hand. Sera saw little more of the wedding than a streak of white gown, but can infer which "him" the princess means: the "enchanted" prince she has heard far too much of.

They stay curled in the loft until Penelope's tears dry up, until Sera's legs are numb and night is falling. Then Sera switches their clothing, draws the crimson hood over the princess's skull, and leads them back – the long way – to their restless horse.

George watches the end of the wedding: the exchange of rings, the kiss. Their daughter will be safe now, despite his ailing body.

And in the next, windowless room: the young woman who so resembles his beloved Kathryn. He could ask her, finally, whether her mother has died or simply refuses to see him, but the difference seems immaterial. And after so many years of keeping secrets, the words have turned to ash on his tongue.

George meets her soon after turning thirty. He's living in a town south of the city, in a shack he built with his own chopped wood. She careens down the road half-carrying, half-dragging her small daughter, and she's dipped in blood like a candle in wax. Underneath the blood, parts of her dress still sparkle and jingle. She's the most incredible thing he's seen in his life.

Three silver wolves hurtle towards her, kicking clouds of dirt from their paws like ocean spray. Wolves so rarely hunt humans; they must have been deliberately starved. He ushers Kathryn and her daughter into the shack as if diverting a stream, and then throws a sizable chunk of salted meat to the wolves, who fall on it like a life buoy.

Kathryn wipes the blood from her face with a wet rag, the girl blows her four-year-old nose into her red cloak, and George stands watch with his axe. Kathryn says they can't linger here; the townspeople have declared her a witch, and the mere act of escape has condemned her. She plans to seek refuge in her mother's house, in the next town over.

George cuts the bells and beads from her black dress and accompanies them.

The house is grander than he expects; Kathryn's mother had employed two servants, one who greets Kathryn fretfully at the front door. The lady of the house passed away a few weeks ago, she says. Ownership has passed to the new husband, a man Kathryn has never even heard of.

They find Kathryn's new stepfather in the master bedroom, sipping an electric blue concoction which trickles down his beard. Whispers of a witch have preceded them, he says; soon the torches will follow. Let him take Kathryn to his isolated country home. Her mother had recently died there, and she can pay her respects in safety.

Kathryn is suspicious from moment one. Eventually, she agrees, largely for the opportunity to investigate her mother's fate. With George's assistance, they acquire a map of this infamous country cottage, and plan in secret for George and her daughter Sera to follow separately.

On arrival at the cottage, George ties Sera's red cloak to a nearby tree and the two of them hide inside the forest. They don't have to wait long. Kathryn bursts through the cottage door, clutching a set of silver keys and gathers Sera into her arms.

Kathryn's stepfather had departed on a day trip that morning, leaving Kathryn with the keys and explicit instructions that unlocking the tower room was forbidden. When she had opened it, she'd found the rancid remains of her mother decomposing on the stone floor. Several additional corpses lined the wall. Kathryn had locked the door extra-tight and gone to keep watch downstairs – if George and Sera hadn't turned up soon, she'd have taken her chances in the forest.

When Kathryn's stepfather returns, George buries a hatchet in the older man's back.

They dump most of the bodies in the river. For Kathryn's mother, they dig a grave in the rear garden under the apple tree. And in addition to mourning her husband and mother, Kathryn feels at a loss; her primary skill is as a chemist, and customers were hesitant to purchase medicine from a woman even before she'd been branded a witch.

While Sera plays on the tower steps, while they sip peppermint tea entwined in the kitchen, they fit the pieces together. If Kathryn must be a witch, they will warp that into a legitimate profession. They'll write the stories to fit – George can barely read, but Kathryn can teach him – and create the demand themselves.

George copies out the text for the third golden book as neatly as he can. Across the bench, Kathryn puts the finishing touches on an illustration of a witch locking up a princess.

And for every villain, the world requires a hero.

Rinaya's wedding night is a flurry of white lace, sparkling wine and purple rose petals. Henry carries her bridal-style into their bedroom and deposits her onto the blankets. By the time he's removed her last necklace, skirt-layer and undergarment she's almost fallen asleep standing up.

Henry folds his own discarded clothes on a nearby chair. From the bed, Rinaya drinks in the lay of his muscles, the foreign angles of his body. She has not been looking forward to this, exactly, but she has always been a curious girl.

Neither of them speak through the act itself. Rinaya can never inhale enough air, although surely she's hyperventilating. There is plenty of pain; they must have ripped or punctured something, and she worries about permanent damage.

Not everything is unpleasant. Above her, Henry's eyes are always intense, and he reads the twitches of her face and the hitches of her breath with relative accuracy. His hands and lips on her body feel nice enough, but between the alcohol and exhaustion they seem anticlimactic. More satisfying is the sensation of joining the adult world in some irrevocable way.

When they finish, Henry stays inside her, and he searches her face and then the room for something he must not find. His face falls before bouncing back into a smile.

Rinaya swallows; her throat feels much too tight. "Have I disappointed you?"

Henry shakes his head. He kisses her once on the mouth and then flops, sweaty and sated, onto his back for sleep.

Upon leaving the city, the princess seems utterly depleted. Occasionally she follows Sera around the cottage like she is tethered to her, watching the familiar motions of the trap cleaning or rabbit skinning with wide, glassy eyes. Occasionally she sits at the piano and plays something morose. Mostly, she sleeps. She curls up in a living room chair, or on the tower's straw mattress, or – if she believes Sera is unlikely to join her, or is already asleep – on her own half of the double bed.

More than two months pass since their return. And one night the princess lifts the bed covers and climbs in under Sera's palpable gaze.

Sera stiffens immediately. Blue eyes settle on her own in the near-darkness. The princess stretches out on her side and says, "This is it, isn't it?"

There are a dozen different things that could mean. Sera stays silent.

"There's so much I'm missing." Penelope's eyes seem clearer tonight. "I think about it, you know. People think I don't think about it. But I had everything planned out. Every detail." Her tongue sneaks out to wet her parted lips. "I know how it's supposed to go."

Sera hasn't blinked since the princess first opened her mouth.

Penelope closes her eyes and gradually lowers her weight, warm and solid, on top of Sera's body. Blind, her hands trace Sera's face, feather-light. Sera understands the princess is not finding her; she is losing her. She is replacing her with someone else.

Her lips come down on Sera's, and Sera doesn't care at all.

She has never been kissed before, but surely no other kisses can incite these feelings; boneless, like her knees would buckle if they were standing up. She is intoxicated. She feels the princess smile against her lips, kissing her again and again.

"I love you," Penelope breathes against her cheek, addressing someone else entirely. Sera resists the urge to arch into her.

Between kisses and nips, they disrobe each other, and the princess never opens her eyes, not once. Sera's brain alternates between perfect, glorious silence and terror that she'll shatter the illusion; with the moan that escapes when her eyes roll into her head; with the mere existence of her breasts as they press into Penelope's. But their delicate sphere of heat and skin does not shatter. Not when Sera's lips part so wide she fears they'll tear at the seams. Not when she trembles beneath the canopy of the princess's hair. Not until Penelope has rolled onto her back and sighs, burying her fingers in Sera's own long, tangled locks.

They both freeze simultaneously. Oh, God. Sera could throw up. She tilts her head to examine Penelope's expression. It will twist into something blank and cold, and Sera will say something she'll regret. She will be left naked and dishevelled and alone.

Penelope's eyes unseal gradually and come to rest on her. "Sera," she says, quietly and clearly. "Please."

Sera unravels completely.

And she uses her scheming tongue and magician's fingers to make Penelope sing.

"I'm sorry it didn't start with you."

Sera struggles to keep tracing patterns over Penelope's ribs. "I understand."

The princess nods against Sera's chest. "Thank you."

Then she raises herself up in the nest of blankets. The cold air rushes in, and losing Penelope's body feels like losing a limb. The princess doesn't turn back as she collects her dress, her underwear, and cradles them in a bundle as she pads naked from the room.

She's going to the tower.

Rinaya supposes her marriage is a pleasant one. She sees Henry most nights, and aside from the occasional strange request he makes no unreasonable demands.

She hasn't bled since her wedding night. Her stomach starts to swell.

Once her pregnancy is undeniable, Henry brings her increasingly outlandish beverages: milk with apple pulp and fox saliva; gourmet beer plus growth potion stirred with raven's wing; venom from a golden-bellied cobra diluted three thousand times. He has her bathe in substances she cannot name. He has a small sample of her blood taken, and insists she wears a rotation of curious pendants: dried canary's eyes and petrified ladybugs.

All for the baby.

Henry says she has to trust him. Henry says he's spared no expense.

While her child grows ever larger, her father seems to be shrinking in his clothes. George's ankle has healed more or less back to normal, but he remains strictly housebound. He vomits regularly and often has trouble focusing on her face. A distinctive rash has broken out on his back, and he lost feeling in his fingers around the time of its onset.

The palace physicians proclaim it the same illness which took Henry's mother and father.

On the day that blood appears in her father's urine, Rinaya extracts her fingernails from her forearm and stares at the half-moon dents. "Has this happened before? Fern never mentioned it."

"No," George grunts. "First time."

"You refuse every suggestion... We can hardly make you worse."

George flops back onto his pillows. "If they couldn't cure the king and queen, they can't cure me. I don't want to spend the last days of my life subjected to experiments. I just want to be left here in peace."

Rinaya moves to curl up on her chair, but finds her four-month belly in the way. Finally, clutching at straws, she says, "Are you familiar with a witch's cottage in the woods? To the south of here, in the north-northeast?"

She expects him to be dismissive; instead it seems she's gained his full attention. With slitted vision, he asks, "What of it?"

The dull spark of hope in her chest flares into a fire. "I'd thought it was just a fever dream, but maybe the witch can save you."

"Witches can't even save themselves," he mutters, but she's already on her feet, digging out his emergency travel pack and a sword sheath.

When she turns back he's leaning on his cane, reaching for her embroidered sleeve. "Rina, this is ridiculous. You won't find what you're looking for. You'll endanger everything. I could never forgive myself if you lost your baby trying to save an old man."

She has no response for that. Instead, she tugs out of his awkward grip and lifts a small, familiar sword from the wall.

Increasingly agitated expressions ripple across George's pale face. "Stop this!" he shouts. "Leave me to die as I am! I forbid you to go to that cottage."

Rinaya steps out of his reach, sliding the sword onto her back. "I'm the queen now."

She feels more alive than ever.

"I'll tell Henry!" he yells, but she's already halfway down the stairs. Underneath the loft, she saddles up George's white horse and races out of the city.

Penelope spots the figure approaching on a white horse and experiences a rush of surety. Many days, she's struggled to climb out of bed, but now she feels a familiar twinge of curiosity and – more potent – desperation. That the Last Chances of yesterday were miniature and melodramatic compared to this final Last Chance.

She flies down the stairs two at a time, hitching her brown slip up around her hips, and grabs a glossy apple from the kitchen bowl. She feels so nervous she aches. With a grimace, she forces her nails through the crimson skin and digs out a chunk of soft apple flesh. It looks passably like a bite. She shakes the almost-rotting flecks of fruit from her fingers and darts out the cottage door.

Her prince hasn't quite arrived yet. Penelope sprints across patches of snow to a nearby tree stump, collapses upon it and plays dead. The mauled apple falls from her fingers to the grass, and a tiny smile twitches on her face.

She will get her happy ending even if she has to claw it free.

Sera hears the thudding on the stairs, the slamming of the door and feels her blood freeze. The princess has not moved with any sort of zeal for months. Sera collects a large knife from the kitchen, pads to the front of the cottage and opens the door a crack.

She sees a pregnant woman in a grubby, expensive-looking gown dismount and approach Penelope, where the princess is lying motionless nearby. No, that's not quite true; Sera can just make out Penelope's chest rising up and down.

Oh, Sera knows this scene. She feels the twin pains of jealousy and loss eat like maggots through her belly. As the pregnant woman glances about, kneels before the princess and kisses her right on the lips, Sera's knife hand quivers and collapses to her side.

The princess pops up like a jack-in-the-box, beaming with the kind of adoration Sera has never been afforded. Loud enough that Sera can hear, Penelope says, "I knew you'd come! You woke me! You *are* my true love!"

Deep inside of Sera, something shatters. There is a physical pain in her heart, like shards of her rib bones are slicing in. Everything in this world is absurd and wrong, and she can no longer care about any of it.

She rips open the door and across the snow, and the other women flinch at the sight of her. "You ridiculous girls! Neither one of you is cursed! There's no such thing as curses, or true loves! Or spirits, or witches. Or any kind of magic." Penelope is gaping at her, and Sera feels a perverse pleasure in ripping away this manufactured innocence. "No effortless curses. No happy endings. You'll gobble up anything. It's easy, like arsenic. A little make-up, chemistry, a bit of sparkle. For goodness sake, I was the witch all along."

She's not even looking at them anymore. Below her, the patchy grass is spinning, and above her the powder-blue sky. Sera hears herself laugh, and it's far from a witch's cackle; more like a death knell. "But no more lies. I can't stomach them. Everything's putrefied into a hideous joke."

And she sags, like the confession has pulled the stuffing from her body, and turns her gaze on the pregnant woman with the sword on her back. "So. Want to burn the witch? Oven gets nice and hot. Playing the hero? I'll play." She offers up the knife, hilt first, the blade cutting lightly into the flesh of her fingers. "My world's ended anyway."

Then there's only the wind howling through the trees.

It's abruptly, painfully cold. When Sera looks down again, she sees her own bare flesh; not a stitch of clothing on it. Her feet almost numb. Her hair damp against her back.

Standing naked in the snow.

The swordswoman doesn't take the knife. Instead, she stands slowly and says, "Can you heal my father?"

Inside, the cottage is quiet and musty, like a mausoleum. The clothed witch boils tea, her face unreadable, and speaks in short, blunt sentences when prompted. The princess slumps in an armchair in a nearby room. Rinaya has had to carry her in bridal-style; Penelope's mind and body seem to have shut down.

They work well together, the witch and the hero's daughter. They ask no unnecessary questions. While the day is still young, Rinaya rides to the nearest town to buy a small carriage and extra horse, and Sera stays home to dribble cups of lemon tea past Penelope's lips.

Rinaya has expected multiple setbacks since leaving the city, but has encountered exactly none. Why Henry has allowed her to run off unhindered – or unaided – she has no idea. As much as the morning's revelations make her head spin, they provide a welcome distraction to her marital suspicions.

The consequences of no magic cascade down on one another like blows. The world is horrifying for different reasons now; not due to monsters and curses, but because of the deaths and suffering caused by believing in them. Because of how steadfastly people can accept any multitude of false things.

Intellectually, she knows she should be furious; with her father, with the witch. But the overwhelming feeling, as she travels alone through the dappled leaf-light and multitude of birdsong, is one of freedom. Of the world unenchanting and coming into focus. That it's entirely reasonable for her life not to mirror the fairy tales, because the tales were never very truthful in the first place.

At sundown, her carriage finds Penelope and Sera by the side of the road. They are both mad as leaking cups, but Rinaya cannot bring herself to think ill of them. The roles they were cast in were more obvious and overwhelming than her own, and they were naturally a better fit for them.

Rinaya half-lifts the witch and the princess inside the darkness of the carriage. How strange, she thinks as she climbs back on top; this is the sanest and happiest she's ever felt.

She flicks the reins.

Sera's boots track dried mud over the stairs. During the past couple of days, she's guided Rinaya through the painstaking process of preparing the appropriate medicine, and the younger woman has caught on admirably.

One last thing to do, to finish the job. Then Sera can think of nothing more to live for.

In the loft with bloodstained sheets, she thrusts an icy, steaming glass towards George's face. "Daughter's orders," she says.

He takes it with trembling hands.

"I told her who I was," she says. "All of me."

"You'd be dead," he says.

"She cares more about you than what you're supposed to do."

The door creaks and Rinaya stumbles through, panting, with Penelope's arm slung around her shoulders. The princess sways about as if feverish. Rinaya deposits her in the chair beside the stairs.

"She speaks?" asks Sera.

Rinaya shakes her head. "Four days of silence."

Sera would feel dizzy with guilt if she wasn't so numb.

George swallows the last drop of medicine, scrunches his face and lets Sera take the glass. She informs him that he'll need another tomorrow.

"Papa..." says Rinaya, leaning over his bed like she's the parent. "You could have told me."

"You'd have been a liability," he says. "Was my burden to bear."

Already feeling extraneous, Sera turns her attention to the window. The king sits on the podium in his city square. To her left, Sera can still make out Rinaya's voice murmuring, "Was it just for the money?" and George's: "Most things, however questionable, are done out of love."

A flurry of movement through the window pane. Sera recognises a blonde figure run across the square towards the king, and a spark of concern she thought long-gone reignites in her chest. Next to the door, Penelope is missing.

Even at this distance, there's something unmistakable in Henry's stance when he spies his sister. When she leaps onto the podium and into his arms, like storybook pictures of reunited lovers.

Sera was aware, intellectually, that Henry must love his sister, but seeing them together...

"Henry had the third golden book?" she asks George, though she's already almost certain.

"Shared," he says. "Between him and..." The empty chair.

Sera has spent hours deducing where the threat in the palace may have come from, ultimately concluding she knew far too little about its political mechanisms to reach an answer. And she's still not sure, not really, but if *she* were Henry, and she'd grown up believing that book of fairy tales...

She flies out the door and down the stairs.

"You take your hands off her!"

Rinaya halts several paces behind Sera, and flinches when Sera's sharp voice booms across the square. On the podium, Henry pulls Penelope closer. His soldiers step forward in perfect synchronization, hands clasped around their sword hilts.

With a flourish, Sera flicks her wrist and clicks her fingers: a burst of flame twice as big as her fist blooms into the air, orange as fox fur, and then flickers out as quickly as it came.

Next to the podium, the string quartet lurches to a halt. Clusters of citizens scramble backwards, bumping into pop-up food stalls and almost tripping over Rinaya's feet. The winter solstice celebration.

Sera's winter dress whirls above the snow. "Stay back or the whole square goes up!"

The soldiers freeze mid-stride. Rinaya closes her mouth, her fingers twitching for her own blade. She clasps them loosely at her stomach.

"You took her!" shouts Sera, loud enough for the whole square to hear. "You took her into the forest and locked her up!"

Henry looks the picture of composure. "I did no such thing," he says.

"But you ordered it."

A smile crosses his lips. "Ah. *You* locked her up. You're not as ugly as I thought."

"Spell," says Sera. "I took her voice and made me young. Made me pretty."

"I might not go that far."

The wind blows out Sera's dark curls and patched crimson cloak, and she looks like an animal; a wild thing. Above the breeze, she yells, "If she wasn't in my tower, she would've been in someone else's!"

Penelope retracts her face from the crook of Henry's shoulder. Henry rushes to cup his sister's cheek. "It's okay, Penny; I never wanted anything to happen to you."

"Then you shouldn't have kidnapped her!"

All around Rinaya, whispers race around the city square. The soldiers pull their swords out another inch. Rinaya feels like her stomach has fallen onto the cobblestones. She won't interfere just yet, not unless she needs to – not while the final puzzle pieces seem to be slipping into place.

Henry keeps one arm around Penelope's waist, extending the other towards the crowd. "Sometimes you have to act for the greater good. You have to do the wrong thing for the right reasons." He cups his sister's chin, but doesn't lower his voice. "Penny. My love. You shouldn't have had to rule alone. You needed a prince. You needed to be captured so that you could be rescued."

Rinaya can barely look at him anymore. She allows her eyes to slip shut.

She hears him continue: "I acted in love so that you could *find* love. I promise. My heart broke when I thought you were dead. I was wrong... But I meant so *well*." In the darkness he sounds entirely genuine. To her frustration and relief, Rinaya believes him completely.

She wants to kick him in the balls. Sweat runs down the back of her neck, and her hands shake through her gloves. She has believed things equally ridiculous. She would've never acted so stupidly – would she?

Her eyes snap open to high-pitched sobbing. Penelope weeps into her brother's chest, her tears running into his navy jacket.

Henry kisses the top of Penelope's head and says, "Were you rescued in the end?"

She manages to nod without pulling her head back.

"Good. *Good*," he repeats. "Wonderful. Is your prince here? He can have my crown."

In a small but clear voice, his sister says, "He died." It's the first time she's spoken since the cottage, and Rinaya wonders whether Penelope's mind has truly snapped. Penelope extends her finger out, inch by inch, towards Sera. "She killed him."

A fresh round of murmurs circle the square, loud as stage whispers.

"That's right," Henry says. He steps in front of his sister, blocking her with his body. "They told me he never came out."

Sera throws out her arms. "He was taking off her dress," she declares.

Rinaya has never heard this part of the story.

"So?" says Henry.

Sera moves even closer to the stage, her arms beating the empty air. "So he was going to take advantage of her!"

Henry twists towards Penelope. "Was he?" he asks.

Penelope shakes her head.

"She wouldn't know," Sera says quickly. "She was asleep."

Henry says, "She would've woken."

Sera laughs, long and dark and loose, and for a second Rinaya expects the older woman to collapse in the snow. "I drugged her!" Sera yells.

Henry frowns and his mouth moves, but Sera drowns him out: "For your precious greater good!" she shouts. "For the love! So I could feed her and talk to her while you kept her locked up!"

When Henry finishes processing this, he says, "This prince you're talking about. About my height, red hair, green eyes? Rare combination around here. I've known him all my life, and he received an anonymous tip as to where my half-sister might be in the forest."

Henry draws a wad of pink and brown material from an inside pocket and shakes it out. It takes Rinaya several seconds to realise her husband has been walking around with a bloodstained nightgown next to his heart.

"He would never hurt her," Henry continues. "If she was clothed in this bloody slip, you don't think he might have looked under it for wounds? To check if she was injured?"

Rinaya waits for Sera to deny this, but Sera doesn't speak, doesn't move.

"I don't know what you're trying to do here," he continues, "but I love my sister." His tone suggests this is all wrapped up. "I wanted the best for her. You've kept her to yourself for months, killed what's probably her only chance for love... Kept her from her rightful place as queen..."

Sera still doesn't move. Henry glances at his soldiers, waves a finger. All eight of them advance on Sera like a single entity. Off to the side, the string quartet raise their bows with trepidation.

Rinaya hesitates only a second. She snatches her sword and leaps in front of Sera, and hears Henry call, "Halt!" and the scrape of armour as his guards comply.

"Rina..." he says.

Rinaya pries open her satchel with her free hand and withdraws her crown. She tosses it onto the stage and it lands with a clink-thump at her husband's feet. "It's Penelope's," she says.

Henry's eyes on her have turned cold as the solstice, and he drops his voice to stop it carrying. "She is your mother only in blood, and not worth our mercy."

Rinaya balks at him. Over the years George has told her various, semi-conflicting pieces of information about her mother's death, but always with such a pained expression that she has learned not to ask.

Sera's fingers wind around Rinaya's forearm. "He means my mother," Sera murmurs, low enough so that only the two of them can hear. "She could be yours, too. I'd believe it."

Rinaya glances behind her to where Sera is studying the snow, splashes of alcohol and a discarded ribbon smeared around their feet. They have different body shapes, different skin tones, but their features are similar – similar face shape, cheekbones, the line of the nose, the curve of the eyes. She believes it.

She turns on Henry: "You kept this from me?"

And he shrugs, so slight she almost misses it. "The time between my finding out and then believing her dead was very brief. I believe you were incapacitated for most of it. Certainly I had yet to meet you properly."

"That's not really the point..."

"I mean to say," Henry interrupts, "that you couldn't go after her. For many reasons."

A drop of sweat runs into Rinaya's eyes, and she rubs savagely at her eyebrows. "No, of course not." Her voice is laced with unfamiliar bitterness. "I can't do many things for many reasons."

She almost asks him where he learned about her mother – from who, and when – but she thinks she knows. There is only one place it could have come from. She will be having a long talk with her father later, his discomfort be damned.

Henry crouches down on the podium to speak to her, to her reach her eye level, as if comforting a small girl. "You have magic inside of you," he says gently.

It does not make her feel gentle. "I have *something* inside of me," she says.

"You have a royal child."

Her free hand automatically goes to rest on her protruding stomach. What a ridiculous mess this is, every strand of it. How naive to think she was exempt from these adults' mistakes; that she had not lived long enough to truly mess things up.

Her baby kicks against her hand for the first time.

Oh yes, she has made her mistakes.

"Henry," she says, over-enunciating every word, "do you love me?"

He rises to his feet and doesn't falter: "I love what you can do for the kingdom."

Rinaya stares at him, expressionless. This is not really a revelation. She is not heartbroken. She is not even disappointed, really. But she does feel betrayed. By consistent, ongoing lies from everyone who is supposed to love her, to be her family. Who have trapped her in increasing layers of expectations and manipulations.

"You're all as bad as each other," she announces, addressing Henry and Sera and even Fern and George, though there's no way he'll hear her from his bed. "And I don't think I agree with your choices, or forgive them, though I do believe you thought they were necessary. And I think both of you," she gestures between Henry and Sera, "have a *great* deal in common."

Rinaya is unused to, and uncomfortable with anger, and also – despite the past few months – with public attention, and she has almost reached her limit with both. She has the strong urge to escape the square and lick her wounds in private, but that would be irresponsible. And then Sera is speaking softly behind her:

"As you said, I tried my best." Dark eyes flick up to meet her own. "If this is the end, then let it come."

"No," says Rinaya, and takes Sera's pale hand firmly in her own gloved one. Even through the glove, she can tell the girl is freezing. My half-sister, she thinks. My sister is freezing.

"Honestly," says Henry, "I would do the same again, probably every piece of it." He adjusts the queen's crown on Penelope's head, evidently deeming the threat neutralized. "I acted out of love for this kingdom, and love for my family. You may discuss personal issues with me, Rinaya, in a less public forum."

He's about to start up the band again.

"Wait!" she barks. "You promise me. Promise you'll look after my family."

Penelope twists in his arms, eyes too large in her head. "Give her what she wants," she says, and Rinaya tucks those words away like a love letter; that maybe she has done a couple of things right, after all.

Henry says, "Fine. My word. As much as that means to you..."

Rinaya is already at the foot of the steps, dragging Sera behind her, up and onto the podium. The crowd trickles back into the front of the square like sand filling a void. Merchants resume distracted transactions, eyes half fixed on their former queen. Sera's hand clamps around her own like a vice.

Rinaya stares into the hundreds of expectant faces and raises her voice: "There's something we need to tell you about fairy tales."

ALL THE FIRST BORN CHILDREN

When they're taken away, all the first born children, at the pointy end of deals struck and bargains made...

When they're wrenched from the arms of weeping mothers and shell-shocked queens and sleeping maidens, take heart: they are most probably alive, here at the house at the end of the world.

The house is entirely white inside: white walls, white carpet, white ceilings with vast white skylights.

Here they are fed, and watered, and healed if they are sick and fixed if they break a bone. Here there are taught not to soil themselves and the basics of human language, and are sedated and encouraged to do not much at all. Here is where the imps and trolls and fairies drop them at the door, still wrapped in their mothers' blood or tears or blankets.

Here are the children who would have been kings and queens, mighty generals and leaders of rebellions, politicians and master thieves, famous writers and inventors and speech makers who changed the course of history. Here at the house at the end of the world they are hospitalised and sterilised and exercised without ever leaving its walls.

When it's taken away, your first born child, because you couldn't spin gold or left the crib unattended or for no reason at all, take heart: these children's potential energy is the strongest force in the world, and it could not be used for a worthier cause.

And when they're taken away, comfort yourselves: we never take second-borns.

THE SECRET DEATH OF LANE ISLINGTON

DAY 1

I first meet Lane Islington when she steps out of the lake, all smeared eyeliner and pointy incisors, and says, "Do you want to be a star?"

DAY 2

A brief history of Lane's life through photos, video and song:

At four in Wonder Woman's cape for Halloween.

At seven as Rizzo in the neighbourhood children's production of Grease.

At eighteen on the cover of her first album, posed on a battlefield, covered with fresh and dried blood and swinging her guitar above her head like a weapon. The ferocity in her eyes almost convinces you that if you threw her into battle with just a musical instrument she would still win. I'm expecting a poster of this on the walls of her bedroom, but the walls are all empty. White.

Lane plays me the entirety of this album whilst she sets up a tiny bedroom beside her own: she squeezes a single foam mattress through a child-sized door and into the cupboard under the roof, which is perhaps two meters by five. Several pillows and blankets follow. The album is very good, in a pop-rock-punk kind of way, and hardly sounds auto-tuned at all; I can see why it went platinum in less than six weeks.

She never calls me Aeris the whole time, only Aer, which most people don't get away with until they've known me at least a few weeks. But she's practically my sister, so I guess she's allowed.

Lane explains that she loves creating music, and that she even gets a thrill out of performing sometimes if she doesn't have to do it often. I watch the videos: she's spectacular on stage or in front of a camera, like her whole self has lit up; I can barely tear my eyes away.

But she wasn't expecting most of the country to recognise her the minute she stepped out of her house, the one she still shares with her mother and younger sister. She wasn't expecting the rapid-fire requests for interviews and talk show appearances and magazine cover shots. Most of those made her want to swim deep under the ocean and never come back.

So she cast a spell to open a portal to the one parallel world, out of an infinite number, where a girl was identical to her visually in every way and near a lake. And she stepped through the portal and into the lake. And came back with me.

Chorus of "Razorblade Girl" from Lane Islington's second album, also entitled "Razorblade Girl" (2018):

So hey, just be careful if you come a little closer
Yeah, I think you're pretty cute
But you might learn that I'm a monster
I won't mean to bite your hand off
Cut your fingers on my skin
A razorblade girl
Just a razorblade girl
So wear your armour if you're going to come in

DAY 3

We work on my walk first: stop swaying my hips, pick up the pace a little, get comfortable walking in Lane's flat Converse sneakers. Lane always wears flats except for some photo shoots, where she's been known to be dressed in heels so high she can barely stand up in them.

"No, you're still leading with your hips," she corrects. "I lead with my head." This is something she learned in acting class a couple of years earlier. Slowly, I shift my body as if a string is pulling me along by my forehead.

"Much better," she says, and turns her attention to my accent.

DAY 7

Lane is out of the house about half the time, which is about fifty per cent less than her producers would have liked, and about fifty per cent more than she would have personally preferred. Largely, she seems to get away with this by saying she's working on her second album, which is true. She's just simultaneously working on a human decoy of herself.

While Lane is away I have hours locked in her room to practice my walk and watch online videos of "How to Perfect Your Australian Accent," which I soon learn I prefer to Lane's personal instruction. Approximating the accent is relatively easy, but most of the internet examples are for broader accents that make Lane laugh. She seems to find my own Clayden accent quite lovely but strange, "as if an English and New Zealand accent got tossed in a blender with some other things."

And I watch Lane's three music videos again and again, fascinated by the sight of myself as an international superstar. I watch her concerts where the crowd surges towards her with love. That could be me – distinctly average Aeris Dormer who has barely been clapped for anything.

DAY 14

Lane declares that I am ready to leave the house.

It's only a ten-minute walk to the milkbar and back, but during that time three groups of people audibly recognise "me," two ask for a selfie and one for an autograph. I've practised Lane's signature for a couple of hours and it's serviceable. She only writes two types of messages alongside her name: "Rock on!" or "Thanks for the support!" which aren't creative or exciting, but they're at least easy to remember.

I've seen snapshots of Lane interacting with her fans before, and although she genuinely appreciates them she always looks a little pained.

I try not to look too out of character, but I can feel my heartbeat speeding, recognise that my eyes are probably dilated, that my cheeks are warm. The entire walk feels like champagne streaming through my veins.

It doesn't matter that they think I'm Lane. Most of them look at me like some kind of goddess. Just breathing the same air as me is the highlight of their day, their week, their year. They tell me I'm beautiful. Back at home, I managed to escape "plain" because my face was symmetrical, but I would never be conventionally attractive. In Clayden, girls are expected to be dark and curvy. Lane and I are both vampire-pale with B-cups.

At the milk bar, the cashier holds up a magazine with Lane as the covergirl. She's dressed as the queen of the amazons, warpaint on her cheeks and arrows in her hands. She pulls it off, utterly, like she'd smash being an amazon if she woke up in their tribe tomorrow morning. The cashier says that it's a good one.

That outing is the best ten minutes of my life. The strange gait, the silly walk; all the preparation was worth it. At the end, I bound up the stairs into Lane's room, embrace her a little too fast, and say, "That was better than sex!"

Which is probably the wrong thing to lead with, because Lane laughs awkwardly, but it hardly matters: I can play her in public again tomorrow.

DAY 16

I pop back into Clayden. Lane summons the portal – the "redial" version of the spell – and we both step through with swimsuits and a change of clothes in zip-lock bags. After squeezing out her hair and changing, Lane stays behind with sunglasses and a crime novel to make sure no-one accidentally passes through the portal in the lake bed, and I go to visit my parents.

Now, my parents have missed me, but not overly so, because I'm a nineteen-year-old adult and they have two children under ten at home to worry about. And they've been concerned by my lack of communication, but it's not unusual for several days to pass without contact between us, so they haven't approached the local authorities.

When I show them their gifts – gold necklaces and diamond rings and jewel-encrusted bangles – any worry they've had about my absence just melts off their faces. I tell them I've dropped out of university and gotten a good, but secretive job across the border. Lane gives me forty per cent of whatever she makes.

It sits heavy in my stomach, this understanding that I could go months without visiting again, and as long as I bring back expensive goods they'll never complain.

DAY 27

Within Melbourne, Australia, Lane is my best and only friend. We paint our nails identically, coordinate nose rings and trade stories of how we got our scars; her ankle scar is from falling through some bushes as a child, camping; mine is from dropping a hot fry-pan. Lane introduces me to her favourite anime and music videos, to fancy coffees and sushi and herbal tea. I teach her the application of winged eyeliner and basic astronomy and how to mix a dozen different cocktails, cross-legged on her bedroom floor.

Neither of us practices magic. I've asked her so many things about sorcery that I'm not allowed another question for a whole month, but I'm not sure there's anything left to ask.

Lane found the portal spell in a library book, but like almost every other spell on earth, no-one could ever get it to work. Lane practised the hand movements until she could do them with her eyes closed, upside down, but it wasn't until she did them whilst menstruating on her ensuite toilet that the portal actually opened. The library book said nothing about blood falling through air whilst facing north. And that's the thing about spells: any fool with a keyboard can write them down, but they don't usually understand half of what made them work: the phase of the moon or a cat crossing your roof or that there's a pregnant woman next door. So they can't be replicated.

Every night there are seven "facts" for me to memorise about Lane on a piece of notepaper, followed by a pop quiz on the ones I've been given the night before. Lane's favourite animal is a puma. Her favourite food is spring rolls. Her favourite word is "aesthetic."

Those are important, but I think I learn more about Lane from just watching her. The way she gets ink all over her hands and lips while she writes her songs. The way she comes home almost mute from a day performing, not because she's lost her voice but because she's too overwhelmed to speak. The way she says things so obscene they render me speechless, but usually flinches whenever anyone touches her.

I mean, except for me, these days. I only sleep in the cupboard under the roof now if Lane's away at night. If I get up before her and she's awake enough to notice, she mutters, "Come back to bed, changeling," until I do and she can nestle her chin in my shoulder.

Lane has plenty of other acquaintances, obviously, if not friends. Her best friend, officially, is Willa Zhang, a Chinese-Australian graphic artist who designed a kick-ass scorpion tattoo for Lane (but which she can't get inked now because I complicate everything), smokes the kind of marshmallow cigarettes they use in theatre shows, and paints her nails rainbow. Lane tells me she sees Willa maybe once a month.

Her best friend, unofficially, is her uncle Trevor, whom she sees every week, religiously, even if she's interstate and their time is FaceTime. After Lane's parents split when she was twelve, Trevor started coming around more; he's the one who taught Lane the guitar, how to read sheet music. In the meantime Lane's father ran off to America and started dating women not much older than she was.

I can hear the clinks of Lane's mother and sister setting their table for dinner downstairs. Lane's perched up here with me, combing the real estate sites, inky fingers warping the skin on her temples in concentration. Thank goodness for the lock on her door, and I've surrounded my mattress with all the colours missing from Lane's monochrome room – tangerines and violets and limes – but that's no substitute for a place of our own.

DAY 36

Every week and a half or so, Lane administers a test on Australian slang.

"I grabbed the torch to find the lollies in the boot of the car before driving to Maccas," I recite. "And never flashlight or trunk, but sometimes Macdonald's."

"And sometimes candy," Lane adds. "Because we're becoming Americanised."

I nod solemnly. "And sometimes candy."

Lane throws a blue jellybean towards my mouth.

DAY 39

I meet men on the internet. I use my real name. We have cyber sex of varying quality and occasionally, when I'm sure I'm alone in the house, phone sex.

I quickly lose interest in most of them. The remainder, when I'm unable to send pictures or meet in person, lose interest in me.

DAY 42

There are photos of me-as-Lane on a celebrity gossip site. I'm carrying a coffee cup around the local shopping centre, all bedazzled jeans and tank top scrawled with "Shhhhh" and sunglasses that cover half my face. This is the most awesome I've ever looked, I think.

"I hope I'm good enough," is what I say to Lane. She doesn't even glance up from her keyboard.

"You look just like me," she says. "So you're perfect."

DAY 57

Settlement is only a week away. Lane paces around a small battalion of moving boxes, quizzing me with potential interview questions (your next album/tour dates/boyfriend/inspiration). I know all the standard answers now – I'm just practising making them sound witty.

I'm concentrating so hard that it takes a few seconds to register the thumps on the stairs. And that we haven't locked the door.

I scramble off the bed and roll under it, bruising my hip and forearm in the process. I clutch my nose against the layer of dust. I'm coated in it already, and force myself to suppress a violent sneeze just as Lane's mother Audrey walks in.

They argue, of course, which is their usual method of communication. I watch Audrey's shiny red heels poke out beneath the bedclothes. She's saying, "This might be the last Sunday we share this home, and it's appalling that you think you won't eat dinner with us. I can't believe I raised such an ungrateful child."

Lane is saying that she'd had five hours of rehearsal today and that she's tired and doesn't want to be yelled at and that she has diarrhoea. Audrey won't take no for an answer. Audrey calls Lane a lazy, selfish little bitch. Lane calls Audrey an unreasonable tyrant. Audrey expects Lane downstairs in fifteen minutes.

Once her mother's footsteps have well and truly faded, I wipe the worst of the dust from my clothes and kneel beside Lane on the bed. I've seen Lane listless before. Bitter, melancholy. But I've never seen her eyes so sad.

She lies us down and wraps my arm around her, the way she likes to sleep even though we usually keep different hours. I don't know what to say.

Lane breaks the silence with, "You go. Be me. I can't bear to look at her tonight."

So I do, because I love her like a sister. I brush the last of the dust bunnies from my hair and hide my blossoming bruises beneath a long-sleeved top and jeans. I even draw on some lipstick – "Bubbleshine Pink" – before I head downstairs.

There are fancier dinner plates than we ever had at my house, growing up. Candles burn in the middle of a beige tablecloth, and each set of shining cutlery has an accompanying embroidered napkin. Lane's sister Imogen is seated in her ballet costume, fiddling with the elastic on her leotard – I wonder if she's a little slow.

"Everything looks really nice," I say. Audrey eyes me like a hawk. Apparently that's not the kind of thing Lane would tell her.

But the dinner progresses fairly smoothly. It's not hard: I ask polite questions, I listen, I try to anticipate their needs. Before Lane was born Audrey had a bit-part on a game show, one of those ladies who spun tiles or opened cases, with a few speaking lines per episode. She's asked Lane for expensive face cream for her birthday ever since Lane was eleven, and complains with Lane doesn't perform household chores "with love."

Audrey wants to be worshipped.

I understand; so do I.

It's not like Lane is an easy person to live with. She has a caustic sense of humour and whenever I get a pimple she insists on popping it herself – immediately. She streams music most of her waking hours and calls me an idiot for the tiniest infractions, like loading a toilet roll the wrong way.

Until recently I didn't even know there was a right way.

But Lane never seems to be good enough for Audrey, so Lane doesn't really try, which Audrey can't stand, and on and on in a malicious cycle.

By the end of the meal, whenever she looks at me, a tiny smile is curling at the corner of Audrey's mouth.

First verse and chorus of "Version of Me" from "Razorblade Girl" (2018):

Hey baby girl, you know, I didn't sign up for this
Her baby girl, I was expecting someone better
You're always so sullen; why can't you smile?
Why can't your compliments go on for miles?
Why can't you love me
Why won't you love me
While I'm screaming at you?

Well, I'm sorry that you were expecting somebody
Sorry I let you down
But you can get fucked if you think that I'll change
Just to keep you around
You think that I'm rude

I think that you'll find
You love a version of me that's only in your mind
You wanted your princess
But I am just the witch
Tough luck

DAY 76

Our new house is two storeys, four-bedrooms, although one of these bedrooms – mine – has been hidden away. Lane has lined the first-floor hallway with bookcases, and while there's a gap for her own matte white door, mine has a bookcase attached so you wouldn't know there was a door at all. The knob can be found behind The Complete Works of Shakespeare and swings inward, to where my windows are almost opaque, like a bathroom.

I give my first interview on The Sam Daley Show, wearing a starry cocktail dress with a faux-bloodstain like a sash. The makeup lady gives me eyeshadow like peacock feathers; I feel her breath on my ear. When I walk on stage the crowd cheers like I've saved the fucking universe: they're on their feet, they're whistling. I want to fall to my knees and bask in it. They're cheering Lane's name, but it's my name now, too. I keep walking, I raise my hand and show my incisors. It's easy now, easy. The audience is a wave of love and I'm up at its peak under the lights and now I'm fucking complete.

When Lane watches the show, afterwards, she says that I'm not as quick and clever as she is, but that I'm more natural – more likable. She's satisfied; I can do most, if not all of the interviews from now on.

Glory, I think, glory, and run my tongue along my teeth.

DAY 78

Lane's door is halfway open, so I pull it the rest of the way and declare, "I miss sex."

Lane is pulling a rockabilly t-shirt over her head. Before her album came out, she'd collected a small handful of both boyfriends and girlfriends, but there's been no-one since.

She only hesitates a moment, and then says, "Fine. It's good for our career. Just no-one awful or ugly. And if you're going on more than two dates with someone, you need to run them by me first."

#

DAY 147

In Clayden, sex had felt a bit like receiving a bunch of likes on a social media post. I got my rush, my validation, even if the experience itself wasn't all that satisfying. It was a small, invisible trophy. I felt worthwhile and full up for a few days afterwards, and then that feeling would dissipate and I would have to find another guy to chase away the circling thoughts of being unwanted.

But it's different as Lane. Everywhere I go, I am watched, I am desired, I am salivated after. I no longer feel a need to collect men as beads on a string. A hook up once every few weeks is more than enough, and it's about my pleasure now just as much as theirs.

I go back to Clayden for my birthday and partially regret it. My parents look excited to see me and buy me a rainbow ice-cream cake to celebrate, even though I'm mildly lactose intolerant and turning twenty years old instead of five. My younger sister has made me one of those paper fortune-tellers that you put your fingers inside, complete with golden glitter glue. My little brother gives me a glossy ceramic horse that he made in art class.

In Melbourne, I display these two presents on the shelf above my bed, even though Lane is clearly unimpressed by their craftsmanship. I resist the urge to tell her to fuck off. Lane herself has gifted me an expensive black and white dress that's much more her style than mine, but I don't think she knows that. And she didn't even wrap it.

We have generally settled into the new house well enough. Lane has installed a camera at the gate, so that she can see anyone who approaches on her phone regardless of whether she's home or not. She's also installed a camera in the living room, attached to a device which throws chocolate Lindt balls at me whenever she presses a phone button. It was originally designed to allow you to watch your dogs while you're at work and toss them treats. I suspect it's more to do with her checking in on me on Tuesday mornings when our maid comes and I'm supposed to be hidden in my room.

I pose for my favourite photo-shoot so far, a triptych of villainous portraits where I am Cersei Lannister, I am the queen from Snow White, I am Lizzie Borden. My face is covered with hundreds of glued-on diamonds, I am wrapped in golden silk on a sea of black apples, I step naked out of a bath filled with crimson paint. I feel so goddamned powerful, my whole body is singing with it, I could practically levitate off the ground...

Right until I walk back through my front door.

DAY 183

Lane beckons me to her piano and starts teaching me to read sheet music. No announcement, no explanation, just pointing to notes and naming them and playing them over the keys. Once I clue in to what she's doing I try to step away, but she grabs my arm.

"No," she says, "it's time. Think how embarrassing it would be if someone showed you some sheet music in an interview – your own sheet music, and you couldn't even say that note was A."

I sigh and grumble and provide some example excuses, but Lane won't let go and eventually I have to admit she has a point and join her on the leather piano stool.

"Okay," I mutter, and press my finger a crotchet. "So this is A?"

DAY 204

It's Halloween: the only day Lane and I can go out in public together. Lane takes me to October "Toby" Johnson's party – he's the lead guitarist of Ninety-Nine Riots and, I am happy to conclude, very cute. Lane is dressed as some anime character named Annalise, in a black bodysuit and blue body-powder, turquoise hair and iridescent makeup. Very alien-sexy. As for me: her plainer cousin, with dyed-black hair and a lace masquerade mask, in a simple violet dress. Literally, I'm introduced as her cousin Madison.

This is the first and only time I will ever kiss Lane. We both drank a bit too much – Lane from the light beers in Toby's fridge with the sunglasses-wearing-panda on them, and me from the novelty of Toby's vodka fountain – and someone suggested a game of spin the bottle. Kissing Lane was fine, I guess, but I'm not super into girls and when we pulled back, Lane had this particularly sharp expression which I interpreted as her wanting a repeat. My life is already at least eighty-five per cent Lane Islington. No need to get romantically involved with her and make it a hundred.

Shortly after that Toby and I end up making out in his walk-in closet. He's a decent kisser and pretty good with his hands for twenty-two, but it doesn't get any further than his fingers between my legs because he hasn't planned ahead. I hate that about guys. His astronaut costume looks great but is a bastard to remove, and there aren't any condoms in his closet. I don't know why he can't just go and get some – surely there are some elsewhere in the house – but maybe he's embarrassed to be caught fucking a nobody.

I bite his neck a few times so he knows that I'm somebody, down a couple of the panda beers and dance with Lane to her first single, "21st Century," because we're that kind of casual narcissists.

DAY 379

Lane receives the phone call on an ordinary day. We're curled up at either end of the couch, so I'm close enough to hear her tone drop from bluster into a cold numbness.

I can never ask Lane to repeat this part, but I think this is more or less what she said:

Trevor was in excellent health for his sixties – in fact he was chopping wood at the time – but he had tooth pain that he had been putting off going to a doctor for. The axe came down, something like an abscess popped in his mouth and he must have breathed in some of the liquid because it infected his lungs.

Lane is getting the call because Trevor is in an induced coma at the local hospital. I barely know what to say. I thought comas didn't really happen to people in real life.

After she relays this story to me in a monotone she seems to come a bit alive again and is going to leave without a jumper on, so I shrug off the hoodie I'm wearing and wrap it around her shoulders before she reaches the door. I'm afraid that's the most useful thing I do that night.

A couple of days have passed and I can see her approaching our house. She comes in, ashen and unwashed-looking, with an old leather book under one arm.

"He died," is all she says before she locks herself in her room.

DAY 383

Four days seems to be the mourning period that Lane's producers will allow.

She's barely left her room since Trevor died, and yesterday she gave me her phone to monitor because she was getting too many texts and voicemails and didn't want to deal with any of them. Her curtains have been permanently drawn, which doesn't seem healthy, but I guess it hasn't been very long and grief is a process. She drags herself between her bed and shower every day, but doesn't actually get dressed in anything but pyjamas, and sometimes she'll reach the kitchen but prefers it when I bring her room service.

"Lane," I say gently to the shape under the covers, "I know you're still feeling awful, but they want you to meet with them about recording the new album. They know the tracks are almost ready and everything."

Lane drags a pillow further over her head. "You know the stuff," comes her muffled voice. "You do it."

I study the mound of bedsheets. It's not like I can force her to leave the house. This is something kind I can do for her when she's feeling like shit, isn't it?

"Okay," I say finally, "I'll meet with them if it will help you. I haven't actually done this part as Lane Islington before, remember? But if I'm a bit weird they'll think it's just because I'm grieving."

Lane makes some kind of sad animal noise in response, and I leave her alone.

DAY 393

Lane ends up saying, "You do it," to a lot of things.

I take Lane's place at Trevor's funeral, which seems like the kind of thing Lane will be furious about later, but she yells and cries at me until I agree. I take her place at the wake afterwards, and at comforting Audrey and Imogen through a weekend of tears and binge-watching Jane Austen movies. I take Lane's place ice-skating with Willa, even though "Lane's" performance on the ice is sub-par. To the outside world, Lane is recovering slowly. In our secret little world of two, Lane doesn't seem to be recovering at all, and I'm starting to freak out a little.

All Lane seems to do these days is watch anime on her tablet, read from the leather book she keeps under her pillow (apparently it was Trevor's favourite), and order food deliveries. When I'm not at home she has the drivers drop the plastic bags inside the gate, and then pilots a drone through the skylight of the upstairs hall, has it pick up the bag and then return to drop the food on her bed. I'd declare this kind of cleverness a good sign, but sometimes she doesn't even go to the kitchen for cutlery; she just eats it all with her hands, even things you'd always think you'd need a fork or spoon for.

When I am at home and she'll let me, I'll sit with her in the dark and watch a show, but she doesn't usually want to talk. She says, "What is there to say? He died," and the first few times I don't have anything to say to that. Later I say, "Yes, but you didn't," and try to coax her out of the house or at least into the garden to get some sun. But that seems to make her shut down into the foetal position instead.

"Lane," I say, after I've brought her the third lemonade of the day, "remember you're actually recording the album next week. That's not something I can do for you."

She calls me a stupid bitch then, for agreeing to record the album at all when I know what sort of state she's in, but – I hope – she also knows I'm right.

First verse and chorus of "My Air" from "Razorblade Girl" (2018):

When life gets hard
And you just want to cry
Just open a window
She'll be there by your side
When life is a burden
And you just want to die
She'll be your shield
She'll wrap her arms around you

My air
When the smog surrounds and the will is fading
My air
When curtains close and I can't leave my room for days
When the lights go out
One by one
Starts at my eyes
Snuffs out the sun
If my lungs give out
If the stars blink out
You are my air

DAY 344

Thank goodness Lane really does record the album. She's sullen when she leaves the house, a dozen rings on her fingers and a hood pulled down over half her face, even though it's not remotely cold. She manages okay in the end, switching into performance mode when she's actually in the studio, even though she has to take more breaks than usual. I'm proud of her, and I tell her as much.

After that she continues to improve a little. She still spends most of her time in her room, but she's taken to making deals with me. She'll spend half an hour outside in the sun if I read aloud to her. She'll keep the curtains open that day if I do an interpretive dance to her entire first album. She'll walk to the milk-bar if I sing her to sleep.

I am a very mediocre singer. I start with a series of nursery rhymes and then switch to a handful of pop ballads at her request. Her eyelids have closed from where they peek out from her blanket fort.

"Goodnight, Lane," I whisper. "Sorry I can't really sing."

She makes some kind of animal noise. "You're not that shitty," she murmurs. "You have a nice vocal quality. You're just very untrained. I'll give you tips."

She's asleep by the time I sneak out the door.

DAY 376

I'm woken at about 7:15 A.M. to distant shouting. I lie there for a few moments, hoping it will stop, but if anything it's just getting louder. If I had to guess, I'd say that it was coming from our front gate.

I clamber out into the hall and knock on Lane's door. No answer. "Lane?" I twist the knob; her room is empty and unusually neat, but her mobile phone is vibrating on top of her bed. She hasn't left the house, then.

I wander around the hallways for a minute, calling Lane's name and listening for signs of life, but there's nothing but that muffled shouting. I don't think that's Lane. I step back into her room and realise the curtains are open. We hadn't even made a deal about that. And there's a note on the bed, next to where the phone is buzzing.

A sudden rush of nausea and adrenaline hits me as I pick up the notepaper.

A –

Thank you for everything. Now it's all yours. Anything numerical you need, I've hidden it behind the bookcase. Don't worry that the new Lane can't play guitar: she's still grieving the man who taught her, and she'll learn it all again in the next few months, anyway. If she's feeling a bit rusty with singing she can take some revision lessons. Don't hate me too much.

– L

I turn over the paper with shaking hands and a churning stomach, but that's really all it says. I stare out the window, as though Lane might just be sitting in the backyard, but there's no-one there. My mind is empty. My feet are rooted to the spot.

Eventually, the noises start to creep back in: the shouting, the steady vibration of the phone. I pick up the phone reflexively. The video stream from the front gate appears from the screen: it's Audrey, and she's screaming for her daughter, and she looks just about ready to scale the fence.

After a moment I press the speaker button. "I'll be down in a minute," I tell Audrey through the gate's speaker-phone, and abandon Lane's phone back on the bed.

On my way downstairs I tuck Lane's note into the pocket of my pyjama shorts.

Outside, Audrey looks furious and coiled, like she's desperate to hit me. That wouldn't be too bad, I think. I open the gate for her.

"You fucking bitch," she seethes, her bared teeth inches from my face. "I thought you might be dead!"

I stare blankly up at her. I know my face should have a better expression on it, any expression, but I can't seem to summon anything. "I'm here," I say.

"You took a goddamn eternity to get down here!" she says. "I called your phone a dozen times. What the fuck were you doing?"

I feel my eyes getting even wider. "I left my phone in another room," I say after a long moment, and that's not even a lie.

Her fist opens and twitches as though she's about to slap me, but then she turns away abruptly before she can. Audrey walks a circle around the front garden. I notice that some of her shirt buttons have been done up wrong, that her lipstick is a little smudged. She pulls her own note out of her bag and thrusts it towards my face. "What is this?"

It's folded so I can't read it. I take a gamble: "I wanted to tell you I love you."

Audrey's hand with the note is shaking violently. There is at least one tear down her cheek now, though you wouldn't know it from the rest of her face.

"I really hate you sometimes," she says, though all the sting has departed. She wraps her arms around me, strong and anchoring. "So you're really alright?"

"I'm not going anywhere, if that's what you mean."

She makes a satisfied hum deep in her throat, and rocks me back and forth, standing up under the morning sun.

After we've had green tea and Monte Carlo biscuits and Audrey has left again, I plod back upstairs to Lane's bedroom. The house feels different, soulless. Where is Lane?

I pocket Lane's phone and drift around the house and gardens. If Lane has truly died, where is the body? I can see no fresh dirt to mark a grave, no bloodstains, nothing out of place. Nothing in the news to indicate her body has been found elsewhere. And I don't think she'd do that, anyway; if it was found by anyone but me, it would ruin everything we'd built.

A breath catches in my throat: when did she stop calling me "Aer" and start calling me "heir?" From right at the beginning, or only the last few days, or somewhere in between? A thousand little moments tie themselves together in my brain. I feel so goddamn stupid. If I'd been paying any attention at all, she'd still be here.

I'm back next to Lane's bed, gazing up at the ceiling. Was that hook always there, with an inch of rope tied around it? It was always so dark in Lane's room lately. Is that drop of blood new, where it's stained the floorboards underneath?

DAY 660

If Lane seems a bit different this past year, well, everyone changes and grows. If she can't quite pull off the fierceness of the warrior attitude anymore, then she can still do pastel goth, avant-garde, dystopian, gothic lolita, street punk, body paint...

If you haven't seen Lane in a gown on the red carpet before, or with coloured hair, call it evolution. If she seems to smile more easily, well, she's been doing this for longer now. Fame affects people strangely.

The second album does even better than the first. Not long after Lane's disappearance, I film the music videos for Razorblade Girl (flying knives, ala Carrie White), Version of Me (I play all the characters: the knight, the witch, and the straw-filled puppet princess), and My Air. That one's the twist to the guts: I didn't even realise it was going to be on the album until shortly before it dropped as a single. The song Lane wrote for me. She seemed embarrassed to play it with even just the two of us in the room, but apparently she'd shared it with her producers and they'd fallen over themselves for Lane's first ballad.

That song fucking haunts me over the first few months. The music video is me as an astronaut, floating through space, the helmet initially full with water but draining as the song continues. Whilst my astronaut lips move through the water, my hands are folding a zoo of origami animals which come to life around my space suit. I don't really know if I "get" the video concept, but apparently this was all worked out with Lane before she went AWOL.

I haven't been back to Clayden since Lane disappeared. I don't think I'll ever go back. Lane was getting awfully good at summoning that portal by the end: she could do it one-handed with her eyes closed, and even move the portal a little through the air. I only tried to summon it once or twice and couldn't even do it right. If there's a chance she's starting over there with the dregs of Aeris Dormer's life, I won't return and screw that up for her. I hope she's doing a better job with it than I did.

They want me to do an international tour next year, and yeah, I guess I'll go. I'm becoming a passable guitar player and a proficient copycat singer. Lane's settling around me now like a second skin.

I've had more than one day where I forget I haven't always been Lane Islington.

DAY 5140

When did life get so goddamned dull? I'm sipping a mandarin vodka beside our swimming pool, an old married lady at age thirty-two. Tied the knot with Toby Johnson three years ago after he'd finally got his head on straight. Released my fifth album twelve months ago and thought it was pretty rocket-fuel-hot, but only my capital-F fans seem to have heard of it. I can even go out sometimes without being recognised. Still gorgeous, but no-one seems to care anymore.

A few bubbles break up the stillness of the pool. I lean forward, narrow my eyes towards the shallows. Tip my sunglasses up just in time to see a surge of water and then a dark head break through the surface. "Holy motherfucker," I whisper to myself.

She emerges smoothly, like the bow of a ship, like a watery goddess. She's wearing a perfectly fitted suit, mirrored aviators and diamond-encrusted fingerless gloves. Even soaked from head to toe, she looks the picture of an ultra-glamorous FBI agent.

The original Lane Islington grins at my dropped jaw and flashes me her pointy incisors.

"Wanna be a star?" she asks.

ABOUT EPHINY GALE

Ephiny Gale was born in Melbourne, Australia, and is still there, alongside her lovely wife and a small legion of bookcases. She is the author of more than two dozen published short stories and novelettes, which have appeared in publications including *GigaNotoSaurus, Daily Science Fiction,* and *Aurealis.* Her stories have featured on the Tangent Online Recommended Reading List, as a finalist in Nestlé's Write Around Australia, and have been awarded *Syntax & Salt*'s Editor's Award.

She has also written several produced stage plays and musicals, including the sold-out *How to Direct from Inside* at La Mama and *Shining Armour* at The 1812 Theatre. Her script *Time Scraps* was a finalist in St Martin's National Playwriting Competition, and *Hearts up Sleeves* won the Five Minute Play award at Dante's.

When not writing, Ephiny currently works as a Project Coordinator for an application development company. Her previous roles have included coordinating a major arts festival, working as the Association Secretary for the Green Room Awards (Melbourne's premier performing arts awards), nine months as a professional wedding DJ, and working as an executive of a university student association.

Ephiny has a Masters in Arts Management, a red belt in taekwondo, and a passion for psychology, fairy tales, and storytelling in all its forms. She also especially enjoys raspberries, Italian greyhounds, playing board games with friends, and wearing clothes made out of unnatural fabrics.

More at ephinygale.com